THE STOLEN BRIDE
KINGS OF FURY
BOOK TWO

GENA SHOWALTER

JILL MONROE

Copyright © 2025 by Author Talk Media LLC

All rights reserved. In accordance of the U.S. Copyright Act of 1975, no part of this publication may be reproduced, distributed, or transmitted in any form or by any means, including photocopying, recording, or other electronic or mechanical methods, without the prior written permission of the publisher, except in the case of brief quotations embodied in critical reviews and certain other noncommercial uses permitted by copyright law.

This is a work of fiction. Names, characters, places, and incidents either are the products of the author's imagination or are used fictitiously. Any resemblance to actual persons, living or dead, businesses, companies, events, or locales is entirely coincidental.

FBI Anti-Piracy Warning: The unauthorized reproduction or distribution of a copyrighted work is illegal. Criminal copyright infringement, including infringement without monetary gain, is investigated by the FBI and is punishable by fines and federal imprisonment. The unauthorized reproduction or distribution of a copyrighted work is illegal. Criminal copyright infringement is investigated by federal law enforcement agencies and is punishable by up to five years in prison and a fine of $250,000.

Cover Created by Naomi Lane

Editing by AZ Editing

Chapter Header by Seamartini through DepositPhotos

Ornamental Breaks by bradnorbi through DepositPhotos

Special Thanks to Cheryl and Heather!

I

"I turn your pet's bad hair day into a paw-some fashion statement!"

Clover Deering,
Owner of Fur-Ever Pet Spa
Where Every Animal Feels Fur-Tastic!

I reached up to flip the OPEN sign in my shop window to closed, accidentally brushing the jingle bell that had rung non-stop for hours. What a day. A German Shepherd peed on my leg after stealing my lunch. A Persian shredded my arms with her razor-sharp claws–now filed, thank you—and a Pomeranian yipped until my last nerve frayed beyond repair.

My lower back and feet ached, and exhaustion saturated every muscle in my body. I reeked of wet dog. Worse, I hadn't eaten in forever—nearly two whole hours!—but right now I was too tired to even slap together a sandwich. Proof I'd reached my limit.

Attempting to fill my bottomless pit of a stomach was

my second favorite hobby. The honor of top spot belonged to rescuing animals in need. One of the many reasons I'd chosen grooming as a career.

I loved Fur-Ever Pet Spa and could only smile at the framed business certificate that hung on the pale blue wall. The shop's first decoration. My hometown of Aurelian Hills, Georgia, offered wonderful entrepreneur resident loans, and I'd taken full advantage, building the pet spa from scratch.

My stomach grumbled, refusing to let me forget my hunger. Okay, so, after I finished my chores and showered, I'd call in a delivery order at Daisy's. The German Shepherd's owner had given me a generous tip, so I could splurge without guilt.

Quickening my pace, I disinfected the check-out counter, stored all leftover complimentary treats in a bag, and swept up any remaining fur. That done, I hosed down the bathing area then put the used towels and comfort blankets through an intense cleaning cycle via the industrial washer in back. In the morning, they'd go in the dryer.

Beginning a day with a messy shop always soured my mood. Satisfied, I switched off the lights and headed for the wooden staircase that led to the second floor. My private retreat and the reason I'd purchased the building. It served double duty as work and home.

A long, hot shower failed to ease my aches. The hydraulics on the grooming table I'd picked up second-hand had stopped working again, forcing me to lift my clients onto the station with physical strength alone. I was stronger than I looked, thank goodness, but even so. Yikes.

I exited the bathroom ahead of a fragrant cloud of steam and entered my walk-in closet. With summer in full swing, I donned a tank top and shorts, then grabbed my

THE STOLEN BRIDE

phone from the charging dock on the built-in dresser, intending to call Daisy's. Oh. Two new voice messages and a text.

I checked the text first and ground my teeth. From Benjamin, my ex-fiancé.

> Benjaboy: I left my favorite game at your place. I'll swing by tomorrow and get it.

I responded:

> No. You're not welcome here. Lose my number.

We'd broken up six months ago. If he'd truly enjoyed the game, he would've realized it was gone long before now. Besides, I didn't want to see him. Every interaction reminded me of my failures. How I had ignored a thousand red flags, doing my best not to make waves, all to keep him happy without ever actually making him happy. How I'd forgotten that I had always desired real, genuine love. The kind my parents had shared. Instead, I'd caved to my desperation to experience contentment and settled for conditional affection. Little wondered I'd constantly felt as if a part of me was missing.

Three little dots appeared in the text thread, and I sighed, anticipating Benjamin's reply. Sure to be a doozy. At least he wasn't waiting the usual three days to respond.

> Benjaboy: Your heart is pure ice, Clo. That's what broke us. You know that, right?

Wow. He never hesitated to go there. My supposed lack of emotion was his excuse for cheating with my (former) best friend. Granted, I wasn't the most expressive of people. But suppressing my emotions was a gift to all, including

3

myself! I'd let loose around him only once, and he'd acted scared of me for weeks.

Pushing thoughts of Benjaman into a shadowed corner of my mind, I listened to the voice mails. Cancellations. Another sigh slipped out. Despite today's influx of patrons, business had slowed the past year, and I was in danger of getting behind on my loan repayments. Every cent counted.

Okay, so, no Daisy's tonight. Tamping down my disappointment—you're welcome world!—I did my best to rally. I had some cheese and crackers in the kitchen. Maybe I'd finish off my jar of peanut butter too.

I returned my phone to the charger. No reason to carry it around, hoping for a longed-for text or a call I wouldn't get. My parents were gone, and I had no other family. Benjamin had won all our friends in the breakup. A blessing, I realized now. Better no friends than bad ones.

As I exited the closet, I braided my wet hair. T minus thirty seconds until I stretched out, closed my eyes and—I skidded to a halt. A man. An enormous man dressed in a black T-shirt, leather pants and combat boots. He sat in a navy blue armchair where I enjoyed playing my violin, mere feet away from me.

The bruiser toyed with the edge of the cozy knit throw draped over the top while sipping a glass of my favorite vodka. The last of my grandma's supply. He stared straight at me.

"Hello, Clover."

"Úristen!" My Hungarian mother's favorite expression burst from my mouth. Fury spilled through my veins, both boiling hot and ice cold, and I balled my hands. Some people had a flight or fight response. I only possessed fight.

Except, in seconds the fury downgraded to mild irritation with a tinge of dismay. Over the years, I'd trained myself to suppress any strong surge of emotion automatically. A process that always left me feeling as if I wore someone else's skin.

"Don't challenge me," the man said, as cool as could be. "My beast won't like it."

I wasted no time asking pointless questions about his so-called beast, and I didn't run. He would pay for breaking into my home and draining my vodka. On a mission to teach him the error of his ways, I kicked, aiming for his smug face, exactly as I'd learned in my bargain basement self-defense class.

Ow, ow, ow! His rock hard jaw almost broke my bones. I'd forgotten I wasn't wearing shoes.

Meanwhile, he absorbed the blow as if I'd merely patted his cheek. He didn't even move to stop a second strike. No, he took another sip of the vodka.

"This is good," he remarked, toasting me.

"I know," I grumbled after stumbling back. Okay, so, perhaps I *should* run.

Yes, yes. *Go!* I turned on my heel and sprinted–nope. I slammed into his hard body and ricocheted backward. But. How had he gotten in front of me so quickly?

"I told you not to issue a challenge," he grated, stepping closer, erasing the distance between us.

"Challenging a madman and escaping a dangerous situation isn't the same thing." As I retreated, I stretched out my arms to ward him off.

He followed me. "I suppose you're right. I'm still irked."

"Who are you? Why are you here?" The backs of my knees hit the chair he'd just vacated, and down I fell. "How do you know who I am?" I huffed.

He crossed his arms over his massive chest. "I have no plans to harm you. Relax."

"Yeah. Believing an intruder isn't on my To Do list." Wait. I knew him. Well, I didn't *know him* know him, but I'd seen him on the news just yesterday. Malachi Cromwell, a former footballer turned action movie star known for his incredible tackles, unbeatable speed and roguish charm. Women all over America melted over his muscles and perfect face. Shoulder-length brown hair with the slightest wave framed heavily lashed, menace-filled amber eyes and a stubborn chin shadowed by a trim beard.

"We're going to talk," he stated, his firm command allowing no argument.

I didn't care who he was or what tone he used. I had zero interest in a conversation. "Sure, sure." I darted my gaze for a weapon, any weapon. An e-reader. Tube of lip balm. Box of tissues. Lavender scented candle. Not exactly helpful. "A talk."

"Your name is Clover Deering. You are twenty-eight years old, the adopted daughter of James and Morgan Deering, both of whom are deceased. Formerly engaged to Benjamin Dolittle, who you only dated because you liked his name."

My attention whipped to Malachi, my cheeks burning. "The part about Benjamin isn't true." Had I liked the thought of becoming Mrs. Dolittle, pet groomer? Yes. Anyone would. Growing up, I'd adored the stories of the little boy who conversed with pets and grew up to become a doctor in San Francisco. "You don't know me, so this, whatever it is you're doing, isn't helping your cause."

"I know you in ways you don't know yourself. You're better off without Dolittle. He did nothing to help you advance the greater good."

Anger flared anew. I'd often heard my parents whisper about "the greater good." And my dreams...

THE STOLEN BRIDE

"Do you comprehend what a sentinel is, Clover?" Malachi asked. "Though you prefer to use the term 'berserker'."

Uh... Had he checked my online search history or library card?

As a child, I'd had a royal temper. Kind of violent, even. Okay, super violent. Anytime I'd gotten mad, toys had gotten decimated. And yes, I'd hurt people. At some point, Mom had begun telling me cautionary tales that featured berserkers gone wild and the consequences they'd faced.

As a teenager, I'd started dreaming of one berserker in particular. A fierce, faceless man in black leather. I always pledged my life to him, then woke up as joyous as I was disturbed, convinced I'd somehow glimpsed a snippet of my future. Which, of course, I hadn't.

Anyway. For the wellbeing of my loved ones, I'd taught myself to bottle and bury my emotions in a never-ending abyss. Rather than act like a berserker, I got my fix reading books about them. From historical texts to romance novels.

So. No wonder Malachi clocked my secret passion. All he'd had to do was glance at the shelf in the living room displaying handmade berserker action figures I'd bought online. A Viking ship model I'd made in the summer between ninth and tenth grade. Or the bear, wolf and boar figurines I'd acquired, the very animals said to be tied to every "rage warrior."

"Clover," my unwanted companion prompted.

"Yes," I said, ready to end this exchange. "I'd bet everyone in the world knows what a berserker is."

He narrowed his eyes, and his lashes nearly fused together. "Tell me."

I licked my lips. "You should leave my house. You won't like what happens if you stay." If I had to, I would unearth and uncork a bottle of rage, and he would pay dearly for his crime.

"Tell me," he snapped. "Then I'll go."

A lie, guaranteed. No way he'd broken into my home simply to converse about fictional immortals. But it wouldn't hurt to keep him distracted while I figured out a way to escape that didn't involve getting blood all over my furnishings.

"Berserkers are mythological warriors who do battle while lost in a trance-like rage," I said. "Once triggered, they slaughter without mercy and nothing can stop them. Some people believe they are possessed. Norse mythology is the most widely accepted origin. Okay. Bye."

"You are only half right. Allow me to set you straight. In the twelfth century, a glowing stone known as the Starfire fell from the sky. It caused the spirits of primordial animals to fuse with ten ordinary men and women. Those individuals scattered to various parts of the world. Now, they and their descendants cohabitate with mortals or live alongside this world in a different dimension. But that's a tale for another day. If we get angry, the beast temporarily gains control of our bodies. If ever we allow evil into our hearts, the beast permanently takes over our minds, too."

"We?" I arched a brow. "You're trying to tell me you're a berserker?"

"*The* berserker. I'm King of the House of Griffin, and you are one of my subjects. I know your birth parents. And your sister."

What the—*what?* He did not suggest he'd learned the name of my birth parents. Or that I had a sister. Information I'd craved for years, hoping against hope to fill my greatest void. But his records were sealed. And other dimensions? Real berserkers who shared a familial connection with little ole me? Please.

I didn't care that Malachi's berserker mythology matched my mother's, a version I'd found nowhere else. Didn't care that he'd moved swiftly enough to count as inhuman. There was a reasonable explanation for everything. I just couldn't think properly during such a high stakes moment. This was a robbery gone wrong, nothing more. Or a psychotic break. A long con?

"I'm giving you one more chance to walk out of my house," I informed him. If he declined, I'd fight my way past him and jump out the window. I might break a bone or two in the process, but his damage would be greater.

In fact, even now my bottled rage rose to the surface of my mind, no digging necessary.

He notched his chin. "I warn you now. Don't do what you're considering—"

Too late. I exploded to my feet, plowing into him with enough force to knock him to the floor. In unison, I bit his ear and raked my nails across his throat.

He growled, irritated, but he didn't strike back.

Without missing a beat, I broke his nose with a hard punch and sprinted for the only window—"No!"

He caught my waist, stopping me. The cork nearly popped off my bottle, anger burning hotter and hotter. I didn't resist its clarion call, erupting, kicking, hitting and clawing, showing no mercy.

With blood smeared on his face, he casually told me, "Viktor Endris is King of the House of Turul, and the only original sentinel remaining. Prophecy says—never mind. You don't need to know that part yet. He's based by the Danube Bend in Hungary, in a dimension of his own, and he's feral. He teeters at the precarious edge of turning."

Turning? Intrigued, I paused long enough to ask, "Turning into what?" A berserker?

"A shifter."

Okay, so, I extended the pause. "Like, a werewolf?" Was this research for a movie or something? Method acting, maybe?

"In Viktor's case, a turul. You'll see for yourself when you give him a wee push and help him over the ledge."

"You're kidding right?" He must be. How was one supposed to push a sentinel slash berserker slash shifter slash figment of a stranger's imagination to welcome evil into his heart?

As I sputtered, the movie star continued. "In exchange, I'll do three things for you. Introduce you to the wonderful world of berserkers. Pay off your debt as well as setting you up with a nest egg. And finally, give you what you desire most. The name of your birth parents and an introduction to your sister. Sleep now."

Sleep? Hardly! But a second later, a sting registered along the side of my neck, curtesy of...his nail? Instant fatigue.

"You have much work to do," Malachi muttered.

A cloak of darkness uncoiled from the fatigue, and I tumbled into a spinning tunnel of nothingness.

MOANING, I fluttered open my eyes. Muted sunlight greeted me, searing my corneas. As I blinked rapidly to clear my vision, memories dawned. The break in. Berserker talk. Or rather, "sentinel" talk. Malachi. A mention of a mysterious prophecy. An offer from the

THE STOLEN BRIDE

movie star and a failed escape attempt. I scowled. Where was I?

Ignoring the ache in my temples, I jolted into a sitting position to study my surroundings. I should be home in Aurelian Hills. Instead, I occupied a forest and perched on lush grass with a large, moss-covered stone behind me. Overhead, sunlight filtered through a leafy canopy provided by big, beautiful trees. Birds harmonized as a gentle breeze whistled through the limbs.

I still wore my tank and shorts, my feet bare. A fresh cut on my hand throbbed. At least the air was warm and wonderfully fragrant with the scent of wildflowers and rich earth.

My stomach churned. Had Malachi brought me here? *Abandoned* me? But I...this...why drop me out in the open? And where was "here?"

I remembered his words. *Viktor Endris is King of the House of Turul. Based by the Danube Bend in Hungary, in a dimension of his own.*

Obviously, there was no such thing as other dimensions. Or berserkers. But. He might be a sick, twisted serial killer. This could be a game of confuse-then-hunt-the-innocent-woman. He was a celebrity, after all. No way he actually expected me to—what had he said? Push an immortal king into allowing evil into his heart. And a Hungarian, no less, like my mother.

Trying to cobble together some kind of plan, I climbed to unsteady legs. "Someone? Anyone but the deranged actor with boundary issues. Help!" If this *was* a hunting game, I preferred to know right from the start so I could turn the tables on my pursuers.

Even if Malachi did, in fact, know my birth parents, even if I had a sister I'd never met, I had no interest in

11

working with the guy. But. Me. A sibling. Was there any greater title?

A deep, guttural roar erupted in the distance, and my blood iced over. Wild animal!

Determined to find safety, I leaped into a sprint, pumping my arms, putting distance between me and the animal. Rocks, twigs, and briars sliced my feet. I didn't care. Where to go, where to go?

Pine, birch and maple trees abounded. Shrubs, flowers and mushrooms too. No homes, huts or people.

Another roar pierced my ears. The predator, whatever it was, had gotten closer. Heart thudding, I pumped my arms faster. Faster still. Sprinting past trees.

Did I hear footsteps?

Every fiber of my being screamed, *Look back!* But I'd seen that movie. I knew what happened when the hapless damsel in distress glanced over her shoulder. She tripped, twisted her ankle, and died. No, thank you.

I should hide. But where? Where?! I scanned. More trees, some bushes, and weird gold flowers. I veered left, intending—"Aaaah!" Strong arms banded around my waist as a powerful body drove me to the ground. I rolled with my captor, eating dirt. To my astonishment, I experienced no pain. Obtained no new injuries.

The moment we stopped, I scrambled to my throbbing feet. He stood too, and we squared off. *Oh, shih tzu.* He towered above me, tall and muscular. Very muscular. He was shirtless, displaying a wealth of swirling symbols tattooed from his neck to the waist of his torn black leathers. Wavy white hair stuck out in spikes around a harsh face chiseled from a block of icy wrath. A thousand threats blasted from eyes the most startling shade of emerald green.

As he looked me over, his nostrils flared, his tether on control clearly fraying. He opened and closed his fists.

My brain nearly short-circuited. Because of his height and muscle mass, he reminded me of the faceless warrior from my dreams.

"The fog is thinning." He spoke in Hungarian.

Oh, goodness gracious. "Am I in Hungary?" I asked, speaking in Hungarian as well. I hadn't used the language in a long while, yet the words flowed from my tongue with ease.

He canted his head from side to side with eerie precision. "Why is the fog thinning?" A question with the force of a threat.

My heart jumped into my throat, my trained defenses having trouble bottling a flood of anxiety. "There is no fog, sir."

He jerked, glaring to the left as if startled by a sound. "Her whispers. I no longer hear them. Do you?"

"Her?" I listened but detected only the rustle of leaves and the call of birds.

"The Valkara." Those incredible, fathomless eyes glazed over. "Find, destroy, happy," he muttered. "Find, destroy, happy."

While he lost his marbles, I resurrected Malachi's words. *He's feral. He teeters at the precarious edge of turning. You will give him a little push.*

If anyone could pass for a legendary rage-fighter, well, it was this guy. But no. No! Absolutely not. Berserkers weren't real. A genuine king didn't expect me to nudge another king into an abyss of evil, thereby becoming a shifter. A turul shifter at that. A mythological bird of prey reminiscent of a giant falcon my mother had described in her stories, said to represent sheer power.

I should go. In no world was staying put wise. But if I ran, this maniac would only catch me again. Guess I'd have to do the supersmart/foolish thing and deal with him head on. Actually, the best path forward might be teaming up. Us against Malachi. Not to mention the predator on the loose! At least the roaring had stopped.

"Look. There's a wild animal nearby," I told him, using my best team player voice while speaking a foreign language. "How about we find a place to shelter?" Hoping to lighten the mood, I added, "You'll be in charge of provisions, of course, because the only fishing I do is for compliments." Eyebrow wiggle. "You can tell me about this Valkara person along the way."

Low growls rumbled in his chest, and I gulped.

"Whoa there, big fella." I held up my hands, palms out. "Let's ease the throttle down a notch or twenty. Okay? Breathe with me. In. Out."

His only response? Growling louder while taking a step closer.

Years of working with aggressive animals kicked in, and I snapped my fingers while making a quick, piercing "spt" noise. Prevention instead of intervention, that's what I always said.

He double blinked, the glaze in his irises fading. His huffing breaths decelerated. "Did you...hiss at me?" Incredulity drenched his gravelly voice.

"No, sir, I *spt*'ed at you. There's a difference." The pooches and kitties I groomed never complained about my methods.

His eyelids slitted. "You have five seconds to explain how an unknown human entered my land, bypassing my securities, or I'll rip out your heart."

The threat lit a fire inside my gut. Suddenly, I had no

THE STOLEN BRIDE

desire to bottle my emotions and play nice. But old habits kicked in, per usual. I displayed no outward reaction as a lie, the truth and a stinging retort raced across my tongue, a photo finish expected...

"I hope *rip out your heart* is just a colloquialism I'm unfamiliar with, because I don't know how I got here." Well, well. Truth won. "A strange man broke into my home and knocked me out. I woke up with no idea where I am or how much time has passed." Hint, hint. *Share the location and date, stranger.*

But he didn't. "Is that so?" he all but purred.

Shudders rolled over my spine. Somehow, that purr was a thousand times worse than his growls. "It is." Time to get blunt. "Where are we? What day is this?"

He stalked a languid circle around me, and I'd never felt more like caged prey. "Why would this strange man bring a mouse to a starved falcon, hmm?"

I gulped. Going to ignore my queries and call me a mouse? Okay. I didn't miss the fact that he'd referred to himself as a falcon, befitting the turul legends. "He told me..." Nope. Mentioning the berserker thing might get me into trouble, giving this madman permission to rage. "He wasn't in his right mind. He mentioned a prophecy." I didn't know why that detail kept gnawing at me, but it did.

When Mr. Growly Pants faced me again, utter stillness came over him. The kind of stillness a predator usually displayed right before devouring a living meal. I licked my lips, doubting another "spt" would help. But he didn't attack. He pinched and lifted my braid, rubbing the ends between two fingers.

"I've added five seconds to your clock," he commanded. "Finish your explanation."

Enough with the timer. "Look, snarls." *Careful.* Only a

fine line divided an attempt to take charge of the situation and incensing the unstable menace before me. As gently as possible, I tugged my hair from his grip. "I want only to return home. Will you help me? Pretty please with cherries on top."

He performed another of those double blinks before narrowing his eyes. "Who are you?"

Now we were getting somewhere. "My name is Clover. And you are?"

"Clover," he echoed and grimaced. "A herbaceous plant with dense, globular flower heads and three-lobed leaves."

So annoying! "Or a strong, independent American woman with pluck and grit." A pet groomer able to afford zero pets of her own, who enjoyed playing the violin to soothe the discomfort of never fully expressing herself. Not exactly someone a legitimate berserker king would choose to complete kingdom business. Not that Malachi was a legitimate berserker. Or a king. "If you're not going to help—"

"I'm not," my companion interjected without hesitation or remorse.

Well, okay then. "Be a dear and direct me to the nearest public area. Then we can say our goodbyes."

"Nem." He leaned in my direction, nothing more, but suddenly he consumed all of my personal space. I gasped, then gasped again when he settled his big, calloused hands on my waist, lifted me as if I weighed nothing, and draped me over his shoulder. "I don't care that you're afraid of me. We will stay together until I sort through my thoughts and decide what to do with you."

2

Before You Attempt to Tame Your King of the Wild, Learn to Harness Your Own Power

–HOW TO TRAIN YOUR BERSERKER
By Elizabeth "Elle" Darcy-Bruce

I hung over the wildebeest's shoulder, limp, my mind performing circus worthy acrobatics to catch up with my circumstances: a hot, growly muscle man was hauling me around as if I were a sack of potatoes while muttering under his breath about irritating invaders. The nerve!

And how dare he accuse me of being afraid of him? I feared nothing! Usually. I mean, had I entertained a twinge or two of anxiety since our initial meeting? Yes. But that proved nothing except my well-honed defenses required fortifying.

"I can walk, thank you," I snipped, scrutinizing the towering trees of the forest, on the hunt for an escape route. The underbrush was thick with ferns and shrubs, blocking any sure path out. "Hey! I'm speaking to you, Carry McCar-ryson. Put me down."

"Nem. You'll run."

"Yeah, well, if you're capable enough to catch me, that shouldn't be a big deal." No reason to deny my intent.

"You shouldn't run," he groused. "My beast will like it."

Malachi had mentioned a beast, too. I pressed my tongue to the roof of my mouth. "What breed is it? Your beast, I mean. Because we *are* talking about a dog or a cat, aren't we?"

My captor stepped over a fallen log. "Did Deco hope your vulnerable maiden in distress act would garner my sympathies? Did he send you to Örök to spy on me?"

"Me? Spy?" I forced a laugh, but the too-shrill notes made a mockery of my casual attitude. "Hardly. I don't even know who this Deco guy is. Or you!" And Örök? Never heard of it. "I just want to go home to my business, before I lose the loyal customers who trust me to keep my appointments."

Maybe someone would be concerned when I failed to open and call the police. Oh, please, please, please!

"I am King Viktor Endris, the decider of your fate. I suggest you tell me everything that led to your arrival in my land. Leave out no detail."

Whoa. All pretense of good humor evaporated. He claimed to be the very person Malachi had sent me to corrupt. But was this Viktor guy also an immortal berserker sharing a body with the spirit of a turul? No. Of course not.

The two men must be working together to, what? Trick me? Produce some kind of blackmarket reality show? But why risk going to jail for a prank or skit?

I must be totally missing the mark. So what *was* this? What, what?

THE STOLEN BRIDE

Proceed with caution. "I've already told you everything I wish to tell you." Yeah. Saving details for later was the smartest play. Curiosity wasn't a bad thing.

"Your wishes have no bearing on this situation," he snapped. "Talk. You won't like what happens if you don't."

"Hey," I barked, tapping his backside to ensure I snagged his full attention. A technique I used when a dog focused too intently on a trashcan, as if imagining an all-you-can-eat-buffet. But, um. Hmm. Viktor was packed tightly beneath his leathers, the muscles delightfully firm.

He missed his next step, but quickly righted. The jostle returned my thoughts to something that mattered. Our conversation.

Onward and upward! "I don't know you, don't trust you, and I'm not sure what you have planned for me. Plus, I'm stressed, hurt, starved, and hanging over your shoulder, Neanderthal style. I'm in *no mood* for snarly dudes with a Tarzan fetish. Gift me with a little grace and you'll reap the rewards."

He puffed up his chest. "I think I liked you better silent."

"Same, caveman. Same. And please note, *you* were the one who rapid fired all the demands." *Why are you antagonizing him? Stop!* "But I will take my own advice, gift you with some grace, and tell you a bit more of my story." I'd dole a detail here and there, keeping him on my hook—for compensation. "First, you gotta put me down."

A deeper growl rumbled in his chest.

Ugh. Did he verge on another eruption? Though he wasn't really a berserker, I needed him to remain calm. Out of habit, only habit, I stroked his lower back the way I did for anxious dogs and cats, cooing, "It's okay, baby, it's okay."

Wait. Hold up. Please tell me I did not call this terror of a man "baby."

He stopped abruptly, going still. My breath caught.

"Hear me well, drágá." With a huff, he hefted me off his shoulder and onto my feet. He glared down at me. "I am no one's baby."

I teetered, knees shockingly weak. The jerk let me fall, never even attempting to catch me. Impact proved jarring, rattling my brain. Probably the reason I couldn't get over his use of 'dear' or 'precious'. I couldn't recall which it was.

A scowl dominated my features as I sat there, glaring at him. "You're no one's baby, but you're someone's worst nightmare, guaranteed."

"Walk," he commanded, stepping over me and continuing on.

Argh! I popped up, dusted the dirt from my rump, and chased after him. My irritation was too sharp to fit into a mental bottle. "We need lessons in common courtesy, I see."

"Yes, you do, but I don't have time to tutor you."

"That's not–" Ow! Eek! Ow! Jagged rocks and razored briars lined the path, tormenting my poor, injured feet. Too bad Malachi had kidnapped me right after my shower while I was without socks and shoes. "I changed my mind. You can carry me," I encouraged, lagging behind.

He kept walking. "You also need lessons in actions and consequences as well."

"Hey!" I called. "I'm *bleeding*."

For some reason, that did the trick. Despite his taunt, Viktor backtracked to clasp my waist and heft me off my feet. This time, he dangled me in the crook of his arm. "You are bothersome, that's what you are."

"Why don't you get kidnapped, and we'll see if you're

all sunshine and roses." A branch scraped my arm, but I didn't dare complain.

"Talk," he repeated.

Guess I was done doling out the story in small measures. Considering I owed him, I had better share. "So, the guy who broke into my home claimed to be a king of griffins or something." I didn't have the mental capacity to weave an elaborate lie I might not remember. Besides, even if Malachi's claims sprang from a well of truth, which they didn't, I still needed Viktor's aid. He wasn't the one who'd abducted and relocated me. Therefore, he was the lesser of two evils. Perhaps he could even help me understand what was going on. "His name is Malachi Cromwell. He's a former professional athlete and current movie star."

"I know who he is. Continue," Viktor added without evincing a single clue to his thoughts.

"Well, he must hate you, because he asked me to convince you to switch to Team Evil in exchange for paying off my debts. And just so you know, I've already refused to cash in." I didn't mention the other payouts. Viktor would hear the longing in my voice. How I desperately yearned to meet my sister and learn the identity of my birth parents. A question that had plagued me since discovering my adoption as a teen. But. I would never, under any circumstances, conspire with my kidnapper. I had standards.

"And? What happened when you refused?" Tension pulsed from Viktor as he tightened his arm around me. "Because the Malachi I know has killed countless others for far less."

An exaggeration, surely. Or maybe he'd confused the actor's onscreen actions with real life. "He knocked me out." Although, I hadn't actually gotten a chance to voice my refusal, had I? "Do you know anything about the prophecy he mentioned?"

Agonizing minutes passed in terse silence, the only sounds coming from Viktor's footsteps as he stalked over brambles.

Fine. "Any comments, elaborations, or feedback about my revelation?"

Viktor began muttering under his breath again. Conversation over. Not the greatest start, but not the worst either. He wasn't as feral as advertised, but he was definitely unhinged.

As soon as the gurgle of rushing water reached my ears, he dropped me and walked off, as if he'd forgotten he carried me. Or that I existed. I crashed into the ground, eating dirt, losing air.

Eyes narrowing, I spit out grains and scrambled to my feet. What the—

Oh. I spun and took in my new surroundings. A rough-hewn shelter crafted from gnarled branches and leaves, blending seamlessly with the dense forest backdrop. A soot-blackened fire pit possessed a single flat rock seat, hinting at nights spent in raw, primal solitude. The atmosphere hung thick with pine and smoke from old fires. Whispers of the wind danced through the canopy of trees above our heads.

"How very...rustic chic," I muttered, trying not to let my inner cringe make it to the outside. "Is this where you live? I bet the rent is fantastic. Kudos to your decorator. Brings open-concept to a whole new level. Who needs walls, amiright?"

Viktor prowled about, his volume increasing as he spoke to himself or to a voice in his head. "Is Malachi working with Deco? Why would he? But maybe. Why don't

I kill the first and imprison the latter, and then it won't matter?"

"Wow. Is execution always your go-to remedy? I prefer to use my master KEY. Keep Educating Yourself." I firmly believed there was a solution to every problem; I had only to find it. Ask questions. Read books. Meet new people. Repeat.

"The girl," he continued. "Is she as clueless as she seems? Why send her specifically?" Pause. "Nem, nem." Longer pause. "Nem! She's everything I despise. Not the kind of female I desire at my side for any length of time. You are."

My spine stiffened. How dare he. He didn't even know me. "You aren't exactly a prize yourself, mister." Dang. Only a three on the burn scale of insults. I could do better. "You're like a cloud. When you disappear, I have brighter days." Not terrible.

Viktor pulled his hair, pounded his fists into his temples, and muttered, "Answer me! What if she's lying? Or being used in a way she doesn't understand?" More hair pulling. "Should I sacrifice her now instead of later?"

Sacrifice me? My fight reflex buzzed, rallying a thousand inner defenses.

Viktor whizzed to me before I could run, dust flying around us. With my chin tucked between his thumb and a knuckle, he forced my gaze to lock with his. "What are you hiding?"

Lots of things. Maybe if I ignored his question the way he ignored mine, he'd forget the whole sacrifice thing. "You're giving me whiplash," I grumbled.

"What. Are. You. Hiding." A second voice joined his, and it was even more gravelly, turning his timbre into a nightmare of aggression. "How did you make the fog thin?"

His confused expression, paired with that jagged, iron-edged tone, ignited something in me. Not fear, but swagger. I didn't tamp it down as I'd always done with Benjamin. Heck, with everyone. No, I went with it, wrenching free of Viktor's grip and stalking a slow circle around him, exactly as he'd done to me earlier. And I liked it. A sense of power dulled the constant sensation of being trapped in the wrong skin.

At roughly six-five, the man towered over me. He also owned muscles galore and rocked lightning-fast reflexes. But he let me do this without complaint.

"Listen and listen well. I don't know a thing about any fog." I stopped in front of him and jutted my chin. "If you're working together with Malachi to trick me into believing berserkers are real, you're going to fail. Let me go."

"Nem. But allow me to assure you, drága." Viktor lowered his head. Rings of neon gold flashed in his eyes, and veins of black flickered directly under his skin, forking like lightning. "Berserkers are very real, and we do not appreciate being challenged."

In a split second, his body seemed to double in size. His facial features sharpened, and his teeth elongated. A prickle of unfamiliar, icy fear raced through my veins. Malachi had told the truth. Berserkers were real, and Viktor might be entering into a rage right this second.

Moisture flooded my mouth, but I couldn't swallow. Years of absorbing my mother's stories paid off, certain details dominating my thoughts. The dos and don'ts of keeping a rage machine calm.

Do not provoke.

Do not stare.

Never, ever run.

However possible, soothe the beast and get the heck out of Dodge.

"Good boy," I rasped, reaching out to pet Viktor's chest awkwardly. Oh, wow. Amazing how hard muscles could feel so soft, covered by such smooth skin. What I couldn't do? Look away.

He glanced at my fingers, then my face, then my fingers, then my face, as if he couldn't believe what was happening.

I couldn't either! Had I really just admired him? *Pet* him? I snatched back my hand. To my surprise, he didn't issue a rebuke, but calmed. Seconds bled together, his breathing evening out. Good, that was good. He "shrank" to his regular massive size, his features projecting confusion rather than anger. The golden rings faded from his irises, and his pearly whites returned to normal.

Thank goodness. Danger averted. Except, I must be in the middle of an adrenaline crash. A cold sweat chilled my skin, and my teeth chattered.

"We should take a time-out." I needed to sit and work on drawing in a deep, calming breath. Needed to think. Organize the thousands of queries swirling inside my head and forcibly bottle my emotions.

But mmm, what was that amazing smell? I darted my gaze and noticed a picnic setup at the edge of his camp, beyond a fallen log, with food spread out over a blanket. A feast fit for a king. My bottomless stomach rumbled.

"Or a meal break," I suggested with hope.

"Eat," my companion snapped. "My men will be grateful someone has finally enjoyed their efforts."

Don't mind if I do. I shuffled over and settled at the edge of the blanket, where I filled the only waiting plate with fresh fruit, slices of rustic rye bread, smoked cheeses and meat crepes topped with paprika sauce. "So you have men."

Good to know. "Where are they?" I'd seen no evidence of others.

"They aren't here."

I rolled my eyes and popped a crepe into my mouth. Oh wow! The delicious blend of flavors exploded on my tongue. After I swallowed, I said, "Well, they know how to feed a girl right, that's for sure."

One of those little snarls left Viktor. He stomped over, plopped onto the other side of the blanket, and reached over to snatch a grape from my plate. After giving another of those little huffs, he ate the green goodness. His brows drew together, and he snagged an entire sprig.

I shouldn't notice the fluid precision of his movements. Nope, I shouldn't. "So. Who's Deco?" Might as well learn the players in this...game? War? "You keep mentioning him, but you've never explained."

Viktor pursed his mouth. "Deco is king of the turul-shifters. My enemy. I hate him with every fiber of my being." His shoulders rolled in. "But I love him, too. We were friends once." He froze with another bite halfway to his lips, as if he couldn't comprehend what he'd just admitted.

Compassion unfurled deep in my chest. "Perhaps he feels the same about you. Torn."

Viktor straightened with a jolt, then glided his tongue over those straight, white teeth. "Do not speak of matters you don't comprehend, and do not mention Deco again unless you wish to lose your head. And do not ask my men about my association with him. If they tell you anything, they will die screaming." He offered the words with great ease, then ate more grapes, all casual-like. "Understand?"

"Yes." Message received. Truly. I even held up my palms in a gesture of innocence. But, um, what did his men know

THE STOLEN BRIDE

that Viktor didn't want me learning? And why did it matter? "Can we talk about berserkers in general? I only just found out they–you–are real, and I have questions." I reached for the only beverage currently available: a bottle with *Brennivin* emblazoned on the label and the words *The Black Death* printed below it. Considering there were no other options... Down the hatch.

Yikes! Awful idea. Just terrible. Lava in a glass. The burn! Far worse than my grandma's vodka. I sputtered and coughed as fire scorched my throat.

Seconds later, warmth spread through me. Mmm. Very nice. I even poured a little alcohol over the cut on my palm, thinking to clean it. "Ow, ow, ow!" I blew on the gash.

"You may eat in silence." Viktor snatched the bottle from my hand and drained the contents. He made a 'not bad' face, and dang it, it was kind of enchanting. Not exactly an appropriate term for a berserker. "I'm busy deciding your fate. I've been told you serve a purpose. For now."

I forgot my pain and how to breathe but not how to eat. I shoveled in another bite. "Told by whom? And any interest in soliciting advice from an outside party before you render your final verdict?" Okay, so, maybe crumbs fell from the corners of my mouth as I spoke.

"I should interrogate you," he said, still so casual-like. "I've found doing so with knives usually elicits the best results."

The *Brennivin* whispered, *He's only teasing*. I chuckled. "You're hilarious."

He narrowed his eyes. "The greater good matters, but you are clearly bait meant to lure me into some sort of trap. You invaded my private land without permission. And your hair." He waved in my direction. "It's too soft."

27

"I'll have you know I paid good money for this blowout." I spoke between inhaling bites, just in case he decided I'd had enough. "But what do my gorgeous polished mahogany tresses have to do with anything?" Man, this food was tasty! So much better than the cheap cheese and stale crackers I'd never gotten to eat after working twelve hours straight and defending my very life from two immortal kings. "And what do you mean, the greater good? Be specific. Please! Someone should tell me *something*."

"But," he added, ignoring my questions and request yet again.

I waited for him to say more, still eating. He didn't. "But you're going a different route?" I asked, hopeful. Again, crumbs might have fallen from my mouth. "You've realized I'm an innocent bystander thrust into a terrible situation through no fault of my own?"

"But. The fog in my head continues to thin, and I'm thinking more clearly than I have in years."

If this was clear-thinking for him, I shuddered to imagine his mud-caked musings. Oh! Was that some kind of chicken and rice dish hidden behind the ball of honey glazed goat cheese?

He rose to his feet with eerie grace. "For the time being, I can use you to my advantage."

I spooned in a bite. Yep. Chicken and rice with a hardy cheese sauce. "How so?"

"Does it really matter?" He offered me a parody of a smile. "I'm keeping you."

3

Get Your Sneak On: More Stealth Equals Fewer Screams

—HOW TO TRAIN YOUR BERSERKER
By Elizabeth "Elle" Darcy-Bruce

"Excuse me? You're keeping me?" I dropped my utensils. "For how long is this so-called keeping supposed to last? A day? Two? And why?" I threw the queries at Viktor, beyond flabbergasted, bordering on discombobulated.

He disregarded my words, because of course he did. Muttering to himself once again, or maybe to the mysterious whisperer he could no longer hear, he pulled a backpack from behind the trunk of a tree and packed up the camp, stuffing a compass, tinderbox, hatchet, sharpening stone and lantern inside. "When the Valkara calls, I come."

That explained nothing! I pressed my hands over my churning belly. "Is she your woman or something?"

"That is my hope, yes."

So he planned to keep me, but he was into her. Typical

guy. "Go, have fun. Don't let your nonexistent door hit you on the way out. I'll be just fine. No worries. Okay, bye."

He snuffed out the fire, chanting, "Find, destroy, happy. Find, destroy, happy."

Ugh. Not this garbage. "As far as mantras go, I've heard better." The sun began its descent, light fading. I didn't know when, exactly, darkness would arrive, but it wouldn't stop me from launching an escape.

Obviously, teaming up was a nonstarter. I wouldn't be aiding either Malachi or Viktor, no matter what prizes they offered. At the right moment, I'd jet. The condition of my feet no longer mattered. Nor did his beast's reaction. Both kings could get bent.

With Viktor preoccupied, I stood slowly, quietly, and backed up. Now might be the perfect opportunity to go. The king never even glanced my way. So, I did it. I spun and ran, dashing around trees. I would find a place to hide. Oh! At the top of a sturdy oak I could wait him out. Maybe he'd already forgotten I existed.

There! That one! The upper branches possessed enough foliage to cover me while notches in the trunk offered anchors for my hands and feet. Pumping my arms faster, I glanced over my shoulder. Sweet goldendoodle! No sign of Viktor. This was better than I'd hoped.

With the finesse of a child, I scaled the tree, yanking myself over different branches. My muscles strained and burned, and bark scraped my skin. A host of stinging cuts registered.

A twig snapped below as I hurled myself across an upper branch and laid as flat as possible while maintaining a firm grip on my anchor. Though I went still as a statue, my heart continued to pound.

Through the thick shield of dewy green leaves, I

THE STOLEN BRIDE

watched as three strangers entered the area. They varied in height, but each man bearing a similar muscle mass to my (former) captor. They'd also opted to forgo shirts, revealing tattooed torsos. Instead of leather pants, they sported loincloths. And, um, wow. Massive wings covered in black feathers tipped with gold arched over each of their shoulders.

I licked my lips. Those wings appeared rooted to their bodies by bony joints. And if berserkers were real, it made sense that turul-shifters were real, too.

Was I about to meet he who should not be mentioned? Viktor's loved-hated enemy, Mr. Deco himself.

The middle warrior sniffed the air and grinned, unveiling a mouthful of too long, too sharp teeth. He smoothed back the strands of his yellow hair, his eyes glinting with a thousand shades of red. "She's nearby, and she's been with Viktor." Like the very king he referenced, he spoke Hungarian.

So. They searched for me. Foreboding arched along my nerve endings, and there was no bottling it. I felt as if porcupine quills pressed beneath the surface of my skin, desperate to break free. Some innate instinct told me these guys weren't interested in having a productive conversation.

Maybe I should have stuck with Viktor.

"Is she his firebrand?" another asked. "Or does the honor belong to the other?"

The firebrand thing roused my interest, but the mention of "the other" piqued my curiosity. Did Viktor have a second prisoner tucked away somewhere? If so, that person might be my ticket home. The much-desired partner to help me navigate this treacherous land.

"Doesn't matter which is which, since they are both

31

ours," the blond replied, and the other two snickered. "Come out, come out, wherever you are, pretty girl," he called. "We're here to aid you. Save you from the big, bad feral."

Hardly! I sensed their malevolence on a cellular level.

I stiffened as a bead of sweat or blood trickled down my temple...my cheek...and hung from my jaw. A single thought consumed me. *Don't fall, don't fall.*

But it did fall, dripping to the ground.

In unison, the trio of warriors zoomed their gazes to my tree and grinned.

"Aw," my taunter sneered. The feathers in his wings rippled, the graceful motion filling me with unease. "Is it scared?"

I gnashed my back teeth. But, um, those wings were for sure real. Which meant the trio was indeed turul-shifters of legend.

"I suggest you move along," I snapped with all the vim and vigor I possessed. "King Viktor is on his way. Will catch up to us any moment."

"Even better." The blond wiggled claw-tipped hands. "Normally I'd fly up, but today I think I prefer a slower route to build anticipation." With a thump, thump, he embedded the nailtips in my tree's trunk and began to climb with fluid agility.

Oh, no, no, no. He would reach me in a matter of seconds. I scrambled upright, thinking about jumping. I could hit the ground and run. Probably break an ankle, too. Not a great plan, but currently my only option.

Wait. My ears twitched, snared by the sound of a familiar growl. Viktor! My onlookers must have heard him, too. Or felt the shocking waft of aggression blanketing the area because wow! Hostility electrified the air.

THE STOLEN BRIDE

The climber dropped, as the other shifters tensed and hissed. Heck, *I* tensed and hissed.

Whoosh! A blur whizzed into my periphery seconds before a powerful body slammed into the blond, tossing him a good distance. The shifter crashed into a tree with such force, the trunk split.

Viktor halted directly in front of the other two, and I gawked. He'd changed again, his bone structure sharper. Harsher. His irises glowed, filled with rings of glittering gold. Just as before, he'd almost doubled in size, and jagged black lines flashed beneath his skin.

He wasn't the only one who'd changed. The shifters sprouted feathers over their skin while their noses and mouths elongated, developing into beaks.

Their transformation seemed to delight Viktor. He didn't huff and puff, as if he'd lost control, but he did exude a savage bloodlust. "You think to touch what's mine," he oh, so calmly stated. Two voices poured from his mouth, one deep and husky, the other deeper and huskier.

I pressed my palms to my stomach. Was this a genuine berserkerage? It must be. Never, in all my days, had I encountered such an inhuman man. And the other guys were honest to goodness birdmen!

"Oh, I dare," the blond bragged as he clambered to his feet. "No mercy!"

The trio dove at Viktor in unison.

Ding, ding, ding. The fight was on. Viktor didn't budge from his spot. Just stood there and swung his arms with incredible speed, delivering one swish of his claws after another. Shifter parts flew, minus their bodies. Arms, throats. Organs. Blood sprayed and gushed as the leftovers plopped to the ground. No one got up. Or moved. Or breathed.

Bile singed my throat, my gaze jumping from macabre sight to macabre sight. The horror of it all. True death, nothing fabricated. Viktor still hadn't budged from his spot. Only difference was, wet crimson now coated his hands.

"I told you not to run, drágá." He didn't glance up at me. "Come down and face your consequences. Stay up and suffer more."

I chewed on suddenly dry lips. "You killed those men. Murdered them right in front of me."

"Ja, and they weren't even my first victims of the day. Come down."

This couldn't be a berserkerage. Not a full one, anyway. He remained aware and coherent, and I wasn't dead. Well, not yet. Even more startling, I wasn't afraid of him. Shocked and disgusted, yes. But not afraid.

Benjamin had nailed it. Something was wrong with my emotions.

As calm as Viktor was, I should go ahead and obey him. But I didn't want to.

When I retained my position in the branch for several seconds, he finally flipped his attention to me. Fury swirled inside irises the same green as the Hungarian forest. The gold rings no longer blazed, allowing me to appreciate the rest of his face. He was handsome. Annoyingly so.

"Come down," he demanded. "If not, I will fetch you."

"Fetch me then." If I was going to spend more time with him, and it looked like I was, I should make my boundaries known. "Until you tweak your attitude, I'm good here, thanks." To prove my words, I got more comfortable, dangling my legs over the branch. "Besides, you shouldn't punish me for guarding myself. That's what you'd want your loved ones to do, right?"

He huffed and puffed big-bad wolf style. But he didn't

THE STOLEN BRIDE

come get me, as threatened. He didn't even mention the fact that I wasn't among his loved ones. Instead, he wiped his hands on his pants as if he hadn't a care.

Hmm. Perhaps defiance was the right MO with him. "What's a firebrand?" Had to be a berserker thing, yet it was a term my mother had never used in her stories. And how had she known such tales to begin with? Had she believed I hailed from Malachi's lineage? Had *she* hailed from his lineage? Had my birth mother? Who raised my sister? If I really had a sister. What about my dreams? What if I'd truly glimpsed the future? This situation proved stranger things were possible. But *me*, bow to someone like this guy? No, thanks.

Not even a whisper rose from my captor.

Fine. We'd discuss something else. "You got any more of that goat cheese? I'd be willing to share it with you out of the goodness of my heart." Dude. No. I couldn't be hungry again after witnessing such a slaughter. But I was.

See! This was the reason I'd been so keen to identify my birth parents. To find out why I was the way I was. And now, Malachi dangled that most enticing carrot in front of my face. But no. Absolutely not. I wouldn't do anything to push a man into opening his life to evil. *That* was evil. Although, to be fair, Viktor might already qualify. Look at what he'd just done!

"Fetching time." Without any more warning than that, Viktor slammed his body into the tree trunk.

Boom! The entire structure shook. Retaining my perch proved impossible. I careened over the edge, falling and flailing.

"Oomph!" My lungs emptied upon impact. Took a second to regain my bearings, but when I did, realization dawned. I hadn't hit the ground; Viktor had caught me.

35

Now he held me clutched against his powerful chest, his grip intractable.

"Making me fall isn't exactly fetching," I grumbled, irritated by his strength. And *only* irritated. Not impressed. Not even a little.

"It accomplished the same goal, didn't it?" He strode forward, stepping on his victims, unconcerned by the disgusting squishing noises.

Well. As far as consequences went, these weren't too shabby, really. Irritation fading, I snuggled up against him, getting more comfortable.

"Yes," he suddenly snapped without provocation. "The only one capable of calming a sentinel from his rages. No."

Confusion set in, and my brow wrinkled. "Um. Okay. Is *this* my punishment? Random word bombs?" Because I wasn't opposed.

"With me, drágá, you will never have to wonder if you're being punished. You'll always know. You asked questions, I answered."

Well. I backtracked through my earlier words to him. "So a firebrand is like a soulmate." How intriguing and very romance novel-esque. But, uh, why did the shifters wonder if I was Viktor's?

No. No way. Nope. That particular query wasn't even worth considering. It was too far-fetched. Besides, the shifters had mentioned "the other," another candidate in the running for such an...illustrious title. The Valkara, I'd bet.

"A firebrand is more than a soulmate. She rouses the world's most powerful force in her sentinel."

Let me guess. "His immortal strength?"

"His unwavering, unbreakable, incorruptible love."

THE STOLEN BRIDE

Aaah. Only something I'd craved my entire life! Viktor must crave it too. I detected a note of longing in his voice.

Bit by bit, my ability to breathe returned. Not exactly a development in my favor. I inhaled the most intoxicating scent: pine needles from ancient woods interwoven with forest dew and dried honeysuckle. Mmm. Surely all that goodness didn't come from him.

Focus. "How do firebrandless berserkers stay calm?"

He glided his tongue over his teeth. "They consume an herb, and it keeps them cold."

Hello! Problem, meet solution. "You should do that."

"I'm too strong for it. Nothing works on me." He waggled his jaw. "However, since meeting you, I haven't neared a rage."

He *must* be kidding. "You seemed to be on the cusp multiple times. Although, yes, you're calm now." Maybe too calm. "What happened?" A roundabout way of asking if *he* believed me to be in the running for his firebrand.

"Everything and nothing." He'd used the same tone and volume earlier, while talking to himself.

Ugh. I bet he was about to launch into another tirade.

"Find, destroy, happy."

Yep. I did my best to lure him back into our conversation. "Where are we going?"

To my surprise, he responded in detail. "Many places. We'll start with my army's camp. There are certain supplies I seek to acquire."

Oookay. Talk about a supervillain tone laden with glee, mystery and suggestion. I opened my mouth to launch into a serious grilling, but he snapped, "Be quiet. The Valkara speaks again."

I waited, listening, but once more I heard nothing. "So, just to be clear, Valkara is the one—"

37

"*The* Valkara," he corrected, a clear warning.

"Right." I pinched the bridge of my nose. *Lord, help me.* "She's the one speaking inside your head, and you want to date her."

"She is perfection itself. Meant to be the bride of the primordial of primordials. *My* bride." He tilted up an ear and scowled. "Too muffled to understand."

His invisible, possibly nonexistent future bride. Got it. Batting my lashes at him, I said, "See Clover nod and smile as if the conversation isn't steeped in absurdity."

"You are certainly bold for someone awaiting punishment for disobeying a direct order from her king, running away without permission, and endangering herself."

Cold infiltrated my veins, an icy tide that raised my hackles. "I'm your *captive*, bud. Not an old friend or new crush or even a tolerated acquaintance. If anything, you should punish yourself for ever expecting me to obey your commands."

"But I won't," he said, almost pleasant now. "You alone will bear the brunt of my irritation."

Okay, that was my cue to stage another escape. This time, I wouldn't fail.

I geared up to slam an elbow into his nose, only to notice we approached a strange glittery wall of air. The corners of my mouth turned down. What the– Dizziness struck the moment Viktor sailed through it. A shock, yes, but the greater shock happened when my vision straightened out. How in the world...

A massive campground stretched before us, the air filled with sounds of clashing swords and pained grunts as hundreds of soldiers trained for battle. An equal number of tents dotted the forest floor. Some warriors competed in an open field, their shouts, calls and trash talk accompanying

THE STOLEN BRIDE

the rhythmic thud of booted feet hitting the ground as still others marched about. A handful of women in old-fashioned frocks performed the fine art of cooking. The scent of roasting meats mingled with smoky campfire, and my stomach rumbled. Nearby, a blacksmith hammered a sword.

As soon as people noticed Viktor and I, every man and woman in the area stopped what they were doing mid-motion. Bows and nods of greeting abounded, as did gaping. Didn't take long to feel as if the heat of a thousand suns spotlighted me.

A beautiful, bearded man with hair the color of a sandy beach and muscles galore rushed over. He said nothing as he kept pace at our side.

In my current position, I was eye level with his torso. What looked to be hundreds of different images covered his skin. From flowers to weapons to household items such as teacups and chairs.

"You're here," the newcomer said in Hungarian.

"Find, destroy, happy," the king muttered.

Groan. I craved information, and there was no way to get it if he kept getting lost in his head. On the other hand, he would never remember my punishment in this state.

But on the *other* other hand, he was currently my only ally amid a horde of what I assumed were immortal berserkers. Not that he was my ally. Still. He'd protected me once. Why not again?

In an effort to snap him out of it, I gently patted his stubbled cheek. "Hey. Snarls. I'd love an introduction to our newcomer."

"This is Prince Boldizsár. Or Bodi," he grumbled without dishing a rebuke for my forwardness. "Bodi, this is

39

my prisoner. Mine!" he added with gusto, squeezing me tight.

Don't roll your eyes again. "So you're brothers," I said. They didn't look alike, though they did possess a very similar eye color.

Viktor pursed his lips. "Princes are chosen for might, not blood."

Intriguing. A berserker fact my research hadn't revealed.

The newcomer missed his next step, his attention riveted on the motion of my hand–eek! I'd kept my palm pressed against Viktor's cheek, absentmindedly stroking the pads of my fingers over his beard stubble.

"You found a female in the forest, majesty?" The prince shook his head, as if he needed a reboot. "And you kept her alive?"

"I told you. She is my prisoner. My exclusive property. Anyone who dares to touch her will learn the true meaning of suffering."

Now that was a plan I could support. I smirked at Bodi. "Yeah. What he said."

The prince blinked with surprise. "I will ensure word spreads, majesty. But if I may be so bold, who is she? Other than your prisoner and exclusive property, of course."

Viktor's hold on me tightened once again. "The more time I spend with her, the more certain I am that she's the one I've been searching for."

4

When You're Just Not That Into Him: How to Say Goodbye and Survive

–HOW TO TRAIN YOUR BERSERKER
By Elizabeth "Elle" Darcy-Bruce

Viktor carried me through camp, his words rolling over in my mind. Me, supposedly the one he'd been "searching for." A wild statement that had come from out of nowhere, considering I wasn't his precious supposed firebrand, Valkara. There was no reason good enough for a berserker king to hunt for a once clueless human pet groomer.

But now I had to give more credence to Malachi's claims. Maybe I did come from a berserker family. Maybe the kings were caught in a generational feud, and Malachi hoped to use me to oversee Viktor's downfall. Now at least Viktor knew of the plan. Perhaps he intended to use me against Malachi. That wasn't just a thing that happened in books and movies, I'd bet.

Or perhaps he simply meant he'd put an ad in *The Immortal Times* for a maid or whatever. No matter his reasoning, this revelation gave me leverage.

Which I needed. Look at all these real life berserkers, with their sinewy muscles rippling and eyes gleaming with primal intensity. Tattoos inked skin of every shade in a plethora of shocking places. I knew this because some males fought naked. All embodied untamed power.

I admit, I grinned at the sight. Basically, I was living a dream come true right now. If not for Malachi's mission and Viktor's, well, everything, I might've asked to vacation here. Except, my business. My bills and obligations. I sighed, my shoulders rolling in. Real life called, and I needed to answer.

Two guards stood in front of the largest tent. Viktor approached, and the pair stepped apart, separating the cloth that hung over the entrance. He soared inside without pause.

Oh, wow. A tapestry depicting an epic battle dominated an entire wall, the needlework so fine I almost smelled the metallic tang of blood and felt the fury of the warriors. A large, weathered wooden desk occupied the center of the space, the surface cluttered with maps and scrolls. The bed was surprisingly luxurious, with overstuffed pillows and genuine furs. Two curtains blocked off an area in the corner. A makeshift bathroom, I hoped.

A step up from the "shelter" in the forest.

Without warning, the king tossed me on the bed. I scowled and sprang to my feet. "Okay, we need to have a serious chat about your manhandling."

THE STOLEN BRIDE

Prince Bodi followed us inside. He stopped at the door, still glancing between us.

"I'm Clover, by the way," I told him. "Clover Deering. Freshly kidnapped and eager to return home."

"How did you and Vik—"

"Report," Viktor snapped, cutting the poor guy off while striding to the desk and riffling through the papers.

The prince shook his head, doing the brain reboot thing again. "The turul-shifters have breached our parameters."

"I know. I killed three of them after I acquired my excess baggage." He pushed the papers aside, not caring when they floated to the floor. "Where's my key?"

I was the excess baggage, wasn't I?

Bodi cringed, radiating guilt and shame. "I'll help you search. I'm sure we'll find it." With barely a pause, he added, "Commander Tibor and his team had eyes on Deco, but he—"

"Deco is here?" Viktor forgot his precious key and strode to his comrade to grip his shoulders and shake. "Tell me!"

"Better be careful," I piped up. "Any mention of Deco can end with the loss of your head. Or so I've been told."

Viktor tossed me a menacing scowl. "Do not insert yourself into a private conversation."

"Sure thing." I held up my hands, all innocence. "For future reference, it's not exactly private when you're standing in front of me."

He didn't seem to register my point as he refocused on the prince. "Respond to my words."

"He is here, ja. Or he was," Bodi corrected. "He vanished inside the stones four hours ago."

Oooh. The stones. What were they, and how did someone disappear inside them? And yes, I listened while feigning disinterest, acting absorbed in the task of giving myself a tour. But if this Deco character had escaped into those stones, I could too.

"For Deco to make it to the stones, I can only conclude I have a traitor in my midst," Viktor grated, easing into a swift back-and-forth pace. "The shifter king must suspect I'm close to finding the key. He seeks to hinder me."

I flittered here and there, picking up items. A Viking helmet with runic engravings. Bundles of dried herbs resting atop a metal first-aid kit. A ceremonial drinking horn beside another bottle of Brennivin. No, thank you. Various musical instruments scattered across the floor, even a Stradivarius. Oh, wow. That was a cool million dollars just sitting there. And hello, my beauties. There was a pile of daggers for anyone to pocket.

Don't mind if I do. I plucked two of the smaller blades free of the cluster and shoved one in each pocket of my shorts.

"What's so special about the key?" I asked my companions, all no *big deal, I don't care one way or the other*. Meanwhile, desperation frothed inside me. Must know! If I could find the key in this mess, I'd have a priceless bargaining chip.

Both men ignored me. "We captured six of his spies," Bodi said. "They're being questioned now. If any are working with our soldiers, we'll know it soon."

Viktor growled, "Not good enough. I can trust no one at such a critical time, not even you. I demand you execute yourself, then everyone else. Leave no survivors." Eyes glazing over, he returned to the desk. "Oh, and when you finish with that, bring the bracelets for my guest. She's earned a prize."

I mean, I wouldn't say no to jewelry. Also, did Viktor have any idea how thoroughly he'd contradicted himself?

THE STOLEN BRIDE

Bodi gave no reaction to the command to off himself. He simply inclined his chin in agreement. "I will see everything done personally, majesty, almost exactly as you desire."

Okay, this was officially weird. "At the risk of inciting further punishment, I'm going to insert myself again. You realize you just told him to kill himself, then kill everyone else after he's dead, right?"

They looked at me as if *I* was the oddity.

Only Viktor responded. "I don't hear the problem. I don't see my key, either." With a noise of frustration, he swiped his arm over the desk, sending everything hurling to the floor. An inkwell shattered, black dye soaking into the dirt. "Where is it?" he roared. "I must have it. The Valkara demands it. The time is now."

Bodi flinched, rubbing the spot directly over his heart as I asked, "You always obey her?"

"Always," Viktor said with something akin to pride. In unison, Bodi muttered the same word with derision.

Did the king love her and the price despise her?

"Majesty," the prince piped up, strained. "Perhaps now is the proper moment to remind you that the key disappeared centuries ago."

Sounded like they'd had this conversation before.

Mumbling under his breath, Viktor stormed out of the tent, leaving me alone with the prince.

I hoped Bodi would follow him, allowing me to do a little more snooping before hitting the bricks. Alas. The prince remained, glaring at me.

Since I was stuck, I might as well take advantage of the situation and try to learn as much as possible. If I needed to strike, I would. Pasting on my brightest smile, I shoved my hands into my pockets and gripped the hilts of my daggers.

45

"So. Do you recall that time your king called me his exclusive property and threatened to hurt anyone who hurt me? Because I do." Man, I hated stringing all those words together, and yet, they didn't taste as foul as they should have.

"Who are you?" he demanded.

"I told you. I'm Clover. Clover Deering. Unwitting and protected prisoner of your king."

"Judging by your accent, you're American, which means you fall under Malachi's domain." He'd spoken in heavily accented English. Now he took a step forward, radiating menace. "Why is an American in our territory? What's your purpose?"

No way I'd share any of those details with him. "Sorry, but that information is above your security clearance."

"I will give you sixty seconds to convince me not to kill you." He palmed the swords crisscrossed over his back. "Does that increase my clearance?"

"You berserkers and your timers." His boiling hostility threw me. What was it about my presence that worried him so much? "Don't you have some executions to oversee?"

The reminder only poured fuel on his anger. "When Viktor battles his beast, he cannot make sense of his thoughts. Unless he sees you again, I doubt he'll remember you exist. That means I can do whatever I want to you, and he'll never know."

"So much for a soldier's loyalty." Well, looked like I'd be fighting my way out.

Inside, I dug for a bottle of rage. Heat pooled in my hands. I curled them into fists and got into punching position. An urge to strike now, now, now, bombarded me.

Whoa! I hadn't experienced this sensation in years, though I'd never forgotten the last time. The day I'd hurt my mom, breaking her arm. She'd bid me to clean up my room, but I'd refused, wanting only to play with a meaningless toy instead. When she'd attempted to take it away, I'd erupted.

I didn't recall what happened after that. I only remembered waking to find my mother crying and in pain, with cuts on her face and one hand hanging at an odd angle. It was then that I'd begun to obsess about berserkers, and even adapted their methods for calming. Deep breathing exercises. Physical exertion to the point of exhaustion. Compartmentalizing.

Eventually, I bottled and buried my emotions instinctively, without thought. Now, I wasn't sure how to react to these urges and feeling. I didn't like them, but I also liked them far too much. I needed to protect myself.

"I am loyal *only* to my king," Bodi spat, *not* attacking me. "He's the sole original in power, his life the most important in this world or any other. Twenty-seven. Twenty-six. Twenty-five."

I kept my dukes up. "Make a move, I dare you."

Gold rings flashed in his irises. He stepped toward me, and I drew back my elbow. I'd go hard and fast. Hopefully, I wouldn't lose my awareness in the process.

Bodi surprised me, abandoning the strike zone before I swung. "Perhaps I'll remind him of your presence after all. If you aren't his firebrand, he'll end you on his own."

"Apparently the firebrand honor goes to Valkara. Excuse me, *the* Valkara."

A muscle jumped in his jaw.

Oooh. I'd noticed his dislike of her before, and this was confirmation. He wasn't Valkara's biggest fan. "I'd love to meet her. Just point me in her direction, and I'll go say hi," I said.

A commotion erupted outside the tent. Shouts for help. Grunts of pain. Rushing, thumping footsteps. The prince and I paused, momentarily frozen.

"Get Bodi!" someone bellowed.

He held my gaze, unfazed. "If you leave this tent, Clover Deering, I will come for you, and you won't enjoy what happens when I catch you."

I snapped my teeth at him. "Like I haven't heard that one before."

He hesitated only a moment more before pursing his lips and hurrying off, leaving me alone.

Okay. All right. A relieved breath seeped from me, and I finally relaxed my stance. Well, as relaxed as a woman like me could get. Obviously, I wasn't letting either man's promise of retribution dictate my actions.

Problem: I now knew more of those turul-shifters occupied the forest. Should I really take off and risk another run-in?

Might be better to wait, just a bit, amass supplies and weapons, and find a map of the forest. And shoes!

Also, what about Malachi's offer? I still had no plans to cash in, but did I really wish to cut ties with the target right now? Although, granted, said target wasn't exactly sane. Viktor flowed in and out of coherency, was execution-happy, and produced more mysteries than Hallmark.

The outside commotion increased in volume, certain Hungarian phrases crystalizing. "No, Majesty." "Please, no." "Don't do this!"

What in the world? My injured, throbbing feet carried me out of the tent before my brain registered my intention. No guards stood at the door, so no one tried to capture me. Fading sunlight spotlighted soldiers congregated around an enraged Viktor, who tossed or broke anyone he could reach.

He reached far too many. They toppled one after the other, broken and bleeding, unable to contain him, even as they worked in tandem.

The sight of him stopped me in my tracks, my heart thudding against my ribs. I'd thought him in a berserkerage before, but no. He'd told me he hadn't yet raged and here, now I believed him.

This was a berserkerage.

He wasn't just bigger; he was monstrous. His eyes were filled with those glowing golden rings, no hint of green remaining. His irises radiated deep cesspools of rage, yes, but mostly hatred. Thin black lines didn't fork or flash beneath his skin, as before, but pooled and layered, resembling feathers. Like the turul-shifters, he brandished long, sharp claws.

Bodi stood out of striking distance, doing his best to calm the king with words. "Let's talk about this, Majesty. I will make it better, whatever it is. Just tell me. That's all you need to do."

Viktor paused and sniffed the air. His attention swung to me and stuck.

The force of his notice sent me stumbling back, as if I'd been kicked. Guess I had a flight response, after all. I should run now. Yes, yes, I should.

Bodi spotted me, too. Anger pulsated from him, and he bellowed in Hungarian, "Leave, female!"

My cue. I spun on my heel and sprinted off. A vicious roar rang out behind me, sending chills down my spine. Fresh grunts of pain followed me, creating a terrible chorus. I picked up the pace, flying through the camp, scanning, scanning, searching for the wisest direction. Right. Definitely right. My breath quickened.

"Nooo!" I screamed when brawny arms clamped

around me. With every ounce of my strength, I fought for my freedom.

A huffing, puffing Viktor hauled me against his powerful body and held tight, but...hmm. He never harmed me. In fact, he didn't even prick me with the tips of his claws.

"Enough, drága."

His delicious scent filled my nose, and I...settled. The danger must have passed. "We all good, Tor?"

"I told you not to run," he rasped between ragged breaths. Once again, he spoke with two voices. His own, and that of his beast?

"Yes, well, I'm not exactly keen to stick around when you're shredding your own men like cheddar cheese."

"Don't be dramatic." The second voice faded. "I only removed a few organs."

Soldiers slowly, cautiously approached us. Well, almost. They halted a good distance away, out of the strike zone. Many wobbled, injured and bleeding. All peered at me in shock. Murmurs of "firebrand" arose.

Not this again! I wasn't Viktor's soulmate, okay. Nope. Not this steel magnolia. Maddened had never been my type. And as he'd babbled earlier, I wasn't his type, either. On top of all that, let's not forget the Valkara, the real firebrand. But...

Viktor's reaction to me. It did explain why Malachi would pick someone as normal as me for such a special, suicidal mission. Though how could he have known I might be in the running for firebrand of the year?

"Put me down," I insisted, wiggling against Viktor.

A ragged moan left him, and I stilled. Either he was injured, and I just couldn't see the damage, or I'd hurt him

THE STOLEN BRIDE

in some way. I didn't like the guy, but I didn't want him to suffer.

"Will you run again?" he demanded.

"Probably. But not right this second or anything." Maybe not the best response, but honest. "I give you my word."

He stiffened. "There's nowhere you can go that I won't find you."

"Just FYI, you aren't helping your cause when you get all supervillainy." Not much, anyway. Because yes, a part of me might kind of...like it. But only a part! The worst part, clearly.

"Majesty." Bodi bypassed those around us, his palms up and out in a gesture of innocence as he neared. "Perhaps you should place the girl under my protection. I'll take excellent care of her, I swear it."

I didn't get a chance to shout, "Liar!"

"Mine," the king snarled, nearly cracking my ribs as he yanked me closer. His nostrils flared, and he bared his teeth at the other royal.

Okay, so, maybe I was his type? I mean, I wasn't unattractive, if I did say so myself. And I happened to dig my personality. Animal lover and violin enthusiast, with an indomitable spirit and an unwillingness to give up when things got tough. Talk about rare qualities!

But what if I *was* Viktor's firebrand, and not the Valkara? Look how calm he'd become. And he'd only dialed up the protection factor.

I mean, it wouldn't hurt to at least test the theory.

"Majesty," Bodi said, gearing up to try again.

"Stay back, prince, I've got this," I announced, then I did it. I made a move, patting Viktor's cheek. "Focus on me, Snarls. Come on. Look at me."

51

He resisted my command, his chest heaving, and I wondered if he was close to losing his temper again. Well, I was already in the fire. I might as well dance.

"Hey! I told you to focus on me, and I meant it." I snapped my fingers in front of his face until his dark gaze found mine at last.

"What?" he barked.

Are you kidding me? "Wow. I try to help, and this is the thanks I get."

His lids slitted. From the corner of my eye, I detected movement. Suspected Bodi and a few others were slipping closer. I stretched out my arm, fingers spread in the classic sign for *stop*. All the while, I held Viktor's gaze.

"Look," I said. "How about we cancel all punishments and return to your place? I'm starving, and I've got some questions only you can answer." I batted my lashes, giving him my best puppy dog eyes. "Take care of me? Please, with a cherry on top."

Silence. Stillness. One moment bled into another, the crowd so quiet everyone might have been holding their breath.

Finally, Viktor scowled and nodded. "We'll be in my tent. Bring us food, and a lot of it," he bellowed, and carried me over the threshold.

See Beyond What You See: When Your Berserker Does Tricks, Dish Treats

–HOW TO TRAIN YOUR BERSERKER
By Elizabeth "Elle" Darcy-Bruce

Viktor dumped me on the pallet of furs for the second time that day and paced. Back and forth, back and forth, agitated but no longer verging on violence or muttering. Rather, he remained silent, which wasn't much better.

At least his size returned to "normal."

As I watched him and waited for the food to arrive, my eyelids grew heavy. Guess the emotional highs and lows, unmitigated stress, constant stream of uncertainty, and mystery drugs had caught up with me.

I fought the fatigue with every fiber of my being, refusing to fall asleep in Viktor's presence. Although, if I *was* his firebrand, I was probably safer with him than anyone else in the world. According to everything I'd read in my studies, berserkers protected what they considered theirs. Proof: look how fervently King Tor had warned his own second-in-command to keep his hands off the royal prisoner. Also, notice how quickly Viktor had ceased raging when I showed up on the scene.

Maybe Prince Bodi wouldn't be so swift to threaten me now. For the time being, I had a bit of power and influence over his sovereign. Except. The Valkara. She threw a wrench in my assurance.

But. Ugh. There was also my reoccurring dream to consider. How I could've seen into the future, I didn't know. If I was, in fact, Viktor's firebrand, he might, just might, be the warrior I pledged to serve. But seriously, me, kneel before him? I still wasn't a fan of the idea. And I didn't even know what "the greater good" was. I did know it wasn't a double chili cheeseburger with a mix of onion rings and french fries, ranch dip on the side.

Dang it, where was the food? My body was probably already eating itself!

I needed a distraction. Again and again, my attention returned to the pile of instruments. My fingers itched to play. Finally I succumbed to temptation, clambered to my feet, and walked to the prized violin. Intricately carved swirls decorated the upper and lower boot.

As gently as possible, I seized the instrument by the neck and body, then got comfortable on the chair at Viktor's desk to test the strings. *Nice*. Perfectly tuned.

After rosining the bow, I gave an experimental stroke. My lips parted as the rich, warm tone of the Stradivarius filled the tent. Never, in all my days, had I heard anything as exquisite or powerful.

Closing my eyes, I played a series of layered notes,

THE STOLEN BRIDE

thrilling at the harmonies. Satisfied with what I heard, I focused on the still pacing Viktor, curious to learn his reaction as I brought to life the serene melody of Bach's *Air on the G String*. Would he calm as I often did?

He ground to an abrupt halt, and at first, he only gave me more scowl. But bit by bit, his expression and posture softened. Ultimately, his lids hooded, giving his entire face a seductive quality. He prowled closer to lean against the edge of the desk and savor the music.

Emboldened, I played and played and played until my body ached. Just in time to notice the sun was finishing its descent, the light in the tent dimming. When the last note faded, I breathed deep and set the instrument aside.

Viktor immediately kicked into a new pace. "Never play again," he growled. "Tell me you understand and you will obey this order."

What? "Why?"

"Because I said so." Another growl.

"Why?" I demanded, unfazed.

He rubbed the center of his chest, remaining silent.

Fine. The reason didn't matter. Better to concentrate on a subject that *did* matter to my continued wellbeing. Something to help me decide my next move. "Be honest. Do you believe I'm your firebrand, yes or no?"

With his back to me, he went still. The muscles between his shoulders bunched, and his hands curled into tight fists. "You shouldn't ask such a ridiculous question. The answer is nem. Absolutely not." He responded in heavily accented English, and I realized I'd asked in my native tongue. "There's no chance. None. Not even the slightest possibility. If ever I'm tied to another, it will be the Valkara." Tension blasted from him, and he snapped, "But maybe."

Aaah! He'd all but admitted it. A part of this slightly

55

insane royal berserker who'd maimed members of his own army for a completely irrelevant motive–just a guess on my end–believed I could be his soulmate. His fated companion. The one he was destined to love, the most powerful force on earth.

I might be the only person in any world with an innate ability to calm him.

Of course, in no way, shape or form did I reciprocate. King Viktor Endris might see me as a possible soulmate, but I didn't view him in the same vein. I believed in the power and necessity of love, yes. And I concurred with his assessment that it was a force unlike any other. Powerful yet sweet. Healing. But I wanted what my parents enjoyed.

They had loved each other without reservation, building each other up, never tearing down. And, as Benjamin had taught me, gifting your affections to the wrong person brought only pain. You gave, they took. You encouraged, they destroyed. Been there, done that. Never again.

The entrance whisked aside, and Bodi strode into the tent. A pair of metal shackles rested in his hands. "I apologize for the delay, Majesty. We doctored the cook and his crew, and they are back in action, preparing the requested feast. I've also found the Bracelets."

You're kidding me. I popped to my feet and shook my head, locks of hair slapping my cheeks. "Hear me now, Viktor. All bets are off if you try to bind me."

"Majesty?" the prince insisted.

Viktor adopted a crouching position, as if he planned to leap onto his soldier and rip off the man's head with his bare hands. Snarls rumbled in his chest, and claws grew from his finger tips. "You heard her. She refuses. Toss the Bracelets."

THE STOLEN BRIDE

Oh, yeah. I was his firebrand all right, on a ring of higher importance than the Valkara, who wasn't. A full-wattage smile bloomed. Smirking, I told Bodi, "Be a good boy and obey your king." For good measure, I flipped my braid over my shoulder. Bravado was a language this man understood. "In case I wasn't clear, take the handcuffs and go."

The prince glanced between us before offering a stiff nod and striding out.

That worked? I mean, sweet! That totally worked.

In an instant, Viktor calmed again. Seeming to forget the entire incident, he kicked into another pace.

What an interesting day this had turned out to be.

Little time passed before the entrance was moved aside once more. I braced for Bodi's return. Instead, a young soldier carried in a tray of food. Finally! From the looks of it, I'd be dining on hearty stew and crusty bread. A meal I didn't have to peel, cut or cook. Bowls I didn't have to wash, dry and put away. Yes, please and thank you.

The perks of being the berserker king's firebrand were kind of fantastic.

The soldier never glanced in his king's or my direction. Just placed the tray on the desk and rushed out.

"You gonna eat?" I asked Viktor.

He muttered a refusal.

His loss. I ate my fill, meaning all of it, doing my best to display a modicum of manners and not shovel in every bite. My companion provided the evening entertainment as he continued to pace, flexing different muscles. What a strange, complicated man.

When I swallowed the last sip of broth, a yawn cracked my jaw, fatigue sneaking up on me once again. I scanned the pallet of furs. Would stretching out in Viktor's presence really be such a bad thing?

Brushing any remaining breadcrumbs from my hands, I returned to the bed. I stretched out, careful not to poke myself with the daggers hidden in my pockets.

Viktor stopped pacing and focused all his intensity on me. Or through me.

"My firebrand," he muttered. "Beautiful. Trouble."

Right back at you, bud. The 'trouble' part, I meant. And yeah, okay, the beautiful part, too. His features were way too harsh when examined one by one, but all together, they dazzled. And those muscles...

Anyway. With a little finesse, I bet I could convince him to return me to Aurelian Hills and force Malachi to share what he knew about my birth parents. If I could make the other king rue the day he'd kidnapped me, even better.

After a while, my lids drifted close, and I didn't resist. I wouldn't let myself fall asleep, becoming vulnerable. Rather, I'd use the time to recharge, so I'd better deal with Viktor. A quick mental and emotional reset...

I DREAMED THE DREAM.

A thick fog enveloped the night sky. Despite the haze, I had no problem detecting the stars. Perhaps because I floated in the ether without an anchor, yet somehow I also stood on solid ground. The hem of my wispy white gown billowed at my ankles.

Before me towered a shirtless warrior sculpted with a wealth of hard-cut muscle. For the first time, I saw his face, and my entire body reacted as if I'd stuck my finger into an electrical outlet. Nerve endings sang.

Viktor Endris.

He said nothing, but then, no words were needed. I knew in the depths of my being. For the greater good, I must place my life in his hands.

Some of the fog around us thinned, and I spotted the weapon he clutched. A long double-edged sword he kept pointed down.

A question drifted through my mind. *Am I willing to die to save him, our loved ones and even our worlds?*

Dream me rasped, "For the greater good, I will do this," and sank to her knees.

Another first: I saw what happened next.

Dream Viktor jutted his stubborn chin and repeated my words. "For the greater good, I will do this."

He raised the sword high in the air, as if he intended to–

Swing.

I awoke with a gasp. My heart pounded at warp speed. I was panting, breath sawing between my lips. Sensing a presence, I jolted upright.

Viktor sat on a trunk pulled next to the bed, twirling two daggers in his hands. Bright morning sunlight filtered through holes and seams in the tent.

I'd slept all night while a berserker played with his weapons a few feet away? Yikes.

The vestiges of the dream faded to mist, to be dissected later. Right now, the king glared bloody murder at me. I poured through my options: run, run fast or run faster.

"Don't," he barked, predicting my decision to go with option three. He set the weapons aside, rested his elbows on his knees, and linked his fingers.

Okay. All right. Without the blades, I didn't mind

staying put and looking him over. He'd bathed, his hair damp and his clothes clean. Today, he wore a plain black T-shirt that covered his wealth of tattooed strength. His eyes possessed no glaze or gold, and his glare became a soft stare.

Unfortunately, the lack of aggression caused me to notice details I'd previously missed. Like how long and thick his lashes were. The perfect frame for those wild green irises. His aquiline nose complimented his stubborn jaw. And his lips. Wow. They couldn't be as luscious as they appeared. Nothing could.

My skin flushed. He was something far better than beautiful right now. He was crazy sexy hot. "Good, um, morning."

Silent, he held my gaze, daring me to look elsewhere.

Trembling a little, I smoothed locks of hair from my face and realized I still wore my tank and shorts. But dang it, the daggers I'd stolen were missing. Well, not missing, per se. He'd been twirling them a moment ago. I recognized the carvings on the handles.

Irritation bloomed. "Are you just gonna ogle me or is there something you'd like to say?"

"After a night spent in contemplation, I have concluded you are not my firebrand," he stated simply.

I almost snorted. "Okay, sugar pop. Whatever you need to tell yourself." Mental gymnastics couldn't hide the truth for long. "What's for breakfast?"

He snapped his teeth at me. "I cannot deny your presence comes with certain...benefits."

"Yeah, you've already mentioned the fog and the whispers, neither of which I understand." But. Hmm. My dream. In it, I always dealt with a fog, too. Could our experiences be connected? "But don't forget, I've seen what happens

THE STOLEN BRIDE

when you're trantruming and I approach. I'm one hundred percent your firebrand."

Shock of shocks, he let the taunt slide. "A thick, agitating fog has enveloped my mind for centuries. Some days it's thicker than others. A necessary evil. Through it, the Valkara helps me see what I need to see. Our relationship. The future." He paused. "The end. Does that ease your confusion?"

"Yes, thank you." Finally! Information for the taking. "I'd argue that there's no such thing as a necessary evil, but that's a conversation for later." As for his relationship, it was clear the Valkara intended to wed him, his firebrand or not. I figured the primordial of primordials was the strongest original, aka Vik, the last of them. Of course she wanted him.

So. If he wanted her too, as he claimed, why hadn't he pulled the trigger already? "To me, you don't exactly look helped by the fog," I pointed out.

He inhaled with authority. "Enough about her."

"No, not enough. As your definite firebrand, I demand answers."

"Very well," he replied without missing a beat. "I'll answer your questions, but in return, you will answer mine."

I noted the satisfaction in his voice and realized he'd herded me precisely where he'd wanted me. "Fine. Agreed." It wasn't like I hadn't already told him all kinds of things, free of charge. "Who is the Valkara that she gets to wed the primordial of primordials?"

A muscle jumped in his jaw. "The guardian of Starfire."

Oooh. "The glowing stone that crash-landed on Earth has a living, breathing otherworldly protector? I should have guessed."

"Starfire wasn't a stone but a collection of eggs encased inside a hard outer shell for travel through the galaxies. In blood and pain, those eggs were fertilized and birthed within us that day on the battlefield."

That made an awful, terrible sense. "So the Valkara is *your* protector, too." A woman who wielded more power over him than I'd realized.

Clipped nod. "Ja." Frown. "Nem. I am *her* protector." He thought for a moment, his frown deepening. "It's complicated."

Exactly what Ben had said about Kami. "What has Val– *the* Valkara told you about the future?"

He pursed his lips. "She has said there are certain things we must do for the greater good."

Oh, yeah. There *must* be a connection between our fogs. No reason to mention it, though, and every reason not to. "I'd love to learn more about that."

"It revolves around protecting our species, our homeland, and subduing the beasts within us."

Admirable goals, honestly. "Does she say, I don't know, just spit-balling here, something like find, destroy, happy?" I took a stab at decoding his meaning. "Find the key, destroy the shifters, and be happy."

His stiff demeanor responded for him, telling me the topic had reached a dead end. But I couldn't gauge whether I'd gotten it right or missed by miles.

I veered, attempting a smooth detour. "Do you trust the Valkara?" She had access to him in ways no one else did.

Silence stretched between us, a clear sign he was done with that line of questioning.

Very well. We'd go with a *new* new direction. "Mind telling me what set you off yesterday?"

A flash of glowing gold in his eyes. "The captured turul-shifters relayed a message from their leader. Deco vowed to take possession of my most valued treasure."

"Meaning me," I said, pressing my fingertips into my sternum. Okay, I got that I was his firebrand and all, but to be touted as his most valued treasure so soon after we'd met—

"Meaning the key," he stated.

Right. Of course. That wasn't upsetting at all. "Not to remind you of a sore spot, but, um, didn't you lose it?"

"Nem. *I* did not." Bitterness drenched his words.

So he didn't, but someone else did. "What's so special about this key?"

"What comes with it," he replied.

More seconds ticked by as I waited for him to elaborate. Or finally ask a question of his own. Silence, only silence.

"We'd both have a much better conversational experience if you provided details in bulk," I said, tossing my arms up. "What comes with the key?"

"Your questioning is done." He stood, the trunk sliding behind him, the daggers falling to the floor. Unconcerned, he rolled his shoulders. "Eat your breakfast, use the facilities." He motioned to the curtained off area. "In the coming days, you will answer ten of my questions."

The exact number of questions he'd answered for me.

He exited the tent. Left to my own devices, I took care of first things first, collecting my daggers, then wolfing down the meal waiting on the desk. A veritable feast of eggs, fruits, juices, lángos and pogácsa. Delicious, but still not satisfying. A third and fourth helping wouldn't have been amiss.

When not even crumbs remained, I checked out the curtained off area, pausing to admire the small, pearl-size stones sewn into the fabric. Sweeping past it, I entered what I believed to be the makeshift bathroom. Except, oh wow. How was this possible? My jaw dropped as I spun. An actual bathroom. Look at all this goodness. Walls covered in mother-of-pearl. A gold toilet. A marble floor with veins of gold. A massive shower stall with Swarovski crystal handles. A mirror surrounded with flowers made from rubies, black diamonds and emeralds. A gold-rimmed sink. Toiletries for every need lined shelves. There was also a stack of folded clothes. A pair of combat boots and ballet flats were tucked beneath the bottom rack, both in my size.

But where was the curtain? The *tent*? There was only a closed wooden door framed by more of those pearl-size stones leading to a mystery location. Hand trembling, I twisted the knob. Hinges creaked, the entrance opening up to—hmm. Back in the tent, the curtain behind me. How was this even possible?

I slunk backward, shutting the door and sealing myself inside the luxurious bathroom. My gaze zeroed in on the rain shower, and I whimpered with longing. A steamy soak sounded as close to heaven on earth as I could get at this point. But there was no way I'd risk Viktor walking in on me.

No, you know what? I refused to bypass this opportunity. Who knew when I'd get another chance? I'd only been here a day, but I was filthy.

As fast as possible, I stripped, washed up under the perfect rainfall of hot water, then dried off with a fluffy towel that remained warm. Zero savoring occurred but hey, no one had interrupted me, and I now smelled of honey and lavender, so I called it a win.

After brushing my teeth, I shimmied into the clean clothes. Perfectly made undergarments the color of a blush, and a delightful knee-length dress in muted gold, with delicate embroidery of bold red and yellow flowers adorning the neckline and hem. Somehow, the garments fit me like a hand-tailored glove.

I also donned a pair of matching leggings. Though the outfit demanded I choose the lace-up ballet flats, I went for the boots after pulling on a pair of socks. Wince. The fabric was soft, but my cuts and bruises protested the contact. I, however, required the warmth. Designer shoes would have to wait for another day.

I retrieved my daggers and hustled into the tent to await Viktor. I expected him to sweep inside with dramatic flare, but one minute passed... ten...fifteen. Noises indicating heavy activity filtered into the tent. Still no Viktor.

I paced and waited. And waited. A soldier arrived with a fresh pot of stew. He didn't look at me or speak, just placed the food on the desk and exited. I was miffed enough to eat every drop, saving none for Viktor.

At dinner time, a different soldier did the same, bringing in a second pot. Again, I ate every drop. When darkness descended, I started pacing again. Still no sign of Viktor. Had he forgotten me?

I should run again, just for the heck of it. But that would be foolhardy. And I was tired. A nap would do me some good. Strengthen me up. Clear my thoughts.

Mumbling under my breath about feral berserkers, I stretched out on the pallet. Sleep didn't come easily, despite my fatigue, but it did come.

Bright and early the next morning, I woke up alone, ready to conquer the day, even willing to bargain about going home for an hour simply to pay my bills. Maybe there was another magical doorway? Except, the day bled into another and another, a pattern emerging.

As a mental clock ticked, I worried about my home and

business, and the animals missing very necessary grooming appointments. I was fed three (inadequate) meals a day, ensuring I couldn't save any nibbles for travel, and left alone until Viktor stomped into the tent to demand I play a song on the violin. He listened from beginning to end, seeming to relish every note. Then he would remind me that he'd ordered me to never play again and storm out. This occurred once every twenty-four hours—at first. By day three, it happened twice. Day four, five times. I tried to converse with him about that trip home, as well as Malachi and the Valkara, but he ignored me, interested only in the music.

At night Viktor might–might!–have snuggled me. I couldn't be sure. He was never nearby when I woke, but the spot beside me was always warm when I woke. As soon as I figured out how I felt about that, I'd ask him.

By the two-week mark, I simmered with frustration I struggled to bottle, my nerves frayed. How many customers had I lost? Had I received a past due notice for my house? Yes, I was given a clean dress and leggings every day. Still fed and watered. But I wasn't allowed to explore. Guards surrounded the tent at all times.

Something had to give. I had a pile of weapons hidden under the bed, but little else to show for my stay. What did Viktor do while I worried about my business and suffered from boredom in this tent anyway? And okay, maybe I wasn't terribly bored. Or bored at all. He dropped off a box filled with romance novels set in my hometown, featuring a quirky cemetery owner and super sexy special agent, plus a series about berserkers. I gobbled them up as if I was dying of starvation.

Still. It was time I did something. Pushed past the point of tolerance, I stomped outside, ready to tell the guards

THE STOLEN BRIDE

where they could go. I drew to a halt instead. They were gone. Everyone was.

I'd been deserted?

Oh! In the distance, a blood splattered Prince Bodi strode around a corner, shouting orders to the men who followed him. "Elek, ready the horses. Laszlo, find my–" He spotted me and missed a step. Confusion twisted his features. Anger and determination followed, hardening his expression.

Dread prickled my nape. Uh-oh. Had Viktor experienced another berserkerage? "Where is he?"

"Did you teleport?" Bodi demanded, aiming for me. "Is that how you escaped Deco?"

"Excuse me? I didn't need to escape him because I've never even met the guy." And teleport? Me?

The prince scowled. "This isn't the time for lies. Come with me before it's too late." Wasting not a second, he snagged me by the wrist and dragged me through camp. Warriors jumped out of our way.

A range of emotions bubbled up, fury burning hotter than them all, a build up from the past two weeks. Heat built in my chest, spreading down my arms.

Inhale. Exhale. Ugh! My usual breathing exercises didn't help.

Maybe if I confronted the newest problem directly. "The manhandling is unnecessary, Bodi. I've been a good little prisoner for two weeks! I'm sure Viktor will have something to say about this. He's grown quite fond of me, I'm certain of it."

"If it means he calms, I welcome a rebuke."

So he *had* erupted again. Great. Just great.

Despite my fury with the prince, I didn't fight him for two reasons. One, I figured he was escorting me straight to

67

Viktor in order to smooth things out. And two, I was curious to know what this had to do with his former friend, Deco.

We wove through multiple tents and many clusters of weapon-wielding warriors preparing for some sort of battle. No one but me seemed to notice the scent of coffee in the air. My mouth watered.

"I could really use a cup of joe before our morning cool down with the big guy," I said as sweetly as I could muster. Which was the angriest I'd spoken to another person in years. But come on! I'd bottled up so much lately, I might explode at any moment.

"You are the strangest creature," Bodi muttered.

By the time we entered a mud hut at the far edge of the campsite, I had calmed enough that I didn't want to drive my fists into his chest cavity. Progress mattered.

Going from sunlight to firelight, I needed a moment to adjust. At the same time, the heat inside me cooled as if it had never been. Which I didn't understand.

When I spotted Viktor, I forgot everything else. He stood in back, panting hard, glaring down at the ground. He wore a ripped shirt and leathers. His arms hung at his sides, his crimson-soaked hands balled into fists. Icy rage blasted from him with the force of a sudden tempest.

My stomach churned with sickness. Around him, men–shifters?–lay on the floor in pieces. What happened?

"She is here, Majesty," Bodi said in a soothing tone he might use with a crying newborn. He gave me a gentle push forward. "Look. Your sweet Clover is returned."

The king's head craned our way with inhuman speed. His glowing gold eyes lit on me. He blinked with surprise, and the glow faded, revealing some of that brilliant green.

THE STOLEN BRIDE

Then he frowned, puzzled. "I don't understand. You are here with me, but you are also with him."

"With Deco?" I willingly took a step closer. "Viktor, I told the truth. I've never met the guy."

"How is this possible, then?" He stretched out his arm and opened his palm, revealing a ring with an opaque stone gracing the center. He shoved the piece down his index finger and from it sprang a...hologram? Whatever it was, the stone projected it, unveiling a smiling man with dark hair, a square jaw, and piercing amber eyes. He loomed behind the woman he imprisoned in front of him, his huge feathery wings solid gold. Though the woman blocked his chest, I knew he was shirtless because his arms were bare. Tattoos covered everything but his face.

This must be the infamous Deco.

"Why would Deco send his men to be slaughtered, all to get this into my hands and taunt me with your loss," Viktor said, still in the grips of his befuddlement, "if you are here with me?"

My gaze landed on the woman, and I gasped, slammed by a bolt of pure shock. Impossible! And yet, I saw her with my own eyes. Or rather, me. I saw me. My doppelganger stood with her back pressed against the shifter's chest, his big, clawed hand poised at her throat.

Trembling, I fluttered my hand to my mouth, but my doppelganger didn't move. Like me, she had dark hair with hints of red. The same gray and brown irises. Same delicate yet defined bone structure, with the same single dimple in her left cheek. She wore a gilded gown that caught the light; the silk swirling around her feet like liquid gold.

Astonishment radiated from her as she looked me over, as if the hologram were actually a live feed. But that couldn't be right. Technology wasn't there yet. Unless it was?

What did I know about anything? Nothing I'd experienced so far should be possible, yet here we were.

"Who are you?" we cried simultaneously. Wow! We possessed the same tone of voice, too, with the same overflow of bewilderment infusing every word.

What! That hologram was, in fact, part of a live feed. "I'm Clover," I said at the same time she said, "I'm Juniper."

Malachi had mentioned a sister. She must be my twin, separated from me at birth. *So many questions.* Even more emotions. Mostly delight, a sense of rightness, and an instant heart-bond I couldn't explain and didn't wish to end. Finally! I was made whole.

Viktor looked between us, understanding dawning in his eyes. Relief followed. "You cannot teleport."

"No." I wish!

Deco laughed with a dark glee. "Now this is an interesting development. I knew she had a sister, not that they were twins." His purring voice scraped my nerve endings raw. "We'll talk again soon, V. I promise you. Tootles." The image vanished.

No, no, no. I rushed over, not yet ready to lose sight of her.

"How is this possible?" I demanded as I snatched the ring off the king's finger. Lightweight. Hot to the touch. No discernible button to push. "Where is she? Will Deco harm her?" I must, must, must reach her. Now, now, now. I had no pride. There were no lines I wouldn't cross. "Take me to her. Please, Viktor. Please!"

He snatched back the ring, unfazed by everything else. "Mine."

THE STOLEN BRIDE

Fine. No problem. Focusing on him, I cupped his shoulders. "Please," I repeated. "I'll do anything."

6

All Out War: When Your Last Resort Is A Battle-Loving Beast

–HOW TO TRAIN YOUR BERSERKER
By Elizabeth "Elle" Darcy-Bruce

"You are here, but she is there." Gold rimmed Viktor's pupils, which constricted to needle points as he looked between me and the ring. "There are two of you. She's your twin."

"Trust me, it's a shock to me, too." I fisted his shirt to gain a firmer hold as my insides sang with joy, fear, and resolve. I truly had a sister. My other half. Juniper. Separated from me at birth.

Taken from me.

Longing and fury collided. Longing won. All my life, I'd missed her as if I'd lost a limb, I just hadn't known it until now. I'd bet she'd felt the same. Who would do such a cruel thing to us?

My adoptive parents had always yearned for more chil-

THE STOLEN BRIDE

dren. No way they would have refused to raise my precious sister. And she *was* precious to me. I wasn't just bonded to her; I loved her with the whole of my being.

"Will Deco harm her?" I asked again.

"Deco is a shifter," Viktor replied. "Malicious. Untrustworthy. Insidious. He is especially motivated to take out anyone suspected of being my firebrand. He won't play nice."

A whimper left me. Screw Malachi. I'd considered recruiting Viktor to go after the guy, but here, now, I didn't exactly care about the other king. I preferred to have Deco's head on a platter.

The decision to work with my captor solidified. "Viktor, I officially sign the roster to join your team." He might not be sane at times—or ever—but he was strong and capable. With my help, he could get this job done and save my sister. "Now, prepare yourself. I'm going to say something you may not like, but I need you to hear it. Are you wearing your listening ears?" I gave him a little shake for good measure.

A bemused glaze overtook his features.

I continued. "Help me rescue Juniper. Please! If you refuse, I'll strike out on my own. And before you rage about losing the firebrand you haven't exactly claimed but hope to keep, don't. Just say yes. When you do, I'll return the favor by helping you find your precious. That's your key," I clarified, in case he couldn't connect the dots. "If there's something else you prefer, now is the time to name your fee. I'll pay it." I'd meant what I'd said. There was no price too steep. I didn't care if I wasted bargaining power. The outcome was too important.

"I will rescue her, yes," he offered without hesitation, and I nearly sagged into a puddle of relief. "And you will owe me anything I desire."

Well. Someone had certainly regained his wits in a hurry. I pursed my lips. "I'm not a hundred percent on board with your wording, but we'll hammer out the semantics on the road. So. Yes. Agreed. You can collect your reward when the job is done."

"I will rescue her," he repeated, his tone hardening. "But you will stay behind."

Ha! "I'm sticking to you like hot glue, bud. And you're gonna get happy about that real quick, because you remember I keep you calm and focused when you're not avoiding me." I gave him a final shake to let him know I meant business. "So? What are we waiting for? Let's go. We're already a day behind schedule."

He said nothing. Nor did he budge.

"Viktor," I huffed. "I've played nice with you so far. Bottled up my emotions and barely let anything leak out. But my patience is thinning rapidly."

"We'll be walking into a trap," Bodi pointed out, reminding me of his presence.

"Yes. We will. A dangerous one. This comes with us." Viktor tossed the ring that had projected the live feed to the prince, as if he didn't trust himself to be its caretaker. "If you lose it, Bodi, you will also lose your head." He kept his attention on me. Weighing his options, as well as trying to intimidate me into staying behind, I'd bet. "I am not afraid of your emotions, drága."

Easy to say while I was calm.

The intensity of his unwavering focus roused a thousand different sensations. Too many jumbled together, ensuring I couldn't pinpoint a single one. But this I knew: I'd never, in all my days, been examined so thoroughly. He studied me from the top of my head to the soles of my booted feet. It felt as if he bore holes in layers of concrete,

THE STOLEN BRIDE

reaching parts of me I'd hidden even from myself. I didn't understand it, and I didn't like it, but I didn't protest.

Concentrate on the task at hand. "I don't care about the danger. I'm coming with you. You'll worry about me if I don't." There was a chance, anyway.

He breathed in deep and told Bodi, "Have my elite ready to leave for the mountains of Fenylith in ten minutes." Still his gaze remained locked on me. "And pack the violin. The prisoner comes with me." He linked our fingers. "You'll play for your passage. To start."

Victory achieved! "Yes. Agreed."

"Are you sure this is wise?" the prince asked his king.

"My compensation outweighs the aggravation," Viktor said, ending any argument then and there. I didn't even mind the insult.

The prince hesitated only a moment more before stalking from the tent to do as commanded.

Tightening his grip, Viktor held me in place. "Let's discuss my rules."

"There's no reason. I can guess them. No running from you, ever, no excuses allowed. Obey your every command and only speak when spoken to." Was this what my dream had always pointed to? Placing my safety in his care? Possibly. The meaning of the dream felt bigger than that, however. And what about the sword? Why raise it and swing, as if to kill me? Which I didn't believe he'd do. Otherwise, I wouldn't be here. "Did I cover everything?"

He stepped closer. "I already know you won't run. You comprehend that I'm the only one capable of succeeding in this endeavor. And you'll obey my every command for the same reason. But I do not, under any circumstances, want you speaking only when spoken to. Nem. I prefer how you've been. I like not wondering what you're thinking."

Whoa. Talk about a sudden, sharp turn and an unexpected confession. "What are your rules then?"

"To start, tell me without delay whenever Deco reaches out to you. And he will reach out. No matter what he tells you, trust me, not him. Also, keep no secrets from me."

Mind blown! Viktor's requests were, like, super reasonable. "I agree, yes, please and thank you. Anything else?"

"Yes."

"Well, I agree to it too, whatever it is. You can explain on the road." I tried to tug him toward the door, but he dug in his heels, remaining rooted in place.

"I'll finish outlining my rules, after I explain what we'll face." He pulled me against him, our bodies suddenly pressed together, and I shivered. His warm breath fanned over my face. "We must journey to the traveling stones. A perilous task in and of itself. Unless Deco is a fool, he won't attack us until we're deep in his territory, a good distance from those stones. Then, he'll put an army around them. We won't get out without a fight. And that comes after the battle for Juniper. Do you really wish to be there when all of that transpires?"

My blood flashed from hot to ice cold. "Yes. I still want to go. You won't change my mind."

He worked his jaw. "I'm unsure how much you know of our kind..." He paused to await my response.

"Of the legends, a lot. But in truth, not so much. I only found out you were real when you did your eye glowing thing." Our kind, he'd said. As if he considered *me* a berserker. What a preposterous idea. I mean, yes, Malachi Cromwell had insisted I belonged to his lineage but come on. I might have a volatile temper, but I wasn't an immortal rage machine. "I've studied berserkers in books and movies and my adoptive mom used to tell me cautionary tales, but I lack a vast amount of background information."

He seemed to absorb even the smallest details of my words, tones, and expressions. "All of us possess the spirit of an otherworldly animal. Beasts that existed before time began. Many hosts never sense it. Some spirits, like mine and those in my elite, are stronger than others. When any of us rage, we feed the beast. If we allow the creature to grow more powerful than we are while in such a state, it takes over. *Evil* takes over, and we want only to tempt others to become the same as us."

"Okay, but what are you trying to tell me, exactly?"

"The shifters live to ruin our lives, make us miserable, and push us over the edge until we become one of them. Or die."

Hmm. Was that why Malachi wished for such an outcome with Viktor? Had *he* turned and now hoped to oversee the same transformation with the other kings?

And now, Deco sought the same, intending to lure Viktor to the dark side. "Based on what you said, I assume Valkara is evil." Right? "Since she guards the primordials, the very evil you speak of."

"The Valkara," he corrected without heat. Then he scowled, his entire countenance tightening. "The beasts aren't inherently good or evil. They feed on our emotions. If we become evil, *they* become evil. The primordials are simply the oldest and most powerful of their line. The Valkara sacrificed her life for us, and you will address her with respect or not at all."

"Sure, sure," I said, patting his chest with my free hand. I shouldn't irritate him. If he decided to back out, I'd be forced to go against supernatural forces all by my lonesome. No, thank you. "So the beasts are as good or bad as their hosts. Noted. But is *she* evil or not?"

"Her love is said to be so powerful, it will affect all primordials and their entire downline."

Well. No wonder he hoped to win her, whether she was his firebrand or not. And that wasn't depressing for some unknown reason. "I hear you loud and clear, Tor. Your final rule. Do not, under any circumstances, tempt you to fall in love with me. Ten-four. Don't worry. I'm not even a tiny bit tempted to fall in love with you, either."

He released a soft growling sound. "You can love me. That's fine."

"Too late." I tapped my temple. "I've already logged the no-falling directive. It can't happen now."

His lips pulled back from his teeth. "Just...stop using your strange abilities on me. *That* is my final rule."

I wrinkled my nose. "You'll have to elaborate. Strange abilities?"

"Ja." His nose wrinkled, too. "Making your eyes flash between gray and brown. It's annoying. And mesmerizing. Also, no more turning the most irritating words into an enchanting spell. Or calling me 'baby' and 'snarls.' No more *spting* at me."

Reeling. Was he, like, already falling for me and just didn't realize it? *Oh, my golden retriever.* I mean, I got that I was his firebrand, and he was predisposed to all the feels with me. But what he described was full-blown attraction.

Not that I'd point that out to him. "You want me to stop being myself. Noted. Just be aware. None of those things are quote unquote strange abilities."

"You have your orders," he insisted before leading me from the tent. "I expect full obedience."

"Ten-four," I repeated.

THE STOLEN BRIDE

Hand in hand, we traversed the campground. Bodi must have told the troops to stand down. The men and women who served under him engaged in battle drills. Commands sounded from here and there, blending with the clang of axes against shields, both wooden and metal.

Atop war horses perched Bodi and nine other warriors. The biggest, baddest, fiercest soldiers in history–the same guys who'd guarded my tent. They wore gold and black paint on their faces, with pieces of spiked, gold-plated armor strapped all over, alongside a variety of weapons.

At the head of the line, an eleventh horse stood without a rider. Viktor released me to mount, then bent down to grab me. I backed up.

"Um. Do you have a car?" I'd lived on a farm as a child, and the two ponies had despised me. I'd tried to ride one once and gotten thrown.

Viktor shook his head. "Fekete Ló is a fine ride."

Wait. "You named your horse... Black Horse?"

"Ja. The area is too dense even for an ATV. Besides, I prefer the old ways. In my dimension, we don't have to worry about drawing the notice of humans, but I'd rather not draw the notice of my civilians, either." With that, he stretched further, snatched me by the waist, and hefted me onto the saddle in front of him.

Now I understood why he'd always included leggings with my dresses.

Speaking of other dimensions, Malachi had mentioned them too. "You have your own dimension. That's nice." I settled in with my back against Viktor's chest. Heat wafted from him, carrying the most incredible scent. He still smelled of pine needles from ancient woods but also fresh mountain air and a hint of citrus instead of rose. Mmm. I

79

breathed deep, savoring this calm before the storm. "But, um, we're in it now?"

"We are. It mirrors the human world but lacks humans, ensuring they are kept safe if ever one of us breaks."

An unexpected kindness from a man I might have, maybe, possibly, misjudged.

With a soft snick and shift of his heels, Viktor urged Fekete Ló forward. The others trailed us. We left the camp in our rearview, soon entering the surrounding forest.

The ride wasn't terrible. To my relief, Fekete Ló behaved himself like a true gentleman.

"How far are the traveling stones?" I asked as we crossed a river, cutting a gentle path through moss-covered rocks. The babbling current harmonized with different bird calls. How deceptive nature's tranquility could be.

"Two days, one night. Give or take a week or three."

I groaned. "I wouldn't be averse to a faster route." The sooner we reached Deco, the better.

"There isn't one." Viktor sniffed the top of my head and tightened his hold on me. "I like the smell of your hair."

My insides fizzed, and my bones softened.

Then he growled. "I thought I told you not to use your strange abilities."

Way to ruin a moment. "That's a you problem, bud. I used the soap in your bathroom." Which reminded me. "How is your bathroom even possible?" For that matter. "How do you always have clothing in my size waiting?"

"Over the centuries, we gathered fragments from the traveling stones, both coming and going. We wove half of those fragments into the curtain and placed the other half inside the washing chamber, creating a doorway between the two. And I assessed your measurements our first moments together, then hunted down an array of clothing."

"First, that was very kind of you. Thank you." I would forever appreciate the supply of dresses, leggings, and boots. "But, um, can you explain the measuring process?" Because he'd nailed it. Even the undergarments.

"Look there. Minks," he said, pointing.

Okay, so, I fell for it. That, I can admit. I looked and got wrapped up in the sight of two super cute minks near the water's shore, watching our procession. I forgot all about my question and his avoidance of issuing an answer. The minks were just so cute.

We ate jerky sticks on the go and stopped to water and rest the horses only twice, but I appreciated each break. Unused to horseback riding, my thighs grew sore fast. They would have chaffed if Viktor hadn't noticed my increasing discomfort and repositioned me, letting me ride sideways while comfy, cozy against him.

Hmm. I liked this. Perfect for propping my head on his shoulder, burrowing deeper into his warmth, and breathing in his incredible scent. "Thank you," I muttered. "This isn't me falling for you, by the way."

He grunted in response, and I liked even that.

His heart beat hard and strong against my temple, keeping me aware of his nearness. When fatigue beckoned, I closed my eyes.

I tried to distract myself from the urge to sleep, occupying my mind with thoughts of the "greater good." Did my sister have the same dream? Did the action of my kneeling before Viktor, offering my life to him, help her in some way? Because that was the only reason I might—might—do it.

As the sun began its slow descent, my stomach grumbled. Concentrating on anything but my starvation became a thing of the past.

"I believe I could set a clock by your hunger," he told me, then signaled to his men. The procession stopped. "Though it would need only one setting. *Always*."

I snorted. "You aren't wrong." But where was this sudden sense of humor coming from?

"Your legs need tending before you attempt to stand," he muttered.

He hesitated before repositioning me, putting my back to him again and settling his big, strong hands on my thighs. As the soldiers set up camp in a small clearing surrounded by tall trees that offered a protective barrier, he massaged my aching muscles. Upon the first kneading, I arched my spine and groaned. Oh! It hurt so good!

"Don't stop," I croaked.

He increased the pressure, and I gasped at the perfection of it. Blood flowed to areas in need.

"You like this?" he rasped into my ear.

"Yessss." So much!

He nuzzled his cheek against mine. "I might *never* stop."

The soldiers erected six tents, created a pit, and started a fire. The setting sun cast the spot in muted shades of purple, red, and orange. So lovely. But when the guys finished, so did Viktor. Despite his claim, he ceased his ministrations when the men settled into a circle around the flames. After dismounting, he popped me off Fekete Ló as if I weighed nothing.

"Good horsey," I praised. My knees nearly buckled.

"I've got you." Viktor held me up with an arm around my waist and led me to a tree near the circle of soldiers. Didn't want me joining the others, hmm?

THE STOLEN BRIDE

I eased to the ground, leaned against the trunk, and stretched out my legs, sighing with contentment. My stomach ruined the moment, rumbling loudly.

Cheeks heating all over again, I grumbled, "Some people say this is the stage of hunger where even horses look good enough to eat."

Fekete Ló whinnied in the distance, and I winced. "Not you, sweetie," I called. "Only the others."

Viktor's eyes glittered with what might have been but couldn't be and surely wasn't amusement. "Quick, Keve," he called, "bring Clover her meal before you lose your mount."

We shared a smile. An actual smile. It lit Viktor's entire countenance, as well as different parts of me. A shock to us both, clearly. Next, he scowled like I'd actually devoured someone's ride.

"Bodi!" he bellowed, marching off. "Figure out why I'm in a good mood so I can end it." He disappeared in the foliage.

I almost shouted for his return. Spend a little alone time with berserkers who didn't view me as their one and only special firebrand? No, thanks.

As a young soldier left the circle to stride over, I prepared to uncap a couple bottles of rage. "Hope you're ready for the best cuisine the forest has to offer," he said, handing me something wrapped in a cloth.

I accepted tentatively. "Is that code for poisonous wild berries?"

A mischievous grin curved the sides of his mouth, disrupting a scar that ran down one cheek. "You are the woman who prevented countless injuries today. I would poison my comrades, but never you."

83

Everyone nodded their agreement with great enthusiasm as he rejoined the group.

Relaxing a bit, I unwrapped the cloth and said, "Yes, well, this hero appreciates a good meal." Hmm. Turned out, the "best cuisine of the forest" was a piece of bread.

I sank my teeth into the outer edge and moaned with delighted surprise. So good! Rich flavors teased my tongue.

"You don't have to be afraid of us," a second male said. He was leaner than the others, almost wiry, with intense eyes.

"Oh, I'm not afraid of you. I feared what *I* might do to *you*."

They all guffawed. "We understand outsiders are terrified of us. But I promise, we don't bite."

"Well, not often," added a third, cracking himself up. His broad-shoulders and booming laugh reminded me of my father, and my chest squeezed.

"Don't worry, guys. I always carry spare chew toys." I put up my dukes to display said toys.

Booming Laugh raised a brow. "She's got jokes, too. That's good, because handling an original isn't the same as handling an average sentinel, neither of which is for the faint of heart. Just ask Deco and Le—"

Another soldier elbowed him in the stomach, and he went quiet.

Oooh. What name had he almost revealed? Leann? Leslie? Levi? Leo? Was this the information Viktor didn't wish me to learn? "Don't worry," I repeated. "I've dealt with something far worse than an original."

"Do tell," Keve said.

"Imagine giving a cat a bath. Now *that's* a battlefield."

Snickers rang out, and I marveled. I'd never experienced such a lighthearted meal. Which was especially wild, considering I was in the middle of nowhere with an elite contingent of legendary berserkers.

"We have some semantics to discuss," Viktor said from behind me.

Yelping, I craned my neck to peer up at him. That someone of his colossal size had crossed a path of twigs making no noise boggled my mind.

Then his words registered, and my heart raced. "I hope you're speaking of the ten answers I owe you, and not the payment for including me on this trip."

"The payment. Ja. That. You owe me *anything* I desire," he all but purred. "Now I require my parameters. The Q and A is next."

Gulp. The wild glint in his emerald eyes suggested I wasn't going to like anything he had to say. "I'd rather save that particular discussion for a time when you haven't murdered your so-called good mood for no reason."

"No need to wait, then. My mood hasn't improved," he grumbled at low volume, ensuring only I could hear as he settled in at my side. "Bodi tells me the only way to rid oneself of such a pleasing sensation is to spend more time with the source and become inoculated."

I wasn't sure if Bodi had done me a major favor or a huge disservice. "Here's an idea. Enjoy it forever, except when you're spanking turul-shifter kings."

Viktor hiked his shoulders in a shrug. "You may provide me with one limit to my payment. Use it at your own discretion."

I could work within those terms. "You can't pick anything that violates my moral fiber. So, as you can see, that's only one limit."

"Accepted. The payment I demand will do nothing to violate your moral fiber."

Hmm. He'd acquiesced too easily. He must not get my meaning. "That includes anything romantic or harmful to myself and others."

I could *feel* his eye roll.

"As if I have any need to demand romance from you or anyone. I'm a king. Women throw themselves at me daily. It's one of the reasons I go to war. To rest."

This time he didn't moderate his volume, and his grinning men all nodded their support of his claim.

First, Viktor had displayed a sense of humor, now ego. I wasn't sure what to think.

"Besides," he added. "I want only to win the Valkara."

I ground my molars. An action my stomach misunderstood, obviously. It gave another rumble. Feeding time again.

Viktor motioned to Keve. The warrior left the circle and rushed over with a second, bigger slice of bread.

"Thank you," I said, digging in. When I finished, I curbed the urge to request a third and leaned against the tree trunk, stretching out my legs. "I'm a fan of that bread. It's almost filling."

"It is Hőskenyér. It provides a sentinel with all the nourishment required to maintain strength on a long journey."

Even better. "I'd love to score the recipe, if it's not some treasured family secret."

"Your world lacks many of the ingredients."

Too bad. I peered at him, intending to say something but... Golden firelight bathed his face, painting his skin with loving strokes. My heart kicked into another mad race as if—No! Nope. No way I was attracted to King Viktor, the feral primal leading Hungarian sentinels, who sought the devotion of an otherworldly woman able to speak into his head. But why did he have to be so gorgeous?

THE STOLEN BRIDE

"Since I have my parameters, I can consider what I wish to demand from you," he said, bordering on gleeful. "For now, I'm ready to ask a few of my questions."

Flutters erupted in my stomach. "Go ahead. Ask," I told him, breathless. "Just know I'll be keeping count."

He canted his head. Quiet again, he asked, "Do you have a male?"

That was what he wished to know first and foremost? How interesting. I may have smiled. Okay, I definitely smiled. He might want that Valkara chick, but he was super into me.

"No. No male. Man. Not too long ago, I was engaged to a mechanic."

Viktor stiffened. "What brought about the end of your relationship?"

Second question, check. "He decided he preferred my former best friend Kami. Well, that, and because I have a so-called heart of ice. Oh, and also because I'm a 'toe-stepper'. Excuse me for speaking my mind and containing my emotions to protect others from my wrath." *Jerk.* "Anyway. I caught Benjamin and Kami together a couple of days before my wedding." Ugh. Had I really needed to share the whole sordid story of my greatest rejection?

Viktor's expression grew pensive. He better not be working up to pity. I was glad Ben dumped me. Gladder than glad. The gladdest. Who wanted to be legally shackled to a lowdown, dirty cheater? Travesty averted—for me. Neither Kami nor Benjamin could say the same.

"You contain your emotions with me, too," Viktor stated, "and you will cease doing so immediately. I told you, there's no need for it."

Maybe. And oh, how tempting was such a thought. To let go. To experience emotions at full wattage. If anyone could handle my temper, it was this man. But I merely shrugged, noncommittal. Could *I* handle feeling things other than rage?

"Back to the fool you almost married. You loved him."

Not a question, but I counted it, anyway. Three down, only seven to go. "I did, yes." I paused, waiting, but Viktor didn't speak up again. "Ask me how he won me over, and I'll tell you."

Viktor didn't take the bait, but he did waste an additional question on Benjamin. "How long ago did this occur?"

"Six months." Not long enough, honestly.

"What do you feel for him now?"

A wee bit jealous, was he? "Relieved that he's someone else's problem."

Five.

Viktor rubbed two fingers and a thumb over his stubbled jaw, pensive.

"Hit me with the next," I encouraged. "I'm ready."

"I'll save my remaining questions for later."

Bummer. I'd hoped to wipe out his entire reserve.

His brow wrinkled. Then he jolted, as if punched by an invisible fist. "She whispers again." Pause. "Yes, yes. Find, destroy, happy," he muttered. "Find, destroy, happy."

Ugh. Not this again. I cupped his cheeks, determined to nip this little episode in the bud. And yeah, okay, prevent any interactions with Valkara. Better his affections centered on me during this journey. "Hey, Snarls. Focus on your firebrand. I want something from you. I *need* it."

A beat passed. Then another. I figured I'd failed. Eventually, his gaze slid to mine. The hazy glaze faded from his irises. "What do you need, drágá?" His voice had dipped.

Ignore your shivers. "To sleep. Be a darling and show me

THE STOLEN BRIDE

which tent is mine." The moment after I spoke, I yawned. Man, I'd had *a day*. "I'm ready for my beauty Zs."

"You're staying in that one." He pointed to the smallest structure and grinned a slow, languid grin that ignited un-ignorable flutters in my belly. "With me."

7

When Your Shelter From the Storm is a Walking Tempest

–HOW TO TRAIN YOUR BERSERKER
By Elizabeth "Elle" Darcy-Bruce

I slept nestled in Viktor's arms.

It happened by accident, but also on purpose. After his shocking yet not even the tiniest bit surprising announcement that I'd be bunking up with him, I sputtered out a breath, producing plenty of sounds but zero words. Eventually, I stopped clutching my invisible pearls while preparing to demand he use his payment in order to gain my cooperation, and sighed. "Fine. Whatever." First, he could force me to sleep outside. Second, he sought to protect me. Third, keeping him close wasn't a terrible idea. "But no making a move. I'm issuing a preemptive refusal."

"I thought we had this conversation already," he said with a humph. "If I want sex, I can get it elsewhere."

"Not with that attitude you can't."

THE STOLEN BRIDE

He opened and closed his mouth, as if trying to say a thousand things at once.

More than a little irritated with him for reasons that definitely had nothing to do with his love life, I patted his cheek. "You don't know this about me, but you're about to learn the hard way. I value my beauty Zs as much as my meals. Precious seconds I can spend in bed are ticking by while you try to do the impossible and think of a comeback that can clean up the damage caused by my truth bomb."

He gripped my wrist and lowered my hand, as if he didn't wish to be touched. Except, instead of releasing me, he dragged his thumb across my palm, sending tingles rushing up my arm.

"Soft," he muttered.

Goose bumps broke out. Okay, we needed to veer to a new track. "Feel free to take the first shift and stand guard."

"We don't require a guard tonight." Wind kicked up, whistling. "A storm comes. Turul-shifters prefer not to fight in torrential rain. They are at a disadvantage. We are not."

To punctuate his words, lightning flashed overhead, and thunder rumbled in a rolling wave.

Ugh. I hated storms. I had lived in tornado alley for years. Losing half my roof was what prompted me to move to Aurelian Hills. "What about the horses?" I'd grown fond of Fekete Ló.

"They'll be in tents with my men."

Another crack of thunder boomed, louder than the first. Tightness spread through my chest. "That's my cue. Get moving or get left behind."

He stood, tugging me up with him, and ushered me to the tent. An astonishingly cozy space with a full-size pallet of blankets that offered a soft cushion far better than the hard ground. The violin waited in the corner.

But. Um. Only one bed, not separate sleeping bags? I might as well be the heroine in a fated mates, enemies to lovers romance novel. "Remember our golden rules," I said. "No falling in love with me or making a move." I toed off my boots. "I'll stay on my side. You stay on yours." I didn't want to play right now. Or talk. I just wanted to sleep. But new cracks of thunder caused even the ground to vibrate, and I swiped out my arm at record speed to link my fingers with his. "For your peace of mind, we'll hold hands so you can be sure I'm not running away." Nervous laugh. "You gotta be well rested for our journey and the battle with Deco, amirite."

Gold rings flickered in Viktor's eyes. He yanked me against him and enfolded me in an almost crushing but amazing embrace. "You'll face down a camp of berserkers without flinching, but a little rain makes you tremble? You know I'm here, ja? I will allow nothing untoward to happen to you."

Okay, so, his incredulity wasn't my favorite. "You might be immortal, but you can't control the weather." Raindrops hit the tent, sounding like pops of gunfire, and I squeaked. "If you've never seen a semi-truck being spun in a dark, twisting funnel of chaos, you don't get to judge my overreaction. By the way, I'm not afraid of anything. I don't do fear. This is…reluctance. There's a difference."

Brighter flashes of lightning electrified the air, raising the fine hairs on my body as he positioned me on the pallet. He stretched out beside me, slid an arm under my neck, and crooked his fingers under my chin to lift my face. "I will hold you like this all night long, making sure you don't fly away, but I, too, insist you make no moves."

I snorted internally, which jostled sore muscles. There was no stopping my outer wince.

THE STOLEN BRIDE

"Is that a hint for another massage?" he asked, his tone conversational, even pleasant.

"No, of course not." But another massage did sound amazing. "Yes. No," I repeated and heaved a second sigh. "Your question borders on a move." And I wasn't exactly unwelcoming at the moment, truth be told. He just, he felt so good, pressed so close. And he hadn't retreated into madness a single time during this conversation. Or mentioned Valkara.

"I won't allow you to keep your emotions at bay, so I'm not your type. I get it." His dry tone grated my every nerve. "You're not my type, either."

Ouch. That stung, considering I was perhaps, maybe, possibly, the tiniest little bit attracted to him. But it was purely physical, so no big deal. "Just out of curiosity, because I'm nosy, what is the Valkara like? Since she *is* your type."

"She's exceptional."

I waited, but he offered nothing more. "That's it? All you've got?" I winced for him. "Your passion for her is extreme."

A scowl darkened his countenance. "Do you want the massage or not? Because if you prefer to suffer during tomorrow's ride, I'll let you."

"Let's say I agree." We'd been side by side for roughly two weeks, and he'd never harmed me. Today, we'd ridden and rubbed together for hours, and he hadn't touched anything he shouldn't. Part of me might...trust him. Ugh. What a terrible realization. "Will you take it as a sign that I'm falling for your charms?"

"I have charms?" He toyed with the ends of my hair, an absent-minded action I enjoyed a little too much. "In return for my extreme generosity, you will play me three songs tomorrow. One to pay for today, one to pay for tomorrow, and one to pay for my efforts."

Of course he demanded another song. "Fine. Deal," I grumbled, rolling to my side to give him better access to my back.

With a quick, smooth motion, he rolled me the rest of the way, onto my stomach.

My insides performed somersaults. Relying on him to rescue my sister *and* protect me from the storm must be doing strange things to my brain; I should have said no to this. But. Come on! Clearly, he wanted this more than I did. So. You're welcome.

With a nudge of his knees, he parted my legs. My breath caught. Too intimate? He crouched between the V he'd created. Even more intimate! My lips formed an O, a protest brewing...until his fingers pressed into the backs of my thighs.

He worked his magic, the ensuing pleasure-pain wrenching groans of surrender from the deepest parts of my being. Oh, yes. Yes, yes, yes. That was good. Magnificent!

"I will play you the best song ever," I vowed.

Once he'd kneaded my thighs into pudding, he shifted his sublime efforts to my calves. My feet. Then my back. My hips. I forgot all about the storm that raged outside, whipping against our tent.

Problem was, I considered things I shouldn't.

How good his touch felt.

Other places on my body he might explore.

Ways to assuage the ache growing inside me.

"You like this." The guttural thickness of his voice registered, and I shivered. "You like *me*."

I did. Far more than I should. A fleeting sentiment

THE STOLEN BRIDE

based on our circumstances, but oh. Oh! He worked out a knot. "In my defense, this is so, so good." Tension drained from muscles that had been overworked for years.

"I know," he rasped, both words containing thousands of nuances, sending new shivers racing down my spine.

"Why do you care if I like you or not?" He *must* like me too.

"I merely made an observation. Now prepare yourself. I'm about to ask the next question in my queue of seven."

"Five," I corrected.

"Ja. I was testing your counting ability."

I snorted. "Whatever, Curious."

He ended the massage and moved to stretch beside me again.

No! There might be another knot somewhere. "I'll give you a sixth question, if you add ten minutes to the massage clock."

"Done," he replied as pleased as punch. He returned to his ministrations and switched to a neutral tone, giving no hints of his inner thoughts. "What's your plan once we have Juniper in our possession?"

Easy. "Hug her. Learn about her life. Hug her again. Sob like a baby. Go home. Hug her some more."

His fingers dug into a knot in my backside, and I groaned. See! "The two of you are on Deco's radar now. The shifter will forever hunt you, whether you are in this world or another. Unless something is done, neither of you will ever be safe again."

Tension resurged, flooding my limbs. "Guess I'll have to do something then."

"You'll require a big, strong, powerful berserker to protect you," Viktor said.

Aaah. "Okay. I see what you're doing here. Trying to

95

scare me straight, get me desperate for your safekeeping, so I'll stick around." Never mind our attraction to each other, the firebrand possibility, and the fog stuff. He must want free concerts. "Admit it."

"You are already sticking around. I'm keeping you, remember. And that wasn't a question, but a command."

"I remember you made such an outlandish claim, yes. Doesn't mean it'll work out for you if I'm unwilling to do any sticking."

He ended the massage again, and this time I didn't let myself request more. I maneuvered to my side, facing him as he stretched out beside me again, linked his hands behind his head, and peered up at the ceiling.

Brighter lightning flashed, momentarily bathing him in a golden halo. With his hair in disarray and his features soft, he appeared sleepy, relaxed, and totally at ease. A good look for him. Very good. My heart actually skipped a beat.

"How do I get you willing?" he demanded with a hint of temper, belying his ease.

I almost smiled. "Is that your next question?" If so, only four remained.

"Ja. And since I just answered another of your questions, it cancels out this go round. You must answer my last question *and* five others."

Dang. He was quick-witted, too. I tried not to be impressed. "I don't know how you can get me willing to stick with you, but I'm happy to offer suggestions." Would I bargain away my freedom for my sister? Yes. There was no way I could defeat a flight of turul-shifters on my own. But that would only gain my outward surrender. I wouldn't be willing on the inside. "I'm really into good moods, being a man's one and only, kindness, meals, and rescuing twin sisters."

THE STOLEN BRIDE

"We shall see," he said, sounding as if he were already plotting my downfall.

"And with that, the conversation ends. Goodnight, Viktor," I rasped, turning from him.

"Cuddle me like you've done every other night." He rolled into me and dragged me against his chest, the big spoon to my little spoon. His arm remained a strong band, keeping me locked in place. Not that I was the teeniest bit tempted to break away. "Better."

Much. "I knew you'd been sneaking into bed with me," I muttered.

"Only because you demanded it."

"Oh, that's what happened, is it?" Other cracks of thunder ebbed and flowed, parts of the tent flapping with the wind, but I didn't care. The rest of the world had ceased to matter. I closed my eyes, breathing deep, trying to forget the residual aches from his ministrations which had yet to fade. What would he do if I twisted around and kissed him?

I'd told him not to make a move. He'd said the same to me. I shouldn't do it. I couldn't. Wouldn't.

But I wanted to.

It was almost a relief when the trials of the day caught up to me. Wrapped in Viktor's heat and scent, I let the sea of nothingness sweep me away. Awareness dulled...

The dream never came.

I wasn't sure how much time had passed when a faint noise woke me. Blinking open my eyes, I tuned my ears.

"Find, destroy, happy. Find, destroy, happy."

Thoughts flickered to life, reminding me of my situation. I stiffened, gaze darting. Viktor. The tent. The storm. It still raged, rain pummeling the cloth walls. Since none leaked inside, I figured the material was waterproof.

"Find, destroy, happy."

I repositioned to take stock. Viktor stretched out on his back, fast asleep. Light glowed from a lantern he must have lit at some point, giving me a full wattage glimpse of his eyes rolling behind his lids and jerking body. Was he trapped inside a nightmare?

My chest constricted. Poor berserker. "Hey, hey," I said, gently patting his cheek. "Wake up for me, Snarls."

He caught my wrist as his eyelids popped open. "Clove. Clovie. Lovie."

Working out nicknames? "Whatever you call me, your treasured firebrand is here," I responded, trying not to adore the final selection but failing. More proof something was wrong with me.

His lips folded in between his teeth. "I dreamed of the Valkara."

I stiffened, not quite as nonchalant about her as usual for some strange, unknown reason I couldn't begin to fathom. "I'm listening."

"The key must be found." He scrubbed a palm over his face.

Or what? He'd be miffed? Total world annihilation would come? "Tell me about it."

"Nem."

I didn't press. Yet. "Tell me about your friendship with Deco then." Maybe I'd glean details about the shifter I could use to my advantage.

Fine! I was simply curious.

"You wish to know more about me, hmm?"

I didn't think I appreciated Viktor's smugness. "Why wouldn't I? Knowledge is power." The best response I could manage.

"I will be kind and tell you how we met." Viktor relaxed into the blankets, toying with the ends of my hair again.

THE STOLEN BRIDE

"Deco was a royal, while I hailed from a court courtesan. We shouldn't have crossed paths, but I snuck into his classroom to learn from his tutors. He spotted me, insisted I join him, and we soon grew as close as brothers."

My brain buzzed. And not only because Viktor was doing this to win me over without trying to hide it. I'd mentioned liking acts of kindness, and now he provided one.

A courtesan mother suggested he might not know the identity of his father. Had he lived his life the way I'd lived mine, always wondering? When the rest of his words registered, I blinked. "I think I misheard you. Did you say he was a royal, not you?" I couldn't imagine Viktor as anything but a leader. The one dishing the orders.

"Unlike most other sentinels, he and I started as humans. He was my king."

Wow. So unexpected.

"My mother kept me at court to teach me how to blend with the upper class. From the shadows, I mingled with the sons and daughters of the peerage."

I sensed sadness in his tone and guessed he'd felt out of place, as if he hadn't truly belonged. "You never thought of yourself as part of the crowd." I flattened my palm over his pectoral. His heart pounded hard, greeting me.

He nodded his confirmation. "I spent much time alone at a marble fountain in the royal gardens. I enjoyed it, at least. The sculptures were intricate, each telling a different story of the kingdom's past."

I pet him, loving when he released a *pff* of breath. Something else we had in common—an interest in history that stemmed from the uncertainty of our own. "Tell me more."

"One day, a group of older boys came up behind me and pushed me into the water. Two held me down." He puffed his chest, seeming to seek deeper contact with me. "The others cheered them on as I drown."

I sank my nails into his skin, as if I meant to pull him from the water even now. "They tried to kill you?"

"Probably only to scare me. To remind me of my place," he said. To my surprise, he clasped my hand, brought it to his mouth, and traced my index finger around his lips. "But as I've learned through my beast, feeding an urge like that only strengthens it, especially in the heat of the moment."

I ached to comfort the boy he'd been and praise the man he'd become. Oh, how I hated our no making a move rule. Because I wanted so badly to replace that finger with my mouth. "Then what happened?" I asked, desperate to know.

"Deco arrived, shoved them off me, and helped me out of the water. That's how he used to be. A protector. Fair. Noble. A future king his men followed without hesitation. When he was crowned, I was his most loyal soldier. He trusted only me at his back. Together, we conquered kingdoms. Then he sent me to scout out the Starfire to discover why it drew warriors from across the globe. I did so and returned months later as the turul king. Stronger. Volatile. Unstoppable."

He released my hand and clasped my knee, forcing it higher. Higher still, until I had no doubt he enjoyed this contact as much as I did.

Not attracted to me? Ha! He absolutely was.

I should respond to his words. Say something in turn. Anything. But I could only pant.

"He wanted to be like me, an immortal berserker," Viktor continued, shifting closer. His gaze met mine, the gold flecks mesmerizing. "The Valkara told me what to do, how to change him, and I did it. It marked the beginning of

THE STOLEN BRIDE

the end for us. I was created by the Starfire itself. He was not. My authority cannot be surpassed and over time, resentment ruled him."

"Sweet Viktor," I rasped. My focus dipped to his lips. Those beautiful, beautiful lips. "Without his best friend."

Agonizing seconds stretched between us.

"You want my kiss, Clover?" He rasped his words, too.

I did. Very, very much. I'd make him forget all about the Valkara. "Maybe."

"Ask me for it, and I'll grant your wish."

My heart slammed against my ribs. Ask him? Yes. I would. Except. Hmm. Why insist on a plea when he could give... unless he intended to use the request against me, asserting the very authority he'd just celebrated. *Do what I tell you, and I'll give you another.*

I stiffened. Was this why he'd offered to share a story from his past? To lead me to this moment?

"You ask *me* for a kiss, Mr. Only The Valkara Will Do," I grated.

Viktor narrowed his eyes and returned his stare to the ceiling. The rain tapered to a soft drizzle, then quit. "Sleep more. It's almost time to rise. We will set out early and reach the traveling stones before nightfall."

My stomach roiled as I deciphered his meaning. By the end of the day, we would enter turul-shifter territory. A treacherous domain filled with shifters determined to trap and kill us. I needed him in ways he didn't need me.

But I'd be one step closer to reaching my twin, so that was okay. There was no way I'd turn back. I'd be careful. Would guard Viktor with my life, because Juniper's depended on his. But I wouldn't consider kissing him again.

I absolutely, positively would not.

8

When Packing For Travel, Snacks Are As Important As Swords

–HOW TO TRAIN YOUR BERSERKER
By Elizabeth "Elle" Darcy-Bruce

Okay, so, I pondered kissing Viktor as we lay in silence. As we rose and readied for travel. As we mounted Fekete Ló and abandoned our campsite. Whatever. I'd get over it sooner or later.

We rode for hours, keeping the same arduous pace as yesterday, doing the same exact things. In other words, we stopped to rest only twice and ate jerky on the road. Despite my obsession with our nonexistent lip-lock, everything felt different between us. Maybe because I had a better understanding of my companion and a new appreciation for his plight.

Loving someone who hated you invited all kinds of hurt. Though I'd adored my adopted family, I had wondered about my birth parents constantly. Were they

THE STOLEN BRIDE

alive? Could they have taken care of me but just hadn't wanted to? Even with such a devastating possibility, I'd still craved a relationship. Hoped, every day, that they would reach out. The longer that hope had gone unfulfilled, the faster it had soured, infecting other things, fueling emotions I didn't like.

Bottling had helped. Something I was a little too raw to do at the moment. In fact, many of the bottles I'd buried in the past threatened to crack.

Maybe I stiffened atop the mount. Maybe I didn't. Either way, Viktor wrapped his arms around me and rested his chin on my crown, enveloping me with his heat and scent. His incredible strength. Though I shouldn't, I relaxed against him. For being such a chaotic guy, he'd been pretty calming lately. Our sizzling sensual tension notwithstanding, obviously.

Here, now, I didn't care if the bottles broke. He'd already expressed his interest in dealing with the complications. Why not let him?

Something to consider.

But not yet. The rhythmic clatters of horse hooves tapped against the forest floor, soothing me further. Despite my rawness, I couldn't remember a time I'd been so at ease, even with Benjamin.

The longer I leaned against Viktor, breathing in crisp air scented by wildflowers, the faster a sense of invigoration bloomed. I began to feel as if I hovered in some kind of timeless moment that had taken place a thousand years ago while simultaneously happening in the present.

I opened my mouth to launch a new conversation, but Bodi trotted over, his horse remaining beside ours.

"No turul-shifters have ambushed us," he announced, as if it were some great surprise.

"What's your point?" Viktor demanded, keeping his arms wrapped around me.

The prince darted his gaze to mine. "Have you considered the possibility the woman is part of the trap?"

You've got to be kidding me. Oh, I got why he might suspect me of lying and working with Deco. But come on! As if I would really put myself into that kind of danger while my twin needed me.

"Ja," Viktor repeated, still totally at ease. "I've considered it. And I will be the one to handle her if so. Me and me alone." A warning dripped from each syllable. "Tell me you understand."

I preened over his possessiveness–Wait. He suspected me of foul play, too, but he was helping me anyway, just in case? Intending to change my mind and win me over to his side? That might explain last night's charm, which must have been more potent than I'd realized, creating some kind of unconscious softening inside me. Look how quickly I'd settled against him, unaware of his dangerous musings.

Well. I straightened with a snap. From now on, I'd be more careful. More guarded. Coming to like and depend upon such an unstable guy wasn't in this year's bingo card. The very reason I should stop thinking about kissing him! I mean, he hoped to keep me glued to his side for the rest of my life, even if he married Valkara. An idea I intended to nip in the bud after Juniper's rescue. My sister and I could forget this other world existed. No more berserker obsession. I'd had my fill. We'd just have to ensure Deco never found us.

Fake our deaths, possibly? Kill the shifter king?

Whoa. Where had *that* thought come from?

"I understand." The prince gave a terse nod and retreated.

THE STOLEN BRIDE

"I'm not, you know," I said and sighed. Except Malachi. His offer.

"Perhaps not wittingly," Viktor replied.

Silence accompanied us the rest of the trip. As the sun descended, the stream of light that filtered through the overhead canopy thinned. Finally, though, we reached our destination. And oh, wow. What a destination it was. People would pay big money to use this area as a wedding venue. Not me, of course, but others. Anyway.

A large circular clearing surrounded a smaller circle marked by ten massive stones reminiscent of Stonehenge, each positioned to resemble a doorway. Flecks of gold and silver glittered in the air, while a dusting of diamond powder coated the outside of every rock. Precious gems rimmed the edges. Rubies. Sapphires. Emeralds. Plus jewels I didn't recognize.

"Anything I should know about these traveling stones?" I asked as Viktor dismounted and helped me do the same.

"Yes. Humans usually die going through them. And if they survive, they often wish they'd died."

What! "I'm human!" And already backing away.

He reached out to clasp my wrist. "Not fully. You are of sentinel blood. Fully griffin with a beast of your own. Which makes sense, since Malachi recruited you."

Wait. I had a lion-eagle hybrid inside me? I mean, yes, Malachi had told me I hailed from his line, but I hadn't considered *this*. The moisture in my mouth dried. "How do you know that for sure?"

"There are many indicators." Viktor moved fast, leaning down to put his face at the base of my throat. My pulse leaped as he dragged his nose up, inhaling deeply. "Your scent is one," he rasped, straightening. Gold rings flashed in his eyes. He released his grip on my arm, but there I stayed,

105

close enough to lean into him. "Though yours is a perfume sweeter than most." His voice dipped. "Deliciously sweet."

I licked my lips and wrung my fingers, each action born from a conflicting emotion. Pleasure versus dismay. "I meant, how do you know I'm not human? What if you're wrong for once and I die?" Who would rescue Juniper then?

"You've already passed through a traveling stone. There's no other way to reach Örök." He linked his fingers with mine and led me to the circle. "And don't forget the doorway in my tent."

Right. Still I reeled. Malachi had risked my life without my permission. He must pay.

The berserkers strapped our supplies to their backs and released the horses, trusting them to return to camp on their own. We approached the stones on foot, everyone halting in front of a different pairing. Tremors swept over my limbs when Viktor took a post at my side.

"Don't be afraid, Lovie." He whispered the words straight into my ear, sending a new tide of shivers cascading over me. A talent of his, apparently. "I will let nothing happen to you, I swear it."

"I'm not afraid. Not really." But the stakes had never been higher. With Juniper, I'd finally found my other half. My missing piece. I needed time with her. "But I kind of am," I admitted. And man, I hated fear.

"I will protect your life with my own." He ruined the beautiful confession when he added, "You still owe me answers, songs, and a reward."

I pressed my tongue to the roof of my mouth. "From sweet as cake to sour as lemons."

"My specialty. Soldiers," he called, and they straightened into attention. "It's time."

After shedding their shirts, they unsheathed large

THE STOLEN BRIDE

blades from the scabbards that hung from the waist of their leathers.

"I'm not going in topless," I warned Viktor.

A rugged smile crossed his lips, there and gone. Just enough to light a fire inside me. "It's purely ceremonial," he said, clasping my hand with his free one. "This might sting a bit." With no other warning, he cut my palm. A small incision with a big well of crimson.

The pain registered, but my adrenaline was too high for me to care. "Was that necessary?"

"You cannot pass through dimensions without blood." He raised my arm and pressed my wound against both sides of the stone, ensuring I left a thick smear of red behind. Then he performed the same act on himself, cutting and pressing. Seeing his blood mingle with mine did something to me. My knees quaked.

"I never shed blood to enter the bathroom."

"The bathroom is within this dimension," he replied.

Oh. Well.

He returned the dagger to its sheath and squared his shoulders. He was just so big, his body so broad, I felt crowded in the best way. The start of a wing tattoo on his shoulder offered a perfect distraction. Not to mention the flawless flesh that stretched taut over what must be rocks. Such power! Oh, the ferocity barely banked inside him. Heat spread over my cheeks. I forgot all about my throbbing hand.

"If you have changed your mind and wish to stay behind, that's no problem," Viktor commented, withdrawing his swords. "I had a contingent of men follow us in case you wished to return to camp. They'll escort you." He didn't wait for my response, just strode into the center of the stone doorway, vanishing in a blink.

The nerve of the man. And the thoughtfulness. The juxtaposition was maddening, exactly like the man himself.

Heart thudding, I rushed to catch up with him. In an instant, a gale force of wind slammed into me. Grains of sand pelted my body, acting as little needle pricks against my skin. Squeezing my eyes shut against the burn, I extended my arms, searching for Viktor. There! I flung myself against his back, clinging to the berserker as tight as humanly possible.

Just as suddenly as the wind kicked up, it died. The storm ended and peace reigned. Breathing deep, I pried open my eyes, relaxed my hold on Viktor, and glanced about, unsure what to expect...

Huh. We stood in front of another set of traveling stones. These were nothing like the others. They looked to be made of rusted metal and crumbling concrete. The sun appeared to be crumbling as well, with bits of it streaking across a dark gray sky studded by oily black clouds. Gnarled snow-capped trees with intertwined, thorn-littered branches surrounded us. An electric current charged frigid air scented with the sharp bite of evergreen.

Mist formed in front of my face with every exhalation. Viktor turned slowly and focused squarely on me, his chin down and his eyes fierce. He panted his breaths.

A prickly sensation rode the waves of my nerve endings, instincts screaming, *Leave. Now.*

I swallowed. He was close to raging out. But why? "Viktor. I need you to dial it down, okay?"

But he didn't. One after the other, glowing golden rings rimmed his pupils, until flames crackled inside his irises. His inhalations became huffs, his nostrils flaring. With him, the mist resembled smoke, making him appear to be some sort of dragon shifter. He opened and closed claw-tipped fists.

Danger, danger! What had caused this fierce reaction? The land itself? Being closer to Deco?

"Viktor," Bodi said, he and the others advancing on us, preparing to subdue the king. Thankfully, they didn't react as he did. They must have used the mystery herb he'd mentioned to keep themselves cold.

Growls rumbled in Viktor's chest, a sign we were one step closer to a full on tantrum.

"Stay back," I commanded the others. Firebrand activated! If words alone weren't the answer, touch was. I flattened my palms against his sizzling chest and glided nearer. Mmm. So warm! "Easy there, big fella. The Clover is here."

He drew in a breath. Released it. His gaze remained hot on me.

"That's it. That's the way," I praised as his tension dulled.

"We should go," he grated. "Turul-shifters lurk all around."

What!

While the soldiers heaved a collective sigh of relief, my fight response cranked to high gear. I scanned the woods with a sharper perspective. No sign of the shifters that I could see. No moving shadows, feathered wings, or glowing red eyes.

A chill settled in the small of my back. If I never glimpsed those glowing red eyes again, it was too soon.

"Formation," Viktor called, and the warriors drew close, encircling us, forming a protective wall. They even radiated heat, saving me from the icy temperature. "Coat."

Bodi pulled a thin cloth parka from a backpack and

tossed it to his king, who secured the material around my shoulders with an ornate clasp at the neck. It was shockingly hot, with a soft fur lining, and oh, I loved it.

After a signal from Viktor, we marched forward, leaving the relative safety of the stone circle to enter this new forest filled with overlarge snakes, spiders and two headed squirrels.

And just like that, I was officially done with the woodland setting.

I remained on high alert, on the hunt for anything suspicious. Near silence provided an eerie soundtrack when compared to the verdant life found in Viktor's lands. Instead of birdsong and the babble of a stream, I detected the hollow crunch of snow underfoot. Rather than the vibrant colors of wildflowers and trees heavy with green leaves, a monochrome backdrop of frost painted a picture of despair.

The only sight I enjoyed sprang from the too brief moments I observed Viktor from my periphery. Though he still hovered at the edge of a break, he provided a visual feast for a starving pet groomer. White hair in utter disarray. Green eyes sharp, watchful. Jaw clenched. Muscles twitching with anticipation, daring an enemy to approach. Aggression pulsed from him.

His sensual appeal was off the charts.

Oh! "Turul-shifter!" I pointed to a winged muscle man perched on the branch of a tree, his eyes glowing bright red. Ebony wings arched over his shoulders, with small horns protruding along each arch. A fur kilt-type garment covered his thighs. His dark hair flapped around ultra-defined features.

None of my entourage reacted. They continued as if we weren't being watched.

THE STOLEN BRIDE

"I don't understand," I said, glancing back. The shifter was gone.

"He's only a scout," Viktor explained. "I want him to tell Deco what he saw."

Ahhh. A war strategy. I liked it. Maybe. Kind of. It showed a confident front.

"Besides," he added, and I swallowed a groan.

Anytime Viktor tacked on an addition to something he'd said, it never ended well for me. I lifted a hand. "No. The conversation is over. Say nothing else."

He shrugged and held his silence, even seeming to forget I walked beside him.

Was he seriously not going to tell me what he'd intended to tell me? "Fine, let's hear what else you hoped to do by letting the scout go free," I said, curiosity getting the best of me.

"Perhaps I'll tell you. Later. With the proper incentive."

"You fiend!" I belted out, and he almost smiled.

Our group climbed a hill, descended it, and came to a river with ice chunks floating along the water's surface. I scanned left and right but found no break or bridge. *Through the slush we go.*

Teeth chattering, I waded across the thigh-deep length directly behind Viktor. Oh, the cold! By the halfway point, the muscles in my legs shook. When we reached the shore, I only wanted to collapse. But I pressed on. I'd probably need another massage tonight.

Fresh goose bumps broke out all over me.

"Very well, I'll tell you without incentive," Viktor piped up, as if I'd insisted. He pointed to a hill. "There's an entire flock of turul-shifters already waiting for us below."

Okay, so, the groan I'd managed to swallow earlier now escaped. "How many soldiers constitute a flock?"

"Only fifty."

What! Heart thumping against my ribs, I palmed both of my daggers. "Fifty against ten is so unfair."

"Ja. They're going to die badly."

I blinked at him, noting the seriousness of his expression.

"I'm ready to ask my next question in the queue," he stated, matter-of-fact, as if we weren't marching into a battle.

Uh. "We should be preparing for war."

"Nem. I'm always prepared."

Was he truly that confident of his victory? He must know something I didn't. "Ask," I croaked, because what else could I do?

"How do you usually calm from *your* tempers?"

"The last one happened when I was a little girl. I got physical and hurt my mother." Shame and guilt coated my voice. "Seeing her pain motivated me to create, well, I call them bottles. I store my emotions in them."

He frowned. "So you've never experienced a true temper as an adult?"

"No." I cringed. "Is that a bad thing?"

"Ja. Because you're about to."

"What—"

A high-pitched, piercing call cut through my response, curdling the blood in my veins.

Our group halted at the top of the hill. Below us, the promised flock stood in battle position, fully shifted and waiting for us. The corners of Viktor's mouth curved into a smile regular people would probably describe as their worst nightmares.

"Whatever you do, no bottling." Lifting his chin, he

proclaimed to the others, "The killing begins in five, four, three, two..."

9

Poison-Proof Your Relationship: Romance Detox Tips

—HOW TO TRAIN YOUR BERSERKER
By Elizabeth "Elle" Darcy-Bruce

One.
My heart thudded. I held my breath, anticipating the attack. I didn't have long to wait. The shifters raced up while we raced down, the berserkers doubling in size while maintaining a tight circle around me.

A shadow swept over our group, and I jerked my gaze skyward. Another flock!

Like the others, they had transformed into half man, half bird of prey hybrids. Their noses and mouths had grown out, creating the world's ugliest beaks. Jet black feathers rimmed with gold covered their wings and clustered in patches along their arms, chests, and legs. Talons tipped their fingers and toes.

I shuddered at the grotesque sight. Monsters!

The berserkers around me hadn't yet noticed the

coming aerial assault. They still faced straight ahead, soon to collide with the foot-soldiers. A scream of warning barreled across my tongue, but it was too late. The flyers descended en masse.

With a gasp, I ducked. The bird-men never crashed into us. Oooh! The soldiers had noticed their approach, after all, and paused to reposition at the last second, jerking their weapons high in the air, ensuring the first line drove themselves through the blades.

Howls of pain pierced the air. Blood sprayed. The starting bell. The foot soldiers reached the fray, and brutal combat erupted. Ten berserkers against ninety shifters. Swords swung. Wings and talons swiped. Feathers rained over the snow-packed, crimson speckled ground.

Viktor remained at my side, but he was in no way stationary. He moved around my statue-still form with astonishing speed, attacking his foes and blocking their strikes with equal fervor. His masterful skill astounded me. Not one enemy blow resulted in my harm, even though I seemed to be the target of every shifter. They challenged the king in clusters, attempting to reach me.

My stomach roiled, but not with fear. As the savagery of battle intensified, anger sparked, burning inside cracking bottles. Suddenly, the daggers I held felt like extensions of my hands. How dare Deco and his army do this? I was so close to saving my sister; I refused to stop now.

Determined and yes, vengeful, I swung at a turul-shifter above us. Viktor decapitated him before I ever made contact. The king wasted no time ripping the heart from the headless body. Golden lights like those in his eyes streaked through the organ, fading, then dying.

"Get down and stay down," he growled at me. "Close your eyes if you must."

"I'm not some damsel in distress," I growled back. The death didn't faze me. Maybe because the creature had attacked us first. Good riddance!

I ran through the moves I'd learned in self-defense class. Use my body as an armory. Elbow, heel, fist, and head. All weapons. Ready, I scanned for my first victim. Him! He looked like he desired a one-on-one tangle.

The eager beaver dodged berserkers and brethren alike, his red-eyes locked on me.

At the half way point, he leaped, tucking his wings against his sides to increase his momentum, becoming a living missile. His feathers shimmered in the weak, wintery sun. I raised my daggers, anticipating impact...

Viktor cut off his head mid-air, then ripped out his heart. Plop, plop. "The day I need your help, Lovie, is the day I deserve to die in battle."

I almost stomped my foot. "I deserved that kill." Yes, it was something I'd never in a million years thought I'd say. But then, why would I ever imagine myself caught in such a situation? Still, I couldn't deny Viktor's utter power as he defended us. A mesmerizing sight to behold. Other women might find him incredibly frightening, but I reveled. So sexy! And irritating.

I readied to attack another shifter– Grr. Viktor struck him first. I huffed with frustration. He'd predicted I would lose my temper, and now I knew why. Because of him! And rightly so!

At least the enemy army dwindled as other berserkers removed shifter heads and hearts, too. According to my mother, it was the only way to truly kill an immortal.

Grunts of exertion blended with growls of fury and hisses of pain. Though tensions and aggression surged, none of the warriors had broken into a berserkerage—yet. I had wondered if they'd partaken of the herb Viktor mentioned, and now I knew. They had. The well-trained soldiers remained cold, Bodi most of all, working in tandem and adjusting their formation as needed.

Argh! A new flock of turul-shifters arrived. Violence escalated as these soldiers proved stronger than the others, managing to injure some of the berserkers.

My gaze collided with that of a particularly big shifter. Another scout? He perched on a branch just outside the raging battle. White hair slapped his inhuman face. His blood-red eyes fit well with a gleeful smile.

With a crook of my finger, I motioned him over. "If you dare."

He merely offered a parody of a smile, staying put.

Out of nowhere, Bodi bellowed a raw and primal sound. Everyone's attention swung to him, even mine. My eyes widened as I took in the devastating scene. One of Viktor's men lay sprawled on the ground, a turul-shifter nearby, cackling as he held a glowing heart in his hand.

No, no, no. The fallen was the young soldier with the mischievous grin who'd offered me the best cuisine the forest had to offer.

Each berserker, including Viktor, rushed his way, but it was too late. The turul-shifter raked his claws through the organ, and the glow vanished, snuffed out. My own heart ached.

Our young comrade's attacker died a nanosecond later. It was then the squad of berserkers began to break with rage, despite consuming the herb. They threw back their heads and spread their arms, roaring into the wintery chill. Their bodies seemed to double again, clothing tearing. Black lines forked across their limbs, and glowing golden rings filled their irises. Razor-sharp talons grew from their fingertips.

Only Viktor seemed unaffected as he fended off attacking shifters.

The metallic scent of blood permeated the air. Cries of rage and pain replaced the grunts and groans. Forget battle. I stumbled backward, ready to run. I could calm Viktor, maybe, hopefully, but not all of his men. And not while Viktor remained preoccupied. Only, I rammed into an obstacle. Or rather, a shifter. He snaked his arms around me, anchoring my body in place while resting the tips of his claws against my throat.

"Thank you for the invite," he squawked in my ear.

I clued in on his identity: the guy from the tree. Every thought in my brain erased but one: *get free!* But as I grappled against his hold, he choked me, stealing my breath.

While Viktor's bigger, badder and meaner-than-before army challenged the remaining turul-shifters, my captor called, "Deco sends his regards, Viktor. By the way, my claws are tipped with vargbane root." He tapped said claws against my throat, threatening to breach my skin.

I gulped. What did vargbane root do?

The king's head shot up as he slammed a booted foot into the face of a limp shifter. Something dangerous glowed in his eyes when he clocked my predicament. One of his arms remained raised in mid-air, ready to descend and remove his foe's heart.

His glowing gaze narrowed on my captor. "Deco wouldn't play with such a substance, even to hurt me."

"Oh, but he would. As would I." Again, the turul-shifter tapped his nails against the column of my throat.

I didn't take time to ponder the pros and cons of my next action; I simply acted, reaching back to slam one of my

THE STOLEN BRIDE

daggers into my captor's thigh and the other into his face. His body jerked against mine, his clawtips cutting me. A surge of adrenaline dulled a flare of searing pain.

Then Viktor was there, freeing me and ending the turul-shifter with swipes of his claws. Pushed past his control, the king kept swiping. Slash, slash, slash. The gruesome sight...

At the same time, his warriors finished off the remaining shifters, who died laughing with delight, as if they knew something we didn't.

But, um, my neck. Each puncture burned hotter and hotter. I rubbed at the wounds, anger and affront draining from me. No longer did the violence leave me unmoved.

Sickness churned in my stomach as I gazed at Viktor, his men, and the blood-soaked battlefield.

Viktor straightened and, glimpsing my horror, pounded his crimson covered fists into his temples, muttering, "Find, destroy, happy. Find, destroy, happy."

I watched in alarm as he slashed at his clothes, his arms, and his legs. Oh, no. If anything, he was worse than when I'd first met him.

"Viktor," I croaked. "Stop."

He didn't stop.

His men did nothing to help him but turned toward me. Bodi looked as if he would like nothing more than to give me the turul treatment and shred my internal organs.

"Yo, Tor," I called, lumbering closer. "Vik. Calm down, and I'll play a fourth song for you."

"Why should he calm down? He's going to lose you and become a shifter, and you're responsible for it," Bodi said, his tone chilling. He bit the blade of his bloodied sword. Another soldier plucked out the shifter claws embedded in his chest, which were attached to a severed hand, and tossed the appendage aside. Both stepped toward me, their intent clear. Punish the interloper. The others looked unsure.

The pair took another step closer. And another. A third joined them and trepidation skittered over me. Despite the agony of movement, I hurled myself against Viktor. The prince was wrong. He wasn't losing me or becoming a shifter. I just needed him to calm!

Contact snapped him out of his fog. He gathered me close with a single arm, throwing back his head, and releasing a wild, otherworldly whistle. His men immediately stilled.

The burn in my neck reached an almost unbearable degree. Beads of sweat popped up over my brow. "Um. Quick question. What's vargbane root?"

A barbaric sound burst from Viktor. "The vargbane root." Anxiety-tinged fury twisted his features as he clasped my chin and angled my head, giving himself a better view of my injuries. Whatever he saw caused the anxiety to spike.

Tremors invaded my limbs. "What? Tell me."

"Won't let you die." He swooped down, setting his lips around a puncture and sucking, then spitting. An action he repeated, as if I'd been bitten by a snake and he sought to remove venom.

His men rushed over, encircling us. Exactly as they'd done when we'd first entered this land.

"Majesty," Bodi rasped, shock and alarm dripping from the title. "You should not do this. You must stop."

But he didn't stop. Not until the last of that sizzling heat cooled in my veins. As he lifted his head, my knees knocked, weakened by relief. Until I realized blood filled the whites of his eyes.

"Viktor?" I breathed.

Releasing me, he stumbled backward and crumbled to the ground. He landed atop a slain turul-shifter. Fresh horror besieged me, and I pressed a hand over my mouth. Reason crested only a split second later. I rushed to him. Or attempted to. His men formed a blockade. To make a bad situation worse, Bodi grabbed me, imprisoning my arm in an iron clasp.

"Do you have any idea what you've done?" the second-in-command demanded.

"I didn't do anything!" I burst out.

"You let yourself be drugged."

"Let myself? You saw the guy with his claws against my neck, right?" I sputtered for a moment. "What's vargbane root?" I repeated.

"An ancient poison able to trap an immortal inside his own mind, keep him asleep, dreaming, and projecting his thoughts for anyone to see while he slowly wastes away, suffering in silence. There's no antidote. No cure. The more powerful the immortal, the faster the toxin works. That is the reason we avoid using it against our enemies, despite its effectiveness. Now, Viktor is as good as dead." Accusation laced his harsh tone.

The blood whooshed from my head, my ears ringing. Why, why, why had Viktor endangered his own life to save mine? That...he...I fought Bodi's hold. "Let me see him."

"Never again. Be thankful you're still alive." To the men, he called, "Carry him beyond the battlefield. There should be a hidden camp."

I could do nothing but watch as the warriors lifted him and carted him from my midst. Along the way, they cast me final menacing glances.

A barbed lump grew in my throat. This was it for me,

wasn't it? "You're going to end my life." A statement, not a question.

"Ja. But only after we end his." Bodi dragged me to a nearby tree, and I didn't fight. "We won't leave our beloved king in such a state."

Shock held me immobile. Viktor. Dying. Killed. Gone forever. The last remaining original. The guy who'd saved me from shifters. Who'd agreed to help me rescue my sister. Who'd calmed for me.

I'd known him only a short time, yet an almost unbearable sadness weighed down my heart.

Bodi yanked a thin silver bracelet from his wrist. The prince shook the metal, its links expanding, somehow pliable and yet strong enough to interlock–to cuff my hands together and bind me to the tree trunk. Out of spite alone, he stole the coat Viktor had secured around my shoulders.

"Why not kill me now?" I grated, tugging at my bonds. Intractable. No slack.

The prince met my gaze. "The amount of suffering he endures will decide the amount of suffering *you* endure."

With the vow hanging in the air, he stalked off.

I bit my lip. Here I was, alone, mere feet away from the field of death. If turul-shifters returned, I'd be a sitting duck.

I laughed without humor. Of course, I was already dead, wasn't I?

10

Lights, Camera, Berserker! Surviving Movie Night

—HOW TO TRAIN YOUR BERSERKER
By Elizabeth "Elle" Darcy-Bruce

The short winter day passed with no visit from the berserkers or the turul-shifters. No food or water, either, though I'd been able to drag a discarded fur over by using my feet. The original wearer no longer needed it.

Despite being forced to remain in a sitting position, hugging a tree trunk, I kept my wits honed. Even as the acrid smell of death worsened and flies and scavengers descended, feasting upon the carnage. Thankfully, I was ignored in favor of the seemingly never-ending buffet.

No matter what, I—refused—to—cry. Deep down, in a hidden part of me, I maintained hope, expecting Viktor to overcome the poison, spank his men for daring to endanger the life he'd nearly died protecting, then rush to my rescue. A prospect as wondrous as it was frustrating. I didn't like needing another person for anything, especially considering a good number of weapons waited only a short distance away, there for the taking.

But dang it, if I had to choose between Viktor's survival and a trip home, give me King Vik. Forget overdue bills and constant internal tension. Return my grumpy, surly berserker. The guy wasn't terrible. On the contrary. He'd saved my life at the risk of his own. And he gave good cuddle. The best. But also, he'd willingly placed himself and his best soldiers in danger to save my sister. From the beginning, I hadn't had to fight for calm; it was just there. Because of him. I'd gotten to (mostly) relax and be myself, and he'd seemed to like me anyway.

If my reoccurring dream was a prediction, as I'd begun to suspect, he *would* survive.

Hope spread, and I clung to it with every bit of my strength. *Please be a prediction.* I just had to get to him. I was the guy's firebrand, after all. An important position. The *most* important. Surely there was something I could do to save him. What was a lethal toxin compared to a determined woman?

Okay, so, I might have sniffled. But sniffling wasn't crying! And, yes, my chin trembled. But no tears streaked down my cheeks. Not more than one. Possibly a couple dozen. Already cracked bottles vibrated.

I racked my brain for any tidbits about healing I might've read in my study of berserkers. Any story my mom may have told me that I'd forgotten. But answers never came, and hopelessness attempted to murder the hope.

A hoarse, broken roar pierced the air, and I jolted. Viktor! He still lived! An answering whimper rose from deep within me. "Keep fighting, Vik," I shouted. He could overcome this. He would! He must. In fact, any moment, someone would remember some obscure cure and release victory cheers.

Awful, terrible silence stretched, and my shoulders rolled in.

When night fell, great darkness cloaked the land. Birds erupted into songs better suited for a horror movie soundtrack. The temperature dropped, the chill drilling into my bones. My teeth chattered. I shifted, using the tree to my advantage, blocking a gust of wind scented with death. Bending my head, I rested my brow against bark. The jagged edges cut into my skin, but I didn't care.

Come on, Viktor. Pull through before it's too late.

Morning arrived with muted rays of light filtering through the canopy of bare tree limbs overhead. I was just about to shout and beg for an update when twigs snapped, signaling the approach of someone—or something. I braced, ready to kick as if my life depended on it. And it just might.

Bodi broke through a wall of branches, his expression grim.

"No!" I bellowed, violently shaking my head. "You didn't. You wouldn't."

"No, not yet," the warrior grated, unleashing great tides of relief inside me. The prince freed me from my prison, but not my cuffs. He jerked me to my feet, and my knees nearly buckled.

Somehow, I remained upright despite a barrage of aches and pangs as he dragged me through the woods. "What happened?" Did Viktor wake up and demand my presence? Had the prince changed his mind about ending my life? I bit my tongue. Or was I soon to die?

Up ahead, a turul-shifter landed on a branch and

squawked, startling me. "Prince Bodi," he called. "Deco's offer is still good."

Bodi stiffened, still saying nothing. We passed the shifter without incident.

"Let's kill him while we've got the chance," I encouraged, looking over my shoulder, but our foe was already gone. Dang it. The more shifters we eliminated, the less danger that surrounded Viktor. "What offer did Deco make you?"

"That's not your concern. Viktor is. He hasn't been the best king for centuries. He threatens us daily, erupts often, and tends to choose punishment over mercy. But his people remain loyal because we remember the ruler he used to be–who he was becoming again with your arrival."

Pain, fury and resolve drenched his words.

"He sought only to make our lives better," he continued. "And he was unbeatable in battle. A brilliant strategist. Innovative. Discerning. Our kingdom prospered like no other. And you took that possibility from us."

He didn't give me a chance to defend myself as we entered a small, hastily assembled shelter, most likely chosen for its southern border of evergreens that provided refuge from the biting wind. Snow had been shoveled to the side, revealing a cold, hard patch of ground and a makeshift pit where a fire blazed.

The remaining elite soldiers formed a protective barrier around the enclosure. Actually, additional soldiers were here. They stretched from the large boulder on one side to the fallen branches stacked high on the other, the different sections acting as walls. Each man stared at me, as grim-faced as his prince. None of them spoke, but neither did I.

Dead leaves and feathers created a bed near the fire

where Viktor rested. He'd been cleaned of all battle gore. He slept shirtless, his lower half covered by my coat.

His expression remained blank, utterly devoid of emotion, humanity... life. My heart and stomach traded places. How still he lay, barely even breathing.

I took a step toward him, but movement drew my gaze to the boulder. What in the world? I pivoted, examining the shocking display. The smooth surface of the rock acted as a projector screen, a scene playing on repeat.

Vignettes of the last few weeks rolled before my eyes. It was like watching a movie based on my past, from the viewpoint of another.

My head spun. *This* was what played on a loop inside Viktor's mind as he slowly wasted away? I watched, transfixed, as he eased beside my sleeping form. I laid upon the pallet of furs in his original tent, wearing my tank and shorts, with my face turned toward him. He reached out to smooth locks of escaped hair from my face with utter reverence, as if he handled something precious.

Our first night together.

I tried to breathe as movie Viktor glided his fingers along my braid. As soon as he finished, he traced the shell of my ear and the shape of my lips, and smiled with pure delight.

My heart pounded in my ears. I yearned to see more of this big, bad berserker being his most gentle, with tenderness and awe stamped into his usually harsh features, but the scene morphed. He now stood with Bodi, the two males face to face. Viktor's lips moved, but I heard no words. Though I did sense the tension between them and the urgency in Viktor's body language.

"Before he broke into a rage after your arrival," Bodi

said, "he made me swear to look after you if anything happened to him."

One of my hands floated to my racing pulse. "Is that why I'm here now?"

"Nem."

On the "film" broadcasted to the boulder, the prince spoke next, and his words, whatever they were, infuriated his king.

"I reminded him of your untrustworthiness," Bodi explained in real life. "Attempted to reason with him about how to handle you. Keep you chained and contained until we'd investigated any ties to Deco. You saw the result of that conversation."

Seriously? Viktor had gone into a rage over the mere thought of my discomfort?

Longing filled me. We *must* save him.

"These two memories play on repeat," Bodi grated. "I believe he is aware of what is happening around him and hopes to remind me of your...importance to him. Since you bring him comfort, for whatever reason, I will allow you to stay with him until the end."

His voice provided a masterclass on fatigue and sadness, and I realized Bodi's hostility toward me originated from a place of deep concern for his king. Some of my hostility toward him evaporated.

"Give him whatever he needs," he added, dour.

Little ole me, important to someone as powerful as Viktor. Did wonders never cease? I mean, yes, I'd recognized my importance to him. But this went beyond that. I wasn't just a desire but a necessity.

I wanted to be flip with the prince, to guard my wounded heart against feelings even now threatening to

THE STOLEN BRIDE

bud, but I was too humbled to try. "I think we all know I'm his firebrand, and he would greatly protest these bonds." I extended my cuffed hands in Bodi's direction.

His internal agitation glittered in his eyes. "Harm him at your peril. That hasn't changed. And I swear to you now, his hurt will be a mirror of yours." Promise issued, the prince unwound the metal from my wrists and stalked out. The others followed.

My heart raced as I rubbed my chafed skin. Rather than stew over the motionless man in need of a miracle, I took a moment to view the newest scene to play over the walls. In it, I sat on the fur pallet in his tent, looking him over as he paced. I leered at him, really.

A stinging burn uncoiled in my cheeks. He'd noticed me noticing him, but *I* hadn't realized it at the time. I'd been too wrapped up in his smoking hotness.

"That's what you're thinking about right now?" I asked and stretched out beside him. "What message are you attempting to convey, hmm?"

His heat enveloped me, and oooh, it was tinged with his decadent scent. I moaned as I wrapped myself around him and snuggled closer.

"Wake up and tell me what you want me to know," I urged. "You can be saved; I know you can. All you must do is pull yourself out of your thoughts."

Right? What had Bodi told me? The victims of vargbane root became trapped inside their heads, Sleeping Beauty style. So. What if I gave Viktor a reason to wake?

I rested my palm on his chest, just over his heart. The organ beat hard and sure, emboldening my theory. This king had a bunch more living to do. He would fight. Now, to offer him the perfect reward...

129

A chance to explain his vision wasn't the golden ticket. What about a threat of punishment? It wasn't a reward, but it might be an incentive. If nothing else, it was familiar to him. "You wake up right now, Viktor Endris. I mean it. Wake up or face severe consequences."

A minute ticked past with no reaction. No matter. Onward and upward.

Threats of harm, perhaps? Surely he'd be eager to protect himself. "I'm sure there's a weapon around here somewhere, and I'm not afraid to use it."

Again, nothing.

I pondered my options, stroking my nails through the smattering of hair on Viktor's chest, and gazed about. Oh! The violin.

"I owe you songs. If you'd like to pretend you want me to stop, as you've done after every concert, you'll have to wake up and make me." Abandoning my place of comfort, a truly difficult task, I gathered the instrument. After settling into a comfortable position, I closed my eyes and played. And played.

I cracked open one eye. The images on the walls had stilled and dulled, as if his mind had settled. An improvement. Excellent. I played some more.

When my arms tired, I let the last note taper to quiet. The scenes on the wall instantly brightened and activated once again. I sighed.

"I'm going to tell you a childhood memory." He liked history, so he might like learning more about me. "You'll wake up, and I'll tell you another." I returned to his side, snuggling closer than before. "See, one day on my walk to school I found an injured chocolate lab. I was only eleven, but I rallied the strength to carry him home. Which should

THE STOLEN BRIDE

have clued me in that I wasn't fully human, now that I think about it, but I digress. I named him Silly Goose. My dad drove us to the vet. Once Goose was given a clean bill of health, I convinced my parents to let me keep him. Goose loved and protected me from that moment on."

Man, I missed my precious Goose.

"If you want to hear about my first date, you gotta wake up," I told Viktor.

Nothing.

Okay, new, new route. "You still have questions in your queue. Do you really want to die with them trapped in your heart?" Nothing. "What if I give you *unlimited* questions? But only if you wake up right...this...second."

One terse minute ticked into another. Nothing.

Frustration brewed. "You can't die. Your cherished fire-brand needs your help," I reminded him, rising to my elbow. I peered down at his beautiful face, my chest squeezing. His expression never altered. "Your men need you, too. Don't leave them stuck under Bodi's command. He's a tool."

Parts of me longed to spew out a litany of complaints about the prince and his treatment of me. But I didn't. Because Viktor was gonna wake up, and I had no desire to taint their friendship.

Look at me being the bigger person. I was pretty amazing.

Still nothing, and my shoulders sagged.

Since Viktor had caressed me while I slumbered, I didn't bother tamping down the urge to do the same. I combed my fingers through his silken white hair, loving the contrast between the colorless strands and my warmer flesh tone.

"If you die, I'll turn myself over to Deco," I warned.

"He'll definitely murder me, but I'll still do it. Unless you're here to stop me. Stop me, Viktor. Please!"

The threat to me, his firebrand, garnered no bodily reaction, either, but the images on the rock came faster. New ones. Viktor carrying me in the forest the first day we met then later spotting me up in the tree. Next came an explicit image of vision Viktor pinning me against a wall and kissing the air from my lungs. My brows knit together even as my heartbeat sped up. This hadn't happened. Wait. Had he *imagined* doing it?

Well, well, well. "Forget the murder thing. Deco and I will probably fall madly in love. I mean, why wouldn't we? My life is basically a romance novel. And you've seen him, right? That face. It rivals yours. And those abs. Mmm, mmm, mmm. The claws and wings! Delicious. Talk about masculine perfection. He's not really a villain, I bet. He's just misunderstood. A royal with an ooey gooey center hiding inside his clay heart. Unless I'm wrong. But if so, you'll have to correct me out loud with words."

Viktor's finger twitched at my side, and I gasped. Ding, ding, ding. We had a winner. Jealousy. Although...

I licked my lips, an idea percolating. I would probably bite off more than I could chew if I followed through, but I had to try, right? Anything to save my ki—*the* king and my sister.

Tracing a heart on Viktor's pec, I purred, "Maybe I'll fall for *you* instead. I know I promised not to, but you're the sublimely sexy king who gets the cutest gold rings in his eyes when he's miffed. By the way, my turn ons are immortals who wake up from drugged sleeps, rescuing damsels in distress together, and food of any kind. Especially chocolate chip cookies. And carrot cake with double cream cheese frosting. And chi tea lattes with extra chi. Oh, what I

THE STOLEN BRIDE

wouldn't give for a dozen cupcakes right now. I went all night without even the tiniest snack."

Focus. Right. "But I digress. We should go on a date, Tor. No, you know what? I'm calling you pudding pop. Or honey bear. Or Sergeant Fox. The only way to stop me from doing this is to *wake up*."

His finger twisted again, harder, and excitement whisked through me. This was working!

"Wake up," I pleaded, stroking his cheek. "Please, pudding pop. Do it for me, your precious sugar cookie. We should discuss our date."

Muscles bunched beneath me. His breathing came faster. Faster still.

My excitement doubled. Tripled! Was it truly happening? Was he awakening?

"Come on, come on. Wake up, and I might ask you for that kiss. A guaranteed five-star experience...if you're using a ten-star scale. But that's only because I've never kissed *you*. You can teach me how to do better. Wouldn't you like that? An opportunity to show me what I'm doing wrong. To give me hands-on tutelage in the art of pleasing you."

His back bowed, and he roared. I jerked upright, unsure whether this was a fit of pain or the moment I'd been fighting for. *Please, please, please.*

He sagged against the blanket, just as still as before. The images projected on the boulder faded to nothing, and I whimpered. Had I killed him?

Seconds ticked by as I wrung my hands. "Viktor?"

His eyelids popped open. He turned his head and met my gaze dead-on. "Don't you mean pudding pop?"

Relief flooded me in an instant, drowning my good sense. With tears welling in my eyes, I threw myself upon him, slinging my arms around his powerful body. "You woke up! You're alive!"

He rolled me to my back, pinning me to the blanket with his weight. Air hitched in my lungs when our gazes locked. Flecks of gold glowed in his green irises.

"You owe me a date and a kiss. Now give me what I'm due."

II

Rise and Roar: Battle-Free Tips for Waking With Your Berserker

—HOW TO TRAIN YOUR BERSERKER
By Elizabeth "Elle" Darcy-Bruce

My heart stopped, or seemed to, only to kick start with fevered anticipation. Viktor smoldered with the most sublime intensity. A true feat, considering white locks fell over his black brows, gracing him with a boyish charm. His gaze remained unwavering, however, and far from boyish.

I licked my lips, adoring the white-hot sear of his skin far too much. "First, I suggested we go on a date and said I might ask you for a kiss. Might." In an effort to put us on equal footing, I said, "Second, you should probably pin me against a wall while I decide if I'm gonna do it or not. That *is* your fantasy, yes?"

"Yours, too. I scented your reaction to seeing the images

even while I slept." He brushed the tip of his nose against mine. "You *want* to kiss me."

A blush heated my cheeks. "Tell me you crave me, and *only* me." Unable to stop the actions, I wound my arms around his shoulders and toyed with the ends of his hair the way he'd done to mine the night of the storm.

His eyelids hooded. "Ask me to kiss you."

Flutters erupted in my belly, making me feel as if I verged on taking flight. A single thread of common sense kept me grounded. "What about the shifters? I saw them on my walk here."

"Deco shouldn't strike for days." Viktor bent his head and nuzzled his cheek against mine. "He's giving Bodi time to kill me."

I frowned even as I nuzzled him right back. "That's not a very shiftery thing to do." But that explained the bargain the turul-shifter spoke of. "I'd think Deco would want to deliver the final blow himself."

"Nem. If Bodi ends me, he'll become a shifter himself and therefore subject to Deco's command. A particularly cruel punishment meant to haunt me after my death. Now, about that kiss you're ready to ask me for," Viktor purred, rocking his body into mine.

I moaned with rapture. Oh, this man could make me burn. I softened against him, asking, "Admit you want me more than the Valkara, and I'll do it."

"I want you more," he growled without hesitation. "Much more. Happy now?"

Yes! And no. I didn't want him to want her at all. But a deal was a deal. I cupped his jawline and peered into his eyes, growing breathless. "Viktor Endris?"

"Yes, Clover Deering." Desperate need flashed in his eyes. He lowered his head, letting his lips hover over mine.

THE STOLEN BRIDE

"Will..." I brushed the tip of my nose against his. "You..." My lids began to slide closed, and I tilted my head to the side. "Kiss..."

"Nem!" he shouted, jolting as if he'd been hit from behind. My eyes popped open. "Not now," he snapped and drove his fists into his temples.

I jolted, too. "Is Valkara trying to speak to you?"

"Ja, and she will stop if she recognizes what's good for her," he snarled, two voices evident. He breathed in, out. "There. She's gone now." His gaze zeroed in on my lips. "Where were we?"

What a marvelous development. He'd chosen me over the woman he'd professed a desire to marry. I smiled up at him. "I was just about to ask you to—"

Activity outside our enclosure reminded me that we weren't exactly private, and my enjoyment evaporated. Judging by the boom of pounding footsteps, an intruder neared our shelter.

Viktor heard them, too. He narrowed his lids. "Someone is going to die today."

By an act of my will, I wiggled out from under him. Just in time. Not only one man, but three entered. Bodi, along with two other soldiers. Each warrior scowled and clutched a weapon. When they spotted their leader alive, awake and aware, they floundered and sputtered.

"Get out," Viktor barked, keeping his focus steady on me as he sat up. The makeshift blanket fell, revealing he wore a pair of black leathers.

"You're awake," Bodi stated wide-eyed, glancing between us. "You ingested vargbane root, but you're awake."

"And busy." Viktor waved in my direction. "I'm in the middle of an intense negotiation."

My cheeks heated once more.

One of the soldiers grinned. All three appeared immensely relieved, despite their shock.

"I'm very hungry," I said, because not a single man here would ever forget that I'd been denied food for an entire night. "Not that anyone inquired about my wellbeing."

Grumbling under his breath, Viktor tore his gaze from mine at last and waved to the exit. "Apologize for keeping her from me, then bring us food. A lot of it."

After a slight hesitation, the soldiers did exactly as commanded, mumbling their apologies and marching out, leaving us alone.

"The kiss you swore to give me will wait." Viktor stood and rolled his shoulders.

I pulled my knees to my chest without a speck of grace. Countless questions frothed, but a clear winner bubbled up. "Why did you risk your life for mine?" He'd known what would happen, yet he'd done it anyway. I mean, I suspected the answer, especially after his most recent treatment of Valkara, but did he?

"You still owe me a reward, and I *will* collect."

"Why?" I insisted, certain the reward had nothing to do with it.

A pause laden with tension. Then, "I have lived multiple lifetimes." He kept his back to me. "You have yet to live one."

"True, but that isn't the reason you did it, either." I highly doubted he'd put any thought into his actions. What he'd done, he'd done on instinct alone.

His hands fisted at his sides. Why wouldn't he look my way anymore?

Bodi entered and stepped aside, a backpack in one hand and the violin case in the other. Soldier after soldier followed in after him, each bearing a different prize. Some brought covered dishes and bottles. Others carried utensils or a piece of furniture. A small square table and two chairs. The scent of a berry cobbler wafted, and my mouth watered.

"Where did you guys get such a feast?" I demanded as they placed two savory meat pies, an improvised charcuterie board, and a platter of some kind of roasted root vegetable medley on the table.

Notching his chin, Bodi grinned. "We're good at pillaging nearby villages."

I didn't return the smile. The man had wanted to kill me mere minutes ago. And the others, well, they'd abandoned me over a misunderstanding. Trust was gone.

The men filed out, while the prince lagged behind to study the king's profile. I thought I detected the barest hints of shame, regret, and affection, but I didn't care. I didn't! Mostly.

"Get out," Viktor told the prince.

Bodi wilted, relinquished the pack and the case, and took off, saying nothing else.

I beelined for the table. "What's the deal with you and Bodi? You're always so angry with him. Not that he doesn't deserve it. I'm curious, is all."

Viktor joined me and lifted the lid from a filched crock, revealing the barley stew I'd had before. It smelled even more amazing. "He's who lost my key."

Oh wow. Okay. Hadn't seen that one coming. "Maybe he sold it. Or traded it. Or betrayed you. Why do you work with him at all?" I asked, as I munched on all the goodies.

"He's my brother."

What! I flattened my hands against the table. "Like, for

real, not just good buddy bros? But you told me you guys weren't related."

"Nem, I explained how princes are chosen. A far more important title than brother. Bodi and I share a mother. Bodi and Deco share a father."

Another bombshell! Bodi and Deco were related. Things began to click. How Bodi never seemed overly bothered by his king's moods. How Viktor relied on him. Their eyes being a similar shade of green.

"Satiate your hunger." Viktor swiped up the backpack before settling on the bed to riffle through his belongings as if he were on the hunt for something specific.

"You're not hungry?" I asked, after consuming half the smorgasbord.

"I rarely am...for food."

A moment passed, and he didn't elaborate or look my way. Maybe he needed a few minutes alone to collect himself. I sure did, even though my previous starvation demanded I eat up his portion, too. But I didn't. Not this time. He must keep his strength up.

"Please eat. I'll clean and change out of my battle dress." Unlike him, I hadn't received a sponge bath, or whatever his men had done. "Is there a pond nearby?"

"Nem. But this is an abandoned bathhouse, eternally guarded by my men."

That explained the extra manpower we had.

He pointed to a shadowy opening near the boulder, the action stiff and choppy. And still he didn't face me. "It's there."

Man, something clearly bothered him. He'd seemed fine just before his men had entered with food.

"Here." He tossed a bundle of clean clothing my way. Garments he'd removed from the backpack. "Wear these."

THE STOLEN BRIDE

I caught them, grateful. "Thank you."

"You are beautiful. And smart," he grumbled out of the blue.

I double blinked. "Um. Thanks."

"And brave," he added.

Was he building up to an admission of feelings? Was this...nervousness? I bit my bottom lip. Perhaps I could help him out. "I find you strong and sexy, especially when you're semi-sane."

His gaze slid to me at last, his pupils huge. "Sexy?"

Cared more about that than the strength? "Very."

Though I expected him to respond, silence filled the air between us.

If he required more time, fine. "See you in a bit, Tor." Almost smiling, I carried my prize through the shadowy opening, trekked a narrow corridor and emerged into a rocky-walled cavern with a natural bubbling spring. Toiletries waited at the edge.

With a giddy squeal, I stripped and entered the water. This time, I didn't worry Viktor would burst in on me unannounced or uninvited. I knew him better. Barging in wasn't his style.

Okay, so, it was his style, but he wouldn't do it to me.

Okay, so, he'd totally do it to me, but not today. Not while he was still a wee bit upset over...whatever he was a wee bit upset over.

As warm water enveloped me, I groaned with delight and savored the decadence of the moment. Enjoyed the scent of lavender and honey as I squeezed out shampoo, conditioner, then body wash. Thrilled when the soft fabric of the tunic and leathers settled over my curves. Oh, la, la. Pants!

I combed my wet hair, secured my boots in place and

gave my reflection a quick check via the water surface. Not bad for a dimension traveling captive. Not bad at all. Now, to face Viktor. We needed a battle plan against Deco. And I required weapons.

I drew in a deep breath and held the air in my lungs before exhaling with gusto and returning to the main chamber.

Viktor was exactly where I'd left him, but not nearly as calm. He sat with his knees raised and his head between them while he pulled at hanks of his hair. "Find, destroy, happy. Find, destroy, happy."

Oh, no. Not this version of the king.

His head snapped up. He went silent when his gaze landed on me. His eyelids narrowed to slits, two gold circlets glowing in his irises. He looked me down and up. Slowly.

New flutters erupted. "Hello, pudding pop," I said with a wave. Uh-oh. I'd meant to tease him, but I'd only sounded flirty. *Get it together.* "For our date, you should bring me daggers rather than flowers. *My* daggers, to be specific." Hint, hint.

He shook his head. "Give a woman a dagger, and she can defend herself until it's stolen. Teach a woman to steal a dagger, and she can defend herself always. I will allow you to keep any weapons you can pilfer from my men."

"Deal." Never mind the shock of receiving a hall pass to grand theft dagger. "Now let's take this show on the road." We had some rescuing to do.

"Nem. We stay and draw the shifters to the camp. According to my scouts, there are many traps beyond this point. Since shifters can attack by air, they like to pepper the land with explosives, pits and a wealth of other destructions."

Disappointment unfurled, but dang it, I understood his reasoning. Part of me even applauded it. "What about my sister?"

"She'll be saved from Deco, I swear it. But first, we will thin the flocks."

"Very well." Guess we should shore up more strength. Time for second breakfast. I swept to the table and sat. He followed my progress visually, but not physically. I removed the lids from the remaining dishes and scooped generous portions onto my plate. He hadn't touched a thing. "Come. Eat with me."

"I'm not hungry."

A reply I didn't like. "You just overcame a life-stealing toxin, Viktor." I held up a peachy fruit, pinched between my fingers. "Come eat, and I'll answer a question free of charge." Then I'd get to ask one for free, as well. "I might even dish another compliment."

Moments passed without a response, his muscles flexing and relaxing on repeat. I didn't break our staring contest, but I did eat the morsel. The sweet flavors hit my tongue. Moaning, I sucked my finger into my mouth. So good!

I offered him a second chance. "Want your compliment or not?"

He glided smoothly to his feet as if propelled by wings. Near me in a blink. I was ill-prepared when he bent down and snagged the treat from my fingers–with his teeth. The softness of his lips registered a split second before the warmth of his breath fanned my skin. Tremors invaded my limbs.

Chewing, he settled into the chair beside mine. As soon as he swallowed, I offered him another bite, which he accepted the same way. Heat bloomed in my cells, radiating satisfaction.

"Not bad," he grunted.

I fed him another and said, "Here's payment. Are you ready? Your skill on the battlefield awed me."

"That isn't a compliment, it's a fact."

"It's both. But I'll also admit you looked beautiful doing it."

His shoulders rolled back, and he raised his chin, the picture of masculine pride. "Better."

I liked this side of him. Bet I was the only person in existence to experience it. "So. Tell me what upset you earlier."

A muscle jumped beneath his eye. "The Valkara says I should kill you now and save myself the trouble later."

"Oh. Well." Wait. Kill me? I sputtered, trying to find the right words. Looked like I had a brand new, bright and shiny enemy. "I've given her zero reasons to target me." Other than stealing her man.

Oops?

Clearly, she wanted Viktor all to herself. Although, I kinda hoped Valkara was imaginary.

"Bet I can guess *when* she gave her newest directive," I said. "Right before Bodi and your men arrived." The moment Viktor had shouted "nem."

"You are correct." He worked his jaw. "But she's given it other times, too. Many other times. Even before I met you."

That he'd known of me before meeting me, just as I'd known of him, pointed to a fate connection I couldn't really deny. "You are the primordial of primordials, and she wants you for herself. Thank you for declining."

"You shouldn't thank me." He canted his head to the side, deepening his study of me.

My flutters took flight, invading other parts of me.

THE STOLEN BRIDE

"You're making me nervous, and I don't do nervous." It was a mild form of fear and an enemy to my beloved calm.

"Are you going to betray me, Love?" he asked with a low, husky timbre.

My breath hitched at the implication of this newest nickname.

He scowled and corrected, "Lovie."

I gulped. Downgraded from Love back to Lovie. The man clearly enjoyed torturing me. "No, Tor. I will not betray you. I have no need to do so. You're the king helping me save my beloved sister. The only warrior able to succeed."

"Let us hope your dedication proves true." He stood as I offered him the next bite. That, too, he accepted, leaning down to wrap his mouth around my entire finger, sending a hot rush over me when he sucked his way back up, taking the morsel with him.

"Good boy," I praised before I could think better of it.

He shifted from boot to boot, his eyes sizzling on me, his expression swinging between wild pleasure and ragged starvation.

My chest clenched. He wasn't used to praise, was he? Oh, his men followed him, sure, but kindness, empathy and encouragement—that he seemed unsure how to handle.

Next, he attempted to adopt a stern manner. "If you value your life, you'll stay here. Finish the meal, eat every bite, and rest. I'll return after I oversee the defenses."

"No!" I shouted, and he frowned. I winced. "Apologies for my volume, but I got hit by a sudden panic bomb. The last time you left me with a promise to return, I remained trapped in your tent for two weeks. I can't do that again. I'll go stir crazy. And shouldn't you avoid going out? The likelihood of Deco's attack increases greatly as soon as turul-shifters spot you."

"I *want* Deco to attack." He slid his knuckles along my jawline, astonishingly gentle. "But I accept your invitation to spend more time with you. I won't stay away for long." He strode from the tent, leaving me yearning.

I stared at the entrance for a long while, excitement and anticipation butting up against foreboding. If the first thing I wanted after Viktor's departure was his return, well, I was already in trouble. Especially now that I knew this Valkara, real or imagined, was attempting to kill the competition.

12

Lip-Lock and Conquer: Bringing Your Berserker To His Knees With a Single Kiss

—HOW TO TRAIN YOUR BERSERKER
By Elizabeth "Elle" Darcy-Bruce

Hours passed as I awaited Viktor. I tried to be a good little shelter bunny, obedient to the warrior who'd oh so graciously agreed to rescue my precious sister from homicidal bird shifters. I played the violin. Paced and mulled over his confession, my reoccurring dream, and a million other things. Searched the sheltered. Swirled around my finger the ring he'd given to Bodi, who'd tucked it inside the pack, as if he'd wanted me to have it.

After a while, my mood soured. If I'd been forgotten again, I would *do murder!* Viktor claimed he didn't want me bottling. Well. We'd find out if he changed his mind when I finally let loose.

I twisted the metal band with more force, hoping and praying Juniper or even Deco would contact me. If the hologram projecting jewelry was dangerous, or some kind of GPS device, the king wouldn't have demanded it be brought with us, so, I had no qualms about keeping it.

Over the course of the day, outside noises filtered into the tent in waves. Sawing. Hammering. Grunting. What were they doing out there, exactly? Oh, I got that they were building traps and defenses. But what kind of traps? What kind of defenses? And how many weapons were out there, being ignored, ready to be pilfered?

Finally, curiosity got the better of me, and I marched to the exit to peer out at the campsite. When I spotted the soldiers, I performed a double take. A shirtless, sweaty Viktor worked alongside several of his shirtless, sweaty men, each sharpening long tree branches into spears they then anchored into the ground and pointed up to the sky.

My gaze returned to the king. Droplets slid over glorious mounds of muscle. White locks stuck to his brow and curled adorably at the ends. He muttered to himself, and though I didn't hear him, I knew what he said. The shape of his gorgeous lips formed three clear words. *Find. Destroy. Happy.*

I still didn't know what, exactly, he meant. He'd never confirmed or denied my suspicions. Maybe I'd nailed it, and he searched for the key, hoped to destroy the shifters, and could then gain happiness. Maybe I was a hundred percent wrong. Either way, his strain had worsened.

With Viktor's promise that I could keep any weapons I stole front and center, I looked over the selection. Some of the men sat before a firepit, sharpening swords, daggers, and arrows.

"Clover?"

THE STOLEN BRIDE

Hearing my own voice but not being the one to speak threw me. Then realization dawned, and I jerked backward, raising the hand with the ring. And there she was. A small, holographic image of my twin. She suffered no injuries that I could see. Bore no chains or restrictions, either.

"Juniper." Love overwhelmed me. Heart racing, I rushed to the pallet to hide myself from anyone who entered. "You are okay?"

"I am. For now." Worry glazed her expression. "Deco has given me five minutes to convince you to sneak away from your king and meet him at a location of his choosing."

So he already knew of Viktor's survival. How many spies did Deco have positioned nearby?

"Four minutes and twenty-two seconds remain," the shifter king called from somewhere near my sister.

Juniper scowled at the sound of his smug, conde-scending voice. "He is literally the worst."

"What happens when I refuse to sneak away?" I asked, understanding his game. Imprison or kill us both, sending Viktor into a wild rage.

"Deco will probably spend another couple of hours describing all the terrible things he hopes to do to me when the time is right, trying to scare me but failing." The picture of stubbornness, she made an obscene gesture at someone beyond the hologram.

Inside I cheered. *That's my twin!* I adored her so much already, but the need to be with her sharpened. "I'm coming for you," I vowed. "On my terms, not Deco's. Nothing will stop me."

"Be careful," she warned, worried again. "He's got traps everywhere. All he's done is brag about them. I've never, in all my days, met anyone more annoying."

"Tell her about the one with the bugs," Deco called, not

149

the least bit upset by Juniper's revelation. "They eat everything in their path, even flesh."

Disgust and horror delivered a one, two punch.

"Tell her I've thought of everything," he added. "Tell her there's nothing she and her band of merry sentinels can do to win."

Oh, how I despised this shifter. "I'm very much looking forward to meeting the two of you in person, but for vastly different reasons."

The barest hint of a smile teased a corner of my sister's mouth. "I'm excited to meet you, too. I didn't know I had a sister, much less a twin. I just knew..." She trailed off, her cheeks pinkening with embarrassment.

"Something was missing," I finished for her.

An enthusiastic nod met my words. "Did you have any idea berserkers and shifters existed?"

"No!" Not in real life. "Did you?"

She shook her head. "Not even a blip. Although there were dreams... Then suddenly Malachi Cromwell showed up at my home. You know, that sporty movie star guy? He told me to ensure King Viktor joins Team Evil for the greater good, then knocked me out. I woke up in a strange forest, and within minutes, Deco had me in his custody."

So the griffin king had known we were twins, and he'd sent us both to do the same job for this mysterious greater good of the berserker world. "He did the exact same thing to me." Questions barreled over my tongue. "This may not be the time or place, but where do you live? What do you do for a living? Are you married? Have any kids? What kind of dreams?"

"Okay, let's see if I can do this in order. Oklahoma. I'm a vet and divorced. No kids. And weird dreams about what I now know is a berserker. What about you?"

THE STOLEN BRIDE

That we'd both chosen a field with animals sparked a little laugh from me. "I live in Georgia, I own a pet grooming business, and I've never been married. I don't have kids, either." But I wanted them. One day. "My dreams feature a berserker, too. He has a sword..."

"Yes!" she cried.

Deco must have said something over the phone, because Juniper's gaze jumped over me again. Her lips parted. "There's another woman here," she blurted and jutted her chin.

"You shouldn't have done that, nyuszi," he said and tsked.

He'd called her 'bunny'. Seriously?

"Fine!" she spat. "As agreed, I'll say nothing else about my cellmate. Whose name is Valkara."

"The Valkara," I automatically corrected in unison with Deco. So. The guardian of the Starfire was real. The woman who whispered in Viktor's mind, advising him to kill me, was being held captive by the shifter king.

I needed to tell Viktor right away. But how would he react? Rage and rush to the shifter, risking an encounter with flesh-eating bugs?

"Do not trust the Val–" The connection cut off before I could finish my warning. I shouted a short, sharp denial. "Come back," I pleaded, shaking the ring. "Juniper!"

A commotion drew my attention to the entrance of the "room." Viktor burst inside a split second later, a dagger in each hand. Huffing and puffing his breaths, he scanned the space. Glowing golden rings filled his irises. Dirt streaked his sweat-glazed body, already double the usual size.

I had never seen a sexier view.

When he ceased his search and settled his gaze on me, I

barely stopped myself from closing the distance and wrapping my arms around him to offer comfort.

He fisted his hands. "No trouble?" he demanded, confusion woven into his guttural tone.

My pulse kicked into an erratic sprint. He'd run to get to me, all because I'd made a noise of distress. Okay, that settled it. I seriously liked this man.

"No, no trouble." I didn't mean to, but I smiled as I stood. Maybe I exaggerated the roll of my hips a little on my walk over. "I'm good." Mostly. He wasn't, though, his breathing still labored. I flattened a palm against his damp sternum, between two of the world's most amazing pecs. "All is well, baby. I mean Snarls. I mean Tor. I promise. My sister contacted me via the ring, and when she disappeared, I overreacted. My sincerest apologies. I shouldn't have bellowed while living in a campground with a group of berserkers. Lesson learned."

He clasped my fingers and lifted my hand, gazing at the ring in the light. "What else was said?" Though he growled the words, I sensed the danger had passed. The intensity in his eyes faded as his fingers entwined with mine. "She couldn't have contacted you without Deco's knowledge."

"Oh, he knew." I was going to tell Viktor all of it. I must. I'd promised to hide nothing from him. If he decided to hit the road before we had a plan to combat those bugs, I'd talk him out of it. "Look. Deco gloated about having more traps for us. You were right about that. One of them involves flesh-eating bugs. He also mentioned he, well...he has the Valkara in his custody."

Tension gobbled up every molecule of air. "Did you see her?"

"No. But Juniper told me the Valkara is her cellmate, and there's no way my sister would lie to me."

THE STOLEN BRIDE

His eyes slitted. "How can you know that? You do not know her."

"Because...just because! She's my sister." My other half. Bonded to me. "Also, I don't like what you're implying."

"I take nothing back." He offered no more on the subject, but I heard the words he kept to himself. *You have spent no time with her. Have no idea about her character, her life, what she believes or loves or hopes for in the deepest recesses of her heart. She might be working with Deco.*

And I got it. After all, he'd loved Deco like a brother, fought by his side, and risked his own life only for the royal to betray him. "Since you aren't freaking out, I can only assume you believe the Valkara isn't a prisoner."

"Just because a woman claimed to be her doesn't mean she is."

"What if the Valkara is the one aiding Deco?" I asked, stepping away and severing contact.

"She isn't."

"You're so certain she's loyal to you. Has she told you she is or isn't a prisoner?"

He worked his jaw. "Since I rejected her last attempt to speak to me, she has ceased all attempts at communication."

Good! The woman wanted me dead.

"But she isn't the prisoner. She's too powerful to be captured. Deco sought to trick us, nothing more." His gaze fastened on my lips and remained. Warm shivers intensified my desires as awareness thickened the air. Seconds... minutes passed and neither of us moved on.

If he didn't do something soon, I'd...I'd...

He shot out his arm, clasped my wrist, and yanked me against him.

Air pffed from me. With my chest pressed against his,

153

and our joined hands positioned behind my back, I was well and truly trapped. And I loved it.

He brushed the tip of his nose against mine. "I suspect the Valkara cannot speak to me because my head is filled with thoughts of kissing you."

My heart tripped over itself. "Is that so?"

He continued to stare at my mouth. Glared, really. "It is."

I glided my tongue over my bottom lip and leaned into him. "And you want me to do something about it, because you're super into me?"

"Very much so," he rumbled, low and soft and husky, dipping his head. His emerald gaze crackled with inner flames. "I'm absolutely *into* you, and you're only making it worse."

I swallowed, then swallowed again. With ten words, he'd snuck past every defense I'd thought I'd erected.

"Same, baby. Same." With a mewl, I rose on my tiptoes and finally did it. I claimed his mouth with my own.

He groaned and opened for me. Then he took over, thrusting his tongue against mine. One stroked the other. The kiss intensified and sped up, as if he'd finally found a source of oxygen and couldn't get enough. As if he'd waited his entire life for this moment. I could only thrill. The sweetness of his taste proved intoxicating, and the heat of his body melted my bones.

Dazed, I poured myself into him, kissing him back with all the passion contained in my body. More little mewling sounds slipped out as thoughts died, one after the other. There was only Viktor and this embrace. This world-rocking, life-changing exchange of breaths.

"Love. Don't stop." His grip on my fingers tightened. Bending his knees, he scooped me up with his free hand. As

THE STOLEN BRIDE

he straightened, lifting me off my feet, I slung my unbound arm around his shoulders, finding balance and pressing ever closer.

On and on we kissed, harder, faster, and it was good, so good. Intoxicating and addictive. Pure seduction. I never wished it to end. But mid-walk to the pallet, he stopped and wrenched his face away with a guttural growl.

For a stolen moment, he pressed his brow against mine. Then he released my hand and set me apart from him, forcing me to let go as well. Our labored exhalations filled the small space between us.

"My mantra," he snapped. "It's the prophecy Malachi mentioned."

Wait. I struggled to understand what he was telling me, until I didn't. "Are you kidding? That's the first thing you think of after kissing me senseless?" I lightly pounded my fists against his chest. "That isn't the way to secure a second kiss, your majesty."

He smirked at me. "As if you aren't already desperate to try again and do better."

Do better? Do better! I sputtered to make intelligent words, and his eyes glittered. He must be teasing me. Because I'd told him to teach me how to kiss him properly while he slept. But, but, Viktor Endris, the mischief maker? *Make it make sense.* Except, dang him, he wasn't wrong! I really was desperate to go again.

"Be serious." Also, how and why was he sexier right now than two seconds ago? "At least give me a critique of my kiss before you launch into a chat about prophecies. Describe an area I should work on. Of course, I will then offer you the same courtesy."

"As if I require improvement." He claimed my hand again, linking our fingers.

Oh, really? "Well, then, give me another kiss and *show* me what I did wrong." As coquettish as possible, I sidled closer while slipping one of his daggers from its sheath with my free hand and hiding the weapon in my pocket. The blade cut through the fabric just enough to catch on the sides of the hilt, letting the weapon dangle and rest against my thigh. To mask my actions, I made sure to pout up at him all the while.

Satisfaction lit his irises, and he couldn't hide it. He lowered his head. "Perhaps one more."

"Oh, never mind," I said with a breezy tone, stepping back. "I'd rather get a tour of the campsite, so I'll know where not to go. Then we should eat."

His eyelids slitted. "You are a craftier opponent than I realized."

I preened with genuine pleasure. "Thank you."

He worked his jaw. "Before we go, there's something you should know. The reason I stopped," he said, giving me a squeeze. "The Valkara spoke a prophecy over each of the original kings. Everything she said has come to pass. Except mine."

Okay. Subject switch accepted and encouraged. "I'm listening."

He braced. "She told me my firebrand will betray and kill me unless I find her, destroy her, and let myself be happy with her sister."

13

Dive In! When To Make Waves With Your Berserker

—HOW TO TRAIN YOUR BERSERKER
By Elizabeth "Elle" Darcy-Bruce

Viktor's words reverberated inside my head as he led me hand-in-hand throughout the camp.

Find her, destroy her, and let myself be happy with her sister.

Was this the greater good I had dreamed of? Kneeling before him and allowing my death by sword to save Juniper?

But. No. That couldn't be correct because...because!

He pointed out the new defenses as we went along, carefree and oblivious to my inner turmoil. This Valkara chick had told the king I would betray and kill him if he didn't kill me first. She must have lied to get me out of the picture.

But. The dream. Which might be an echo of Juniper's. I gulped. And what if the prophecy pointed to *her* death?

But. She wasn't his firebrand. I was. I'd already proven it.

Unless we both were?

"This is particularly effective for skewering any and every turul-shifter who attempts to descend from the air," Viktor said, pointing to the spears anchored into the ground, with their sharp tips aimed skyward. How delighted he sounded. "As you know, berserkers cannot fly, but we enjoy hobbling those who do. You'll see."

"You're in a good mood again, and it's weird." Especially considering we'd just discussed my murder. "Excuse me for being unable to let this go, but how are you supposed to marry the Valkara and also be happy with your firebrand's sister?"

"One will be my partner, the other will be my muse."

His muse?! "That doesn't even make sense!"

"Agreed." He continued as if the incongruity was perfectly normal. "The pillory holds a shifter in place. Makes it easier to remove their hearts and heads. The only true way to kill a turul."

I eyed the wooden frame made up of splintered planks and shuddered. A horizontal board slashed through the center, three holes designed to secure a shifter's hands and neck.

We came upon another wooden frame, with a single long arm. Men rushed around, securing a basket to the end of the arm with thick, coiled rope. So this was what all the hammering was about.

"The basket is filled with hot oil, rocks, and tar that will knock the shifters out of the sky and ground them." Delight turned to glee.

THE STOLEN BRIDE

As much as I appreciated the tour of medieval horrors, I couldn't help but lose track as my brain returned to the threat of my death. A concept I didn't quite have the bandwidth to carry, but tried, hoping I wouldn't glitch. Every time Viktor had chanted his mantra, he'd contemplated killing me, and yet, still, he'd saved my life and kissed me. Another incongruity.

How could I stay with him? But how could I leave him when I needed his aid? But how could I accept his aid, relying on him for my and my sister's protection?

What if he decided to strike? I mean, could I change his mind? Probably. If he gave me a chance. But. I couldn't, shouldn't, shrug this off. She who did not deserve a "the" in front of her name would do whatever it took to get me out of the way. She'd wanted this man for centuries.

I'd had an enemy before I was even born, and I hadn't known it.

"This," Viktor said, motioning to a series of trenches filled with spikes that soldiers were currently covering with dense brush, "is where we—"

"Wait," I interjected, wrenching my fingers from his. "Normally I would be beyond curious about your war hobby, but I find I'm a little too perturbed right now."

Frowning, he faced me. "What's the problem?"

He did not just ask me that. "You! Obviously. If you think I'll betray and kill you, why did you save my life by endangering your own?"

He shrugged, as if the topic were no big deal. "Never cut what can be untied."

Great. Wonderful. "That's a profound truth, sure, but it's hardly reassuring. You can change your mind and decide to make the cut at any moment, ending my life."

"Ja. But only because the same can be said of anyone, anywhere, about anything."

Argh! "Are you asking me to trust you or to suspect everyone else of plotting my harm?"

"Both." A white lock fell over his brow, and a corner of his mouth curled up. "Perhaps this will reassure you. I find I...like having you around. You taste delicious."

Double argh! He just had to go and mention my other conundrum. The hottest kiss of my life.

How could I have locked lips with a man who considered killing me on the daily? Who might chose another woman, as Benjamin had.

I admit, I wasn't the easiest person to hang with. Or the safest. My wealth of internal bottles hadn't shattered yet, but I now believed detonation was only a matter of time. Those cracks...

His men halted their work to watch us with unabashed interest. My cheeks heated. But end the conversation? No.

"While the sentiment is appreciated," I said, "I need a stronger assurance of my long-term safety. I refuse to date someone plotting my death. It's a quirk of mine. Cut Valkara from your life. Don't speak to her ever again."

If Viktor didn't convince me that my welfare mattered to him, I might have to rethink Malachi's offer. Which constituted a betrayal, didn't it? I gulped. Maybe I'd present an un-pass-upable bargain to Bodi. Help me save my sister, and I'll return to my old life, leaving Viktor in my dust. That should delight the prince.

My ribs squeezed, but I didn't back down.

Viktor scowled. "She is a necessary part of my existence. But I can promise you that you won't like what happens if you run from me again, drágá."

And back to square one we go. Disappointment and anger

THE STOLEN BRIDE

engulfed me. "Keep making threats, and I'm guaranteed to run. I'd be a fool not to."

He stepped closer, erasing my personal space. Bending, putting his nose level with mine, he grated, "You are arguing with a berserker king. I'd say you are already a fool."

We remained just like that, close, so close, breathing in the other's panting breaths. His intoxicating scent did its thing. Thoughts fragmented and blurred until a single urge lingered: Get another kiss.

What was wrong with me? How could I crave the male who hobnobbed with my greatest enemy?

Although... A teeny tiny sliver of hope flickered. As his firebrand, I wielded a considerable amount of influence. The most powerful ability any person could possess, in fact: the chance to change his heart, the only way to permanently change his mind.

If I took the time and applied myself, I could win him over. Make him see Valkara as his enemy too. She might be necessary to his existence, but I was, too. More so!

Calm him during a temper—check.

Wake him from a supernaturally induced sleep—check.

Snatch his allegiance from a supervillainess who whispered evil commands into his head—checkmate?

Of course, there was a good chance I was only deluding myself, rationalizing to obtain something a part of me had always desperately desired.

Viktor's patience reached its limit. "Roland, tell Clover what I do to prisoners who attempt to escape," he commanded without looking away from me.

"You disembowel them, Majesty."

"Wow. Another threat. What a shocking development I never saw coming." I notched my chin. "You need to get new material, baby. I'm only attracted to men who bring their A game."

Low growls rumbled in the king's chest. "You are only attracted to *me*." He lowered his head, putting his narrowed gaze level with mine. "Say it. Say *I am only attracted to you, Tor*."

"Agree to cut Valkara from your life."

"Viktor?" Bodi called, distress dripping from his voice.

Still, the king didn't attention his attention from me. "Whatever it is can wait. I'm in the middle of reminding my captive how big, strong, and scary I am."

With a flick of my wrist, I flipped my hair over one shoulder. "I've seen scarier."

His nostrils flared as if I'd kneed him in his happy zone. "That is a *lie*."

"Viktor," the prince repeated, all kinds of concern in his voice. "Something comes."

Both Viktor and I whipped our focus to the right, where the soldiers stood statue still, fully alert, peering into the distance. When I spotted the object of their enthrallment, I blinked. A thick gray cloud rolled across the land, coming closer and closer. Pinpricks of crimson flashed within it.

A low buzzing sound reached my ears and foreboding crept over my spine. "What is it?"

"I am unsure," Viktor replied, his tone as ominous as the cloud.

A herd of wild deer burst from a thicket just in front of the cloudy veil. The slowest of the bunch got swallowed by the haze, and its screams of agony pierced the air. My stomach bottomed out, the urge to sprint almost too strong to resist.

"Do I see...bees in the midst of the gloom?" Bodi asked.

Oh, no, no, no. The blood in my veins flash-froze. I'd bet

THE STOLEN BRIDE

my entire savings those "bees" were flesh-eaters. "Deco said he'd thought of everything," I croaked. The shifter hadn't just laid traps for us–he'd sent one. Had indeed planned for everything, as advertised.

"Go, go, go," Viktor shouted, grabbing my hand and racing me through the camp. "You know what to do."

We took the same path we'd used to get here, going in the opposite direction of the cloud. His men did the same and split off into groups of two, taking different routes.

"We need to get underground," I said between huffing breaths. My heart pounded against my ribs with increasing fervor. "The trenches you dug. We can fit between the stakes and cover ourselves with dirt."

"Nem," Viktor growled as we sailed over the rugged terrain. "Grab any weapon you can."

"Already did. I took yours," I confessed. "There's a dagger in my pocket."

"Oh, yes. I remember."

Ha! "No, you do not."

Once we cleared the campsite, we picked up speed. Heading for the traveling stones, where turul-shifters probably awaited us? Nope. We veered right, entering a dense cluster of trees and thickets.

The sound of rushing water hit my ears, and his plan crystallized. I approved. We headed for the ice-filled river, our best chance for survival.

A tide of adrenaline surged through me, and I pumped my arms faster. My feet responded in kind. Viktor's, too. We picked up speed again.

"Dive," he commanded, following his own order.

I obeyed, crashing into the frigid liquid, losing my hold on the berserker as the shock of cold seized my muscles. A thousand stings pricked my skin. No need to swim. The current dragged me along a rocky river. I put up no resistance, holding my breath as long as possible. When I could tolerate the burn in my lungs no longer, I fought my way up, already bracing for the danger that awaited me. My head breached the surface. I sucked in oxygen.

No bug attacks. Had we passed the danger zone?

Took some doing, but I struggled against the dangerous current and twisted, glancing behind me. The line of fog had reached the shore but hadn't braved the water. My relieved breath came out as near frost. We should exit the river now or die of hypothermia. But where was Viktor?

"Oomph!" Pain reverberated through my entire body as the force of water slammed me into a boulder. Impact spun me around and around and around. I flailed my arms in a desperate attempt to grab on to something, anything. Icy water shot into my nose, clogging my airways.

I fought to inhale even the slightest tidbit of oxygen and failed. My limbs grew heavy and weak. My world darkened. With the last of my strength, I cut through the current and lugged myself onto a fogless part of the shore.

As darkness took over, I sagged over the dirt. *Where are you, Viktor?*

I AWOKE from a dreamless sleep with a start. Memories overtook my awareness. Approaching bugs. Long distance sprinting. A tangle with the river. Viktor! My gaze darted here, there. Still no sign of him.

Worry instantly gripped me. Where was he? What happened to him?

Using my elbows, I pulled myself up the riverbank

THE STOLEN BRIDE

edged with a layer of frost. A single animal track criss-crossed through the surrounding snow, but nothing human, err berserker, err birdlike. A light mist free of bugs hung in the air, and judging by the fading sunlight, hours had passed since we'd fled into the dangerous water. Where was he?

At least I could breathe. And the ring, my one connection to Juniper, hadn't slid from my thumb. Wait! A crunch of brittle leaves and ice sounded. Footsteps. Someone approached. Viktor? A shifter? Another kind of predator?

Unwilling to risk it, I scrambled to stand, intending to hide...where? Too late. A grinning Deco strode from the shadows. Instant fight response. I palmed my pocket dagger and rooted my feet in place. No doubt his acolytes perched all around us.

"Hello, Clover." Not quite as tall as Viktor but equally muscled, he painted an imposing picture. Like many of the other warriors, he'd opted to go shirtless, letting those solid gold wings arch over his shoulders freely. A hooked horn grew from each joint. Black leathers covered his tree trunk thighs. Metal spikes protruded from his combat boots. The perfect complement for the numerous weapons strapped to his powerful body.

"Where's my sister?" I demanded, tightening my hold on the hilt of the blade.

"Not here," he said, speaking in Hungarian as he stopped just out of reach. "Nor is Viktor, I see. Too bad. I so look forward to killing you in front of him. Well, no matter. I'll relay a message instead."

"Ah. Is the big, bad birdie still jealous that his second-in-command is stronger, more powerful, and so much hotter?" I infused each word with enough taunt to irritate even the most patient of souls.

165

His smug expression never altered, but ripples of irritation swept over the feathers in his wings. "Tune your ears. My message is dire—for you. Four of Viktor's elite decided to join me rather than die at my hand. I'll be unleashing them in the morning, letting them hunt you."

Four? So. They'd traded their honor to keep their lives. That was gonna hurt Viktor badly, whether or not he admitted it. Especially if Bodi was among the four. Was he?

Deco continued with his taunts. "If your precious sentinel king wishes to save *your* life, he must come out of hiding to do it."

Viktor wasn't in hiding. No way, no how. He was an attack first and question later kinda guy. Which meant, what? Nothing good, that much I knew.

But no. Absolutely no harm had come to him. He was fine.

My hand curled into a fist. He better be fine.

"You're lying to me. Trying to break me down." My dream pointed to a future event. Therefore, Viktor still lived.

"I never lie sometimes," Deco replied, nonchalant.

Anger uncoiled in each of my cells, and I snapped, "I believe you're too afraid of hurting me to do the job yourself."

What are you doing? Begging the villain to attack?

I didn't know and wasn't sure I cared. The words burst from my mouth before I could think better of them.

A fresh smile bloomed over the turul-king's face. "Oh, sweet Clover. I can kill you, no problem. In fact, I'm eager to. Allow me to prove it."

Blink. He stood directly in front of me, his fingers wrapped around my wrist, driving my dagger into the spot

THE STOLEN BRIDE

beneath my left clavicle. Searing pain exploded inside me, yanking a cry from my deepest depths.

Deco kissed my brow like a father to his daughter. "If I don't get to witness Viktor's anguish, I'll be forced to live forever with regret. A fate I hope to avoid. But. If he's a no show tomorrow, I'll just have to ensure the horror of his firebrand's death is a tale that haunts him for the rest of time. A worthy trade, I think. Ja, a worthy trade indeed."

"You will pay for this." I heaved the words between ragged breaths. Blood trickled from the corners of my mouth.

"Whatever you need to tell yourself, galamb."

"Pigeon?" I grated.

He booped my nose with the tip of an index finger, yanked out the dagger and tossed it aside before sauntering off, whistling under his breath. "By the way," he called. "If you survive, you're invited to a ball I'm hosting. It's black tie and lasts until I'm no longer amused by it. Hope to see you there. RSVP if you can."

My knees buckled, and I dropped. With a hoarse cry, I pulled off my shirt. A Herculean task. Hands trembling, I pressed the material into the wound to staunch the flow of blood. The cold helped. But.

What was I going to do?

14

Rage On! Handling the Heat When Others Can't

–HOW TO TRAIN YOUR BERSERKER
By Elizabeth "Elle" Darcy-Bruce

I couldn't stay here.

My brain screamed, *Find Viktor.* Yes, yes. Viktor. He was the difference maker, and he was alive. I refused to believe otherwise. Think about it. He'd survived centuries at war with the shifters; a rushing river didn't have the power to end him. And he wouldn't abandon me on purpose. He absolutely would not. Even though I'd spoken of running again.

My stomach twisted. What if he hoped to prove a point? Let me wander about on my own until I admitted how desperately I needed him.

No, that wasn't his style. He liked to keep his "mine" close. There was a greater chance the vargbane root had screwed with his immortality.

THE STOLEN BRIDE

Oh no! I'd forgotten about the root. What if he truly had died?

High octane trepidation and sorrow leaked from the cracks in my bottles. Tears welled and dropped, blurring my vision. Sniffling, I wiped my nose with the back of my hand. Even the thought of being without Viktor shredded me.

What are you doing? Enough! There was no reason to borrow trouble. Vik wasn't dead, and that was that. I would hide and heal, and he would find me. Plan made. As I lumbered to my feet, pain and weakness nearly felled me. With sheer determination, I persevered and reclaimed the dagger.

Hemorrhaging what little strength I possessed at record speed, I stumbled forward. I kept my wadded up shirt pressed into my wound with one hand and clutched my weapon with the other, ready to defend myself from any shifter I stumbled upon.

I crested a hill, my knees almost buckling with relief when I spotted a village. A village meant food, warmth, and maybe even rudimentary medical care.

Kicking up snow behind me, I charged forward as fast as my abused body allowed. Hmm. Frost clung to the cracked, weathered walls of abandoned cottages. A door to a former store creaked on its hinge, ominous in the wintry wind. Its roof was partially caved in under the weight of ice and dead leaves.

Okay, so, this wasn't the safe space I'd imagined. But maybe that was a good thing. Residents might have gladly turned me over to Deco.

With a tired sigh, I exited the village and plodded forward. A gust of glacial wind hit my face, but the bite didn't sting quite as much as I expected. Maybe my senses were dulling as I neared death.

A humorless laugh bubbled up.

"What's so funny, baba?" an unfamiliar voice called.

Ack! Shifter! I scanned ahead. A turul perched high in a tree. He watched me with a wicked grin, his dark hair slicked back, his features sharp. "I'm not your baby," I grated.

"You'll never escape us," he taunted, as smug as Deco.

Fury sparked. *Don't waste energy engaging with the enemy.* I hurried on as fast as my abused body allowed. Not that I made it far before spotting another shifter. And another. And another. They lurked everywhere and none missed the opportunity to threaten me.

"I'm gonna love ripping you open."

"Are you a screamer? I'm excited to find out."

"I like your face. Maybe I'll wear it."

I kept going, my fury burning hotter and hotter. But it wasn't my usual fury. There was a righteous tinge to it. Like, how dare they think they had any power over me. I was Clover Deering, firebrand to a king. *The* king.

Bottles shook. Soon, my blood graduated from a low simmer to a high boil. To my immense surprise, each new level of heat strengthened me, making my steps surer. The pain dimmed before vanishing completely. I glanced down. Blood no longer dripped from my wound. The edges had even begun to knit together and close.

What! Was I actually healing supernaturally? Oh, not as quickly as the berserkers on the battlefield, but far swifter than humanly possible.

Malachi's proclamation whispered through my mind. *I am now King of the House of Griffin, and you are one of my people.*

Viktor's confession followed. *You are of sentinel blood. Griffin.*

THE STOLEN BRIDE

Well, well, well. I tugged my crimson-stained shirt into place. How fitting. Look at the blood-soaked dog groomer who also happened to be part berserker. Excuse me, sentinel. Exactly as Malachi and Viktor had claimed.

Maybe I didn't need to hide from the turul-shifters. Or my emotions. I could do battle. And what better place to do so than the camp where Viktor and his men had worked so hard to mount a defense? But which direction was it?

Even when the last bit of light snuffed out, I kept going, listening for the river. Dried leaves and snow crunched beneath my boots, blending with the haunting call of owls and other critters I didn't want to know about.

Glowing red eyes seemed to hover here and there, there, there. I tightened my grip on the dagger. How good was a turul-shifter's night vision?

I entered a silvery, moonlit clearing and ground to a halt, struck by a bolt of shock. Ten shifters waited on the other side, standing wing to wing, forming a wall of menace. Nine males and one female, each a picture of confident power. The worst part? Four of those males were former elites, exactly as advertised. They pawed at the ground with their bare feet, almost as feral as Viktor had once been. Unlike their former king, they couldn't contain their desire to kill me.

Outrage consumed the whole of my being, my bottles shaking harder. "How can you do this? You were chosen by him. Trusted."

They didn't seem to register my words.

I couldn't blame Deco for this. No matter what he'd done, these men had always had a choice. Welcome the evil or fight it. They'd caved. But I *would* punish Deco for it. Soon. First, I must survive this encounter.

The guy in the middle—the jerk who'd expressed a

171

desire to wear my face—popped the bones in his neck. "King Deco has realized it'll be more fun if Viktor comes out of hiding and finds his future queen scattered throughout the forest. We concur."

I hurled past the future queen comment. So they'd found no sign of Viktor either. That wasn't good. Deeper cracks spread through my bottles. If anyone deserved to feel the sting of my wrath...

Then. That moment. A bottle shattered. Then another and another. An icy inferno of rage deluged my entire body, and a red haze enveloped my mind. My senses heightened.

Suddenly, the fine hairs on my neck and arms detected a slight alteration in the direction of the breeze. The first of many changes I experienced. Before, I might have only noticed the pine fragrance of the trees and the sweat from the shifters. But now I scented their emotions. Hatred proved strongest, as acrid and sharp as sulfur.

My sights constricted to the threat before me. The pulse beat at their necks. The narrowing of their pupils. The bracing of their muscles. My own muscles bunched, ready for action. If a fight was what they wanted, it was a fight they'd get.

I didn't care that I was outnumbered and outgunned. I was glad for it. More shifters to kill. And I wanted to kill. I no longer saw living beings, but shadowy prey. Ten feature-less targets.

The rest of the world ceased to exist.

I purred, "When I kill you, and I will, I'll use your bones to build my first throne." My voice! It was mine, but not. Deeper, throatier, with the hint of a second speaker.

The goad hit its target: their control. Amid grunts, growls and huffing breaths, the shifters surged forward, teeth and claws bared. As they erased the distance between

THE STOLEN BRIDE

us, I sprinted to meet them in the middle, running faster than ever before. I could almost taste death—*needed* to taste it.

Just before reaching the strike zone, I leaped into the air as if I had wings of my own. An action no one expected. My aim: the soldier in the center. I slammed into him, knocking him to the ground. Before I registered a command from my mind, I plunged my dagger into his eye. His throat. Heart. Except, the blade got stuck in his throat and I ended up driving my fist through his chest. Driven by instinct, I wrapped my fingers around his heart and yanked.

His back bowed, and he roared. Then he went still and silent.

I felt zero emotion as I dropped what I held and whipped my attention to the others. First, they stopped, obviously confused. When they spotted what remained of their teammate, they comprehended what just happened. Any remaining hint of amusement evaporated.

Must I remove his head, too, to truly end his immortality? Might as well, just to be sure the death took. But that would happen a little later.

I gave the remaining nine a smile and a nod. 'Come hither' in berserkerspeak.

With snarls and high-pitched calls, they converged on me.

Once again, I moved without conscious thought. Ducking. Dodging. Spinning. Kicking. Biting. Elbowing. Always slashing my claws with abandon. As flesh tore beneath the razored tips, hot blood splashed over my skin. The elixir of life. Animalistic noises rose from me.

If a turul-shifter injured me, even once, I didn't feel it. Was this what Viktor and his men experienced in a berserkerage? Sign me up for more, because I never wanted it to end. With every kill, the ice cold reshaped into sublime pleasure. By the time the last shadow fell, motionless, I floated on a bed of euphoria. But. No more? I needed more! Now, now, now.

I spun, searching, searching—there! Another featureless target. I might have grinned. I did walk...jog...run toward it. But wait. A golden light flickered from the darkness. My steps slowed. And that fragrance. Familiar. Comforting. I stopped and canted my head. The flickers grew brighter and wider and lasted longer.

Inside me, the ice melted, downgrading my euphoria to curiosity. What was this? Oh! A man. A very large man. With white hair, green eyes, and harsh features set in an expression of ragged concern.

As soon as his identity clicked, the remaining red haze broke apart and lifted. Viktor! He was alive and well. Crying out, I threw myself into his powerful body. He caught me, wrapping his muscular arms around me and holding on as if he feared I might fly away.

"Where were you?" I demanded. "What happened?"

He buried his nose in the hollow of my neck and inhaled. "My head hit a rock in the river, and I was dragged into another coma-like state. Since I'm the first in history to wake from vargbane root, I didn't realize I'd have to fight my way free of it when next I slept. This time, I drowned over and over before I woke." He shuddered against me.

I pulled back only far enough to cup his face and—*sweet golden doodle*! My hands. They were covered in blood, and I'd smeared him with it.

I tried to wipe his cheek, but only added more crimson. Horrified, I wrenched from him and stared down at my hands. My mother's most prevailing warning whispered

THE STOLEN BRIDE

through my mind. *What you do in a temper cannot be undone when you calm.*

I squeezed my eyes tight, remembering her broken arm and my vow to never get angry in such a way again. Dragging in a shuddering breath, I geared to look over my shoulder and survey the battlefield.

"Do not," Viktor commanded, and I went still, my body obeying him of its own volition.

Stiffness invaded my limbs. What had I done, what had I done? "I moved without thought. Or training! I...I..." I'd taken down ten accomplished and trained soldiers as if we were children playing a game.

"That is the sentinel instinct, and yours is stronger than most. Listen to me," he added. Another command. He'd never used such a sharp tone with me, even upon our initial meeting. "You experienced your first break. Any moment, you will become extremely fatigued. Do not fight it. Understand?"

No, I didn't understand, thank you very much. How could he know what I'd—all at once, my muscles gave out. I sagged, and he caught me, ensuring my head rested on his shoulder.

Sleep crooked its finger at me, but panic refused the invitation. I needed to move my body or, or, or. I didn't know! Couldn't think. Wanted...must... Argh!

"Shh, now," Viktor comforted, combing his fingers through my hair. He carried me to the river, cooing all the while.

As he tenderly cleaned off my battle gore, my brain blipped. The perfect opening for calm, which created the perfect opening for sleep. Lights flipped out one by one.

He finished up and swept me into his arms once again. "There's a good Love. Just let yourself drift away."

175

Yes. Drift away. What a wonderful idea. "'Night, Tor," I murmured, greeting the darkness with a smile. Then came the nothingness. No dreams, no present, and no future.

I AWAKENED GRADUALLY, blinking open my eyes. Cocooned in warmth, I dragged in Viktor's scent. Pine needles, forest dew and roses. Mmm. How I loved being in his arms. I stretched out on my side, cuddling deeper into him as he slept on.

Wait. Memories huffed at the edge of my thoughts, reminding me of bulls champing at the bit to throw a cowboy to the ground and stomp his bones to powder. They bucked themselves to center stage, one after the other. The bugs. The river. Deco. His promise to send his men after me. My break and the aftermath. Viktor's reappearance. Everything except the atrocities I committed on the battlefield.

How vividly I recalled the berserker king's worn expression, though, and shuddered. Did he know four of his men were among the dead, thanks to me? He must. He was a details guy.

At least I didn't have to worry about being hunted by traitors. But. My bottles. They were gone. I was raw inside. Vulnerable in a way I'd never been, battered by emotions I'd denied for far too long. Guilt, shame, fear. More anger.

Tears filled my eyes. I didn't try to rebottle everything, just let it all flow through me.

Eventually, I eased up, doing my best not to jar my companion. A fire raged in a crumbling hearth a few feet away, woodsmoke filling...I gazed around. A cabin. Above me, a roof sagged from the weight of time, gaps in the planks revealing patches of sky. Viktor must have carried me back to the abandoned village and found a place for me to sleep off the aftermath of my berserkerage. I mentally punched myself for giving him one more burden, especially after he'd battled against the effects of the vargbane root not once, but twice.

Needing reassurance that my sister had lived through the night, I lifted my hand to activate the ring. To be honest, I was also a teensy bit curious to learn if Deco raged over the loss of his ten warriors at the hands of a berserker novice.

Oh no! The ring was gone. I patted my pockets. Not there. Had I lost it when I broke? I must have. My shoulders rolled in, and I blinked back another round of tears. Argh! I hated, hated, hated this new emotional Clover. And now, Juniper couldn't contact me.

Movement drew my attention to the side, and dread slapped me. A scene played over the walls, like a movie projected onto a screen. Viktor had sunk into another vargbane root coma. Would this happen every time he slept now? Poor Viktor. I stroked his fevered cheek. At least I knew he could battle his way free, both with and without me.

What scene did he showcase today? With both anticipation and regret, I left the warmth of his side, stood and tiptoed over for a closer study. Hmm. Okay. I pressed my palm over my roiling belly. I doubted he meant to broadcast this one. He stood in front of a stunningly beautiful woman with strawberry blond hair and clear blue eyes. She wore a royal gown of shimmering emerald, a match to his eyes. The bodice sparkled with countless tiny gemstones while the skirt billowed around her ankles. A crown of gold adorned with glimmering jewels rested atop her head. She grazed the tips of her nails over Viktor's bare chest.

My back stiffened. A former love interest?

The projected Viktor gave a sharp shake of his head and backed up. A negation to whatever she'd said as well as her touch. The refusal didn't deter her, and she tugged at the buttons of her bodice. Scowling, he gave another shake of his head and seemed to bark curses at her. She only worked the buttons faster. He reached out to stop her.

A wingless Deco strode into the room, spotted them, and blanched. When he gained his bearings, he stormed their way.

Oooh. This must have occurred before he'd signed on for Team Evil.

He got in Viktor's face and shouted. Viktor shouted right back. Small pinpricks of red dotted Deco's irises, soon forming a ring. Then another and another, until his eyes glowed. Within seconds, Deco launched at Viktor, swiping and snarling, wings budding from his back. The shifter king fought with the intention of murder while Viktor defended, never delivering a killing blow. Though he could have. Multiple times. I imagined growls echoing as the pair clashed in a primal rage.

In the wild frenzy, they slammed into the beauty—and she did not survive the encounter. She dropped, blood trickling from her mouth, her eyes dulling until no life remained inside them.

The men froze, the wrath between them momentarily forgotten. Then Deco dove to his knees and did everything in his power to patch her wounds. But he failed.

My hand fluttered to my throat as the war between the

THE STOLEN BRIDE

two men began to make sense. Deco's desire to hurt Viktor's firebrand, whatever the cost. Viktor's resistance to end his enemy. One sought vengeance, the other redemption.

15

Finding Your Cinderella Moment When Every Dance is a Killer Tango

—HOW TO TRAIN YOUR BERSERKER
By Elizabeth "Elle" Darcy-Bruce

I knelt beside the still sleeping Viktor, a sultry softness invading places inside me no other person had ever reached. I understood the King of Turuls so much better now. His unraveling. How he'd grown feral to separate himself from the pain of his friend's loss. The guilt of accidentally killing the other man's beloved. Depending on the powerful Valkara to help him. No doubt believing he didn't deserve a happily ever after of his own.

I traced my fingers along the line of his strong jaw. Brighter flashes peppered the walls, as if my action inspired a new line of thought. A different scene danced there, the edges tattered as if it had been dragged through a briar patch. I saw an untamed forest, the ground carpeted by tangled roots, moss, and fallen leaves. An unnatural light shrouded a grove the size of a football field, pulsing with colors.

A massive stone occupied the center, letters of an ancient language carved into the sides. Atop it balanced a spherical object that radiated an otherworldly energy I could almost feel. The outer shell glimmered with a mother-of-pearl exterior, with deep cracks stretching from top to bottom, dividing the object into ten distinct sections. Each glowed with a unique hue.

This must be the Starfire of legend. Which meant what I was viewing happened over a thousand years past. Lifetimes ago.

Viktor's legacy.

My own.

I began to shake. A crowd encircled the stone, a varied group from every walk of life. Nobles, soldiers, peasants and everything in between. Mostly men with a handful of women woven in here and there. Viktor stood near the front.

In the sky, dark swirling clouds gathered above their heads. No one seemed to notice, yet tensions mounted. Wind whipped through the grove, scattering leaves and debris. Rain started to fall, soon pelting them. Still, the crowd inched closer to the Starfire, utterly transfixed.

Through the memory, I experienced the almost irresistible force luring everyone forward, hoping to touch the stone. In real time, my own hand lifted.

A bright flash of lightning raced across the scene, temporarily blinding me. Did the lightning come from the sky or the Starfire? With it came a surge of primal rage. Wave after wave of aggression. Unimaginable fury. Despite the lack of audio playback, I heard the curses bellowing between spectators as their bodies convulsed and their eyes flashed with neon rings. Viktor's gold. Another's green. His red. Hers blue. Purple. Blue. Shades in between, all the colors found on the Starfire.

I suspected what came next and shuddered. A red haze that fine-tuned the senses. An ice-cold force that took over and blotted everything else out. The need to cause death.

Except, the scene blurred and faded as war erupted, as if Viktor couldn't remember the slaughter. Or hated facing the moment he first broke.

No other scene took its place. Maybe that was a good thing. As much as I wished to learn more, I knew we couldn't stay here forever. Deco still prowled just out of reach, seeking my death as his vengeance. He'd probably sent a new group of shifters to hunt me. Plus, my mission hadn't changed. I must rescue my sister as quickly as possible, which meant I needed a plan. And my partner.

I returned my gaze to Viktor. Hazy light from the crackling fire bathed him. Yet again, he appeared almost boyish, with his hair spilled beneath him, his features relaxed, his lips soft. Mostly, he struck me as beautiful. A complicated commander with a fierce spirit, a brusque manner, and a downright sizzling vibe.

Gently patting his cheek, I said, "Snarls. Tor. Baby. Vik. Pudding pop." I should give him a better nickname. Something as good as Love. Err Lovie.

No reaction.

Should I offer another kiss? A sure-fire guarantee he'd wake up.

No, no more promised kisses. Only spontaneous ones. But not right now, when I desperately required a bath, a toothbrush and industrial strength toothpaste. But yes, I craved another kiss. The guy revved my motor, and I could deny it no more. Since Benjamin's betrayal, I'd been rela-

THE STOLEN BRIDE

tionship shy, but looking back, I understood my former fiancé did me a huge favor by leaving me for Kami. Our marriage would've crumbled at some point. I would've remained on edge, and he would've continued to be blamey, nothing ever his fault, always mine. Honestly, he had demanded too much while giving too little.

Viktor gave as much as he took and then some, and he didn't nitpick the small stuff. I didn't feel as if I walked on eggshells around him.

On the surface, however, he seemed to share Benjamin's worse trait: a desire for another woman. But Viktor didn't really want Valkara. I knew he didn't. He just wasn't aware of it yet.

"Wake up because I said so," I told him, continuing to pet his face. "I'm hungry." The words slipped out without thought, and I realized they were true. "I'm famished, actually. Ravenous. Do you know what I crave more than anything?"

He jolted with a roar, his eyes popping open.

Grinning from ear to ear, I pumped my fist toward the caved-in ceiling. "I did it! I woke you without making promises. I'm a miracle worker!"

"What do you crave?" he asked, perfectly at ease, as if we'd been in the middle of a conversation. His gaze slid over me as he grazed the pad of his thumb along the pulse in my throat, igniting flutters in my belly. "Is it me? It's me, isn't it?"

I marveled at the sight of him. He was just so relaxed. So sane. No hint of feralness. No trace of any kind of upset. This was a side of Viktor I had only experienced in glimpses.

"Maybe, baby," I replied. "Oops. I'm not supposed to call you baby."

His eyes crinkled at the corners. "I protested the endearment only because I liked it so much."

"If that's true, you like a lot of things too much," I retorted with a tone as dry as the desert.

A slow lifting of his lips suggested he might be about to smile... My chest clenched and my breath hitched. Yes! He did. He smiled, and it lit his entire face.

"What's even happening right now?" I gasped out.

I remained dazed as he brought my hand to that indulgent smile and kissed my knuckles. "I'm embracing my good mood. You are my firebrand. The best firebrand in the history of firebrands. Am I saying firebrand too much? You are immortal, beautiful, and scary fierce. And my firebrand. You will not die, so I won't lose you and become a shifter. Firebrand."

I detected a note of superiority in his expression, as if he truly believed his words. "So you accept it now? You're done fighting my importance to you?"

"Ja. I do. I am." In his sprawled position, the Hungarian berserker king was relaxation itself, and oh, it looked amazing on him. His eyes did that hooded thing, and when he ran his bottom lip between his teeth... hello, romance novel hero!

This seemed almost too good to be true. There had to be a catch. "You telling me you won't heed the Valkara's warning to kill me before I supposedly kill you?" Which I could maybe, kinda, sorta do now. I'd raged out. Shredded powerful shifters with abandon. Although, I felt no different today. Didn't feel any kind of beast, griffin or otherwise, prowling around inside my head.

His smile dimmed, and I nearly whimpered, already mourning its loss. "She made a mistake. That's the only expla-

THE STOLEN BRIDE

nation. You won't harm me. I'm the only one able to calm you from your rage." His statement filled the airwaves, echoing within my mind. "You will never betray me. Never wish to leave me." His confidence intensified with each new sentence. "Not just for the greater good, but for me specifically."

Oh, no, no, no. We weren't going there. He had a fire-brand, but I did not. Nope. Not me. "I was surprised to see you, is all. It startled me from my anger."

"Try again. Sentinels in a rage-trance do not get startled. They don't feel a thing."

Stubbornness kicked in. I opened my mouth to deliver a very reasonable explanation for the incident, but came up blank. I went with the ridiculous instead. "Well, for all we know, I'm the most powerful berserkatrix in the history of ever." And with that, how could I not fully accept what I was? An immortal-ish warrior, capable of unleashing untold fury upon my enemies–and others, if I wasn't careful.

Although Viktor could certainly hold his own. A fact that thrilled me. "We should go. Deco might send a new hunting party after us." Surely the shifter king had learned of Viktor's recovery by now.

"Ja, we will go. Now that you're able to heal, we'll risk the traps and air strikes and head to the turul fortress to finish this war." Viktor kissed my brow, shocking me. He stood and helped me to my feet. "There's a hot spring nearby, and it's on our way."

I clasped his hand, and all but dragged him toward the building's exit. "How far is the spring?"

"Just over the ridge."

So close! We walked outside, entering the wintry, gray terrain, and I shivered.

"You have questions about the memories you viewed, I'm sure," Viktor said.

So many. "Let's start with the woman."

"Very well. I will preface this by saying I dislike discussing it. But you are...you. So I will." He didn't give me a second to process his amazing words before rolling full steam ahead. "That was Deco's wife, Lena, from once upon a time." He grimaced slightly. "The three of us grew up together in Deco's palace. Before her romantic relationship with Deco began, she and I shared a dalliance. But when I confessed my love, she did not return the sentiment."

Ouch. Rejection hurt, no matter which way you sliced it. "Please. Go on."

He shoved a branch out of our path. "She didn't want Viktor, the bastard child of a courtesan, but Deco, the king, and she won him. They married before he turned sentinel, and he loved her dearly."

Viktor's resentment over his human lineage rang loud and clear. "Who we are born to physically doesn't make us what we are." Keeping pace beside him, I reached out to tap his chest. "It is what's in here that counts. And besides, your mother lived in a time when women had few options. It sounds like she did everything she could to ensure you not only survived but thrived."

He swallowed. Then swallowed again. "You defend my character. And hers. That isn't something anyone has done since..."

His words trailed, but I knew what he'd almost said. No one had defended him since Deco, all those centuries ago. Perhaps no one but Viktor himself had ever justified his mother's actions. He'd lost so much, and now, the bulk of his pain revolved around what happened to Lena.

"Until becoming a sentinel king, I hadn't realized Lena

cared only about power and status. When I seized my crown, Deco served as *my* second. Jealousy ate at them both."

The pain in Viktor's voice tore at my soul. "My ex was that kind of guy. Jealous of anyone with more than him."

"I will kill him for you. I'll make it as painful as you wish." His childlike eagerness to please struck a chord in me. "Nem. Allow me to rephrase. I'll make it as painful as *I* wish."

"That's so kind of you. Truly. But he's irrelevant. I'm more interested in you." Heat scorched my cheeks. "I mean, your past. And Tor, if it makes you feel any better, Lena and Deco were miserable the entire time they were hating on you. No one can be happy with that kind of mindset."

He thought for a moment, nodded. "Lena's envy fed Deco's. Days and weeks and months of whispering in his ear, vilifying me at every turn. When she struck, we'd never been so divided."

Once two best friends, closer than brothers, suddenly enemies on opposite sides of a war. "Tell me what happened next." Oh, I remembered Vik's vargbane root induced dream, but I had no idea what led up to Deco storming Viktor's way. The pair shouting, swiping and snarling at each other in a wild frenzy.

He rubbed the back of his neck. "Lena lured me into a private area off the ballroom and admitted she loved me. She claimed she had always loved me, but had feared angering Deco and sentencing me to death. If I would slay him, we could be together. I rebuked her and told her I would end *her* if ever she threatened his life again. That I would watch her closely and if I suspected she so much as pondered Deco's demise, I would take action against her.

She said I didn't know what I was missing and started stripping."

"Oh, Viktor. That's awful."

"Ja." His lips compressed in a grim line. "She knew what I didn't. Deco hunted for me, intending to challenge me. She'd finally convinced him to try. He came upon us while I attempted to stop her seduction, which ensured he raged. You saw what happened afterward. But I've never ceased hoping…"

I could guess. "You think Deco and the others can be saved, though it's never been done." That was why he hadn't attacked the shifters unless they'd attacked us first. He couldn't save them if they were dead.

"I know they can be recovered. I only need my key. The Valkara told me ten keys arrived at the same time as the Starfire, landing in different parts of the world. Each of the original kings were to find ours and return them to her. I found mine, only to lose it. As soon as I discover it again, she can use it to revert turul-shifters to their natural state."

Well. No wonder he was so determined to have that key in his possession. And yet, something prodded at me, ringing an internal alarm. "I don't want to burst your bubble, but that sounds a little too good to be true." A scam in the making. A long con. "You're confident she's on the up and up, even though she threatens the life of your firebrand?" I'd asked before, but maybe phrasing it a new way with this new info would get him thinking along the right line.

"*You* seem too good to be true, yet here you are."

Then. That moment. A part of me fell a little in love with him. But just a little, so it wasn't a big deal. I'd probably get over it in a day or two.

As we continued forward, I linked our arms and rested

THE STOLEN BRIDE

my head on his broad shoulder. I'd let the subject of Valkara rest for now. "I need to tell you something." He'd trusted me with his past. Now, I would trust him with my future. "I've had a recurring dream most of my life. Juniper has, too, though I'm not clear on the details of hers."

He stiffened but said, "I'm listening."

Here goes. "In mine, I'm standing in the sky, surrounded by fog. I kneel before a powerful warrior. You."

His eyes lit with interest. "Now I'm *really* listening. Kneel, you say?"

Men were such simple creatures. "Yes. In the dream, I tell you I'm doing what I'm doing for the greater good. You say the same. You're holding a sword and you lift it as if to remove my head. Just as you swing, I wake up."

His hold on me tightened. "I meant it when I said I wouldn't harm you, Love."

"And I believe you." Now. "But the dream means something." I winced and gave voice to my most awful suspicion. "Even if I've been seeing Juniper all this time."

"You don't have to worry. I won't harm your twin, either. As for the meaning of the dream, give me a day or two to ponder."

Between one step and the next, our surroundings transformed. The air lost the crisp bite of winter, replaced by muggy heat scented with lush greenery and blooming orchids. The landscape changed, too.

Where once empty branches stretched toward the cloudy sky, now dense foliage and towering trees did their best to block out a bright golden sun. The crunch of snow and dead leaves was replaced by buzzing insects and the melody of birdsong.

I remained on alert for any signs of a turul-shifter scout,

GENA SHOWALTER & JILL MONROE

but to my surprise, I spotted none. Didn't mean they weren't out there.

"Where are we?" I asked, not missing the bite of frost one bit.

Viktor led me forward, our boots sinking into spongy, rich earth and moss. "This dimension has four parts. Each embodies the essence of a season in the mortal world. We have entered spring."

The sound of soothing water splashing against rocks reached my ears. Excitement bloomed as we rounded a corner. Spotting a gorgeous crystal pond complete with a tumbling waterfall, I stopped. Steam curled from the water's surface, coiling around a mini-rainbow. Three types of fruit dangled from tree branches, each a different color.

A veritable paradise. There was no stopping my mewl of delight. "As much as I'm looking forward to a warm bath, I'm dreading wearing these dirty clothes again."

"About that. I sent a soldier to a nearby village while the rest of us worked on camp defenses. He had orders to confiscate specific things and leave them here." Viktor squeezed my hand before releasing me to pluck a plum-size red berry he offered to me. "This will soothe your appetite." He selected a golden grape type fruit and offered it as well. "This will refresh you." He merely pointed to the blue apple-like fruit. "That will liquify your bowels."

I snorted. "Thank you for the warning." Marveling over his thoughtfulness, I took a bite of the red berry first. Mmm. My eyes slid shut in surrender. What incredible sweetness. A bead of juice ran down my chin as I devoured the rest of the treat and popped the golden grape thing into my mouth. Oh, wow. Even better! He wasn't kidding about being refreshed. I didn't think my mouth had ever felt so clean.

THE STOLEN BRIDE

"If you don't have any of these trees in your realm, get some," I advised. Even indulging every day wouldn't be enough. "Well, not the bowel liquefying one, of course. The others are perfection."

"They only grow here, but if you want to rule this dimension, I will gift it to you after we secure your sister." He gently dragged his knuckles over my jawline, as if he hadn't just rocked my world. "Your happiness leads to mine, apparently."

I peered up at him, mind boggled. When he decided to go all in, he went *all in*. "I thought you didn't like happiness."

"I suppose it's an acquired taste."

My lips quirked at the corners. "I'm ready to bathe. Join me?"

"You wish to bathe together?" His eyes widened ever so slightly. "If you insist." He kicked off his boots, dropped a million and one weapons I hadn't known he carried, and tugged at his clothing, disrobing to his briefs.

His speed impressed me, but his body... *Hello, gorgeous.* My heart attempted to jump out of my chest. The man utterly dazzled. Muscles cut with steel. Tattooed skin on display.

"No one will sneak up on us. I'll remain aware. The very reason I'm still partially dressed," he added with wry humor.

I trembled as I stripped to my undergarments as well. He watched unabashedly, even licking his lips like a big, bad wolf. No reason to wonder if he liked what he saw. His body let me know big time. Huge time.

"I'm definitely keeping you," he rasped, looking me over from head to toe.

I almost asked him to kiss me, but I had a feeling once

we started, we wouldn't be able to stop. Especially dressed like this. Gulping, I backed into the water. "You can't keep me without my permission."

"Then I will get permission." We maintained our eye-lock as he prowled forward, following me. "I'm confident of it."

Warm water swallowed my feet. My calves. My thighs. Soon I was submerged to the navel. The soothing liquid delighted sore muscles while Viktor's hot stare melted everything else.

"I look forward to your efforts." My trembling redoubled as I swam to the waterfall, where I found a wealth of toiletries. "One day, when we're not in enemy territory, on a mission, we're going to enjoy some water play." Splash around and paw at each other, letting hands slip and wander. But that day was not today. The sooner we reached that fortress, the better. I rubbed the center of my chest, where my bond to Juniper tingled as never before. She must be nearby.

"Agreed." Viktor followed me still. "One day we will play. Today, we focus on cleanliness. You are very dirty." His voice dipped. So did his eyelids.

"Oh, I am, am I?" Never mind the bath he'd given me yesterday.

"The dirtiest."

I didn't protest as he soaped me up. And, okay, yes, his hands did wander. Mine did, too, when I returned the favor. The scent of jasmine and lotus enveloped us. I relished our closeness, leaning into every touch. Aches only he could rouse blazed to life, need for him nearly a tangible force.

Only the intensifying tingle of the bond stopped me from going further.

"We better go," I said, before I gave in to temptation.

THE STOLEN BRIDE

He kissed my brow, and we exited the water together. "Our clean clothes are in a pack next to that S shaped tree."

I stalked to the pack, dug inside, shed my wet underwear, and wiggled into my new outfit with a growing sense of alarm. The gauzy material was soft, luxuriant—and indecent. A translucent bodysuit was pink as cotton candy with a built-in panties and bra, spaghetti straps, and a cutout midriff. Basically a genie costume, with a sheer skirt flowing from the cinched waist rather than a pair of pantaloons.

Viktor donned a soft black shirt and black leathers. Fully covered!

"Your soldier failed you," I muttered. I looked myself over with a grimace before sliding my feet into my combat boots.

"Nem. He acquired almost exactly what I requested."

My gaze zipped to him. "You did not specify I go into battle like this."

"Correct." He gently chucked me under the chin. "You are missing the ruby choker and diamond toe rings."

16

When Nothing Adds Up: Nix the X to Solve For Y

–HOW TO TRAIN YOUR BERSERKER
By Elizabeth "Elle" Darcy-Bruce

Viktor steered me through the jungle. With an unofficial-official boyfriend I trusted and my heart no longer weighed down by thousands of emotion-filled bottles, I was able to do something I'd never done. Relax and soak up the ambiance. There were more flowers than I'd ever seen in one place. They scented the air with sweetness. Lush plants dripped with delicious-looking berries and razor-sharp thorns. Colorful birds and howling monkeys swung from vines.

Despite my ridiculous outfit, I had pep in my steps.

"Where are the shifters?" I asked, ducking under the branch he moved out of my path. I remained ready for an attack, but I saw not even a hint of the enemy.

"I think they realized they require a new strategy with

THE STOLEN BRIDE

you, now that they comprehend you are capable of a rage-trance. I'm certain they'll regroup soon. I only hope we reach Deco's fortress before it happens."

I didn't mean to, I really didn't, but I smiled. The thought of powerful shifters—the enemy—needing to redo their war-plan because of little ole me, well. Talk about a confidence boost! On the other hand...

"I don't want to break again." I despised not recalling what I'd done. The loss of control. The endless icy cold, where every thought died before my opponents.

"What you felt, that is what the shifters experience all the time. Or so the Valkara explained to me long ago."

I grimaced. How terrible to live out immortality in such a way. Never satisfied. Never experiencing joy or peace or love. Always hungry for the misery of others.

Grrr. Was I seriously feeling sorry for the creatures who had attempted to murder me? I switched my focus. "Is Valkara still silent?"

"Ja."

Good. "And how do you feel about that?"

"I am...unsure."

Well, that was better than before, when he'd only welcomed her.

He slung his arm around my waist and helped me over a fallen log. "I've never required her aid more, but even apart from you, the fog remains thin now. It is the mist that carries her voice."

"You hate the fog," I reminded him. Hint hint. If the fog was awful, it stood to reason that Valkara was too.

"Ja," he repeated, "but it serves a purpose. Just as the fog you experience does, which may come from her."

I heaved a sigh. "Yeah, I've had the same suspicion." But

did that mean I should ignore my dream? Treat it as Valkara propaganda?

Tension exploded from him, as if he'd been hit with a bomb. "I think, perhaps, she hopes to convince you to accept death by my hand. What I don't know is what she will do when I refuse."

When, not if. The reassurance brought a cascade of warm honey over my soul. "I won't ever accept that death is the answer," I assured him. "Not even for the greater good." So yes. I should ignore my dream. "The two ideas aren't even compatible."

"Agreed."

I beamed up at him, and a sharp, electric awareness turned even the air I breathed into a caress. I noticed the confidence in his stride. The glint of sunlight against the bronze hues of his skin. How he flared and fisted his fingers, as if imagining all the ways he yearned to touch me.

He must have experienced a similar reaction. In unison, we increased our pace, attempting to escape the growing cognizance between us.

Nature's romantic serenade didn't help. Distant calls harmonized with the gentle rustling of leaves and the low rasp of our inhalations, creating a carnal chorus meant for lovers. We came across many of Deco's traps, but Viktor sussed them out before we tripped one.

Without warning, he spun in front of me. I crashed into his big body, bouncing back. His powerful arms shot out, slinging around my waist to keep me close and upright. For balance, I flattened my hands against his pecs. His heart raced, and the heat of his skin radiated through his shirt.

"Is something wrong?" I trembled with anticipation as he backed me into a tree.

"Ja." He planted his hands near my temples, caging me

THE STOLEN BRIDE

in. His attention slid down the curves displayed oh, so vividly in my barely-there pink ensemble. "I haven't yet marked you. But I want to."

My breath caught, trapping his incredible fragrance in my nose. My head. Mom had told me about a mark between berserker mates. A cut on each person's palm, the mingling of their blood, a kiss, and an unbreakable bond no other warrior could deny. The greatest gift a sentinel could give his woman, forever protecting her from other immortals if ever they were parted.

"Let me," he demanded, letting his lips hover over mine. "I sense no threat in our vicinity."

"I...shouldn't." The refusal required every ounce of strength I possessed. Gliding my palms up his chest, I said, "Creating a permeant tie when we've only just met is foolish."

Far from upset by my response, he set his beautiful mouth at my ear to whisper, "Why delay the inevitable?"

In that moment, he was kindling; I was flames. Heartbeat a storm of thunder and lightning, I tossed caution into the wind. Forget waiting for the right time to enjoy him. Danger smanger. "Kiss me and I'll think about it." And probably nothing else.

Understanding the assignment, he swooped down and melded his lips to mine. I opened without hesitation, welcoming the thrust of his tongue. His groan of pleasure filled the air around us.

We devoured each other. His taste transcended perfection, and I couldn't get enough. As little mewls and growls erupted in my chest, sublime power pulsed from him.

He liked my reaction to him.

"I want to make you mine in all ways," he rasped.

"You are temptation itself." Emboldened, I sank my

197

fingers into his silken hair, clinging to his strength. He gripped my hips and yanked me closer, only clothing separated us.

The kiss turned fevered, spinning out of control, becoming a fiery exchange I never wished to end. Thoughts realigned, each centered on a single word: *More.*

But. Footsteps. Nearby. Shifters?

With a ragged roar, Viktor wrenched his face from mine. We both panted, breath sawing between us. Actual claws sprouted from the tips of my fingers.

"It's only Bodi." He traced his thumb over my cheek, studying me as if I were some kind of exotic creature worth more than anyone could afford. "At the first opportunity, we'll pick this up where we left off."

My claws retracted—something I'd consider later. At the moment, I was a little too drunk on him to do anything but nod.

When Malachi had found me and thrown me into this unwanted adventure, I'd been alone with no idea of my lineage. Now I had a sister and a possible firebrand within reach.

There. I'd admitted it. I might have a firebrand, too. Something else to consider later.

Bodi emerged from a thicket. Gashes littered his face and torso, and crimson streaked his skin. Leaves were scattered throughout his sandy golden hair. He stopped when he spotted us, grumbling, "If your goal is to cross the terrain without drawing notice, you're failing. I heard you a mile back."

"What happened to you?" Viktor demanded, releasing me. "I ordered you to go home."

He had?

The prince swiped his tongue over a scab on his upper

THE STOLEN BRIDE

lip. "A contingent of shifters has chased me nonstop since the incident at camp. Rather than do battle at the traveling stones, I've gone in circles, slaying my tail one by one. I just killed the last shifter an hour ago."

Poor Bodi. "Don't worry. I'll protect you if other shifters show up." I flipped my hair over my shoulder. "Excuse my humble brag, but I'm kinda really strong now."

The prince didn't spare me a glance, but arched a brow at his brother. "She broke then?"

Guess the pair had discussed the possibility. "She did," I answered for him.

Viktor's chest puffed with pride. "I'm her firebrand. I calmed her rage."

His delight affected me as staunchly as his kiss, and I nibbled on my bottom lip to halt a smile. So I'd only known him a short while. I wanted a chance with this man. Wanted to be with him today, tomorrow, and forever. He'd saved my life. Protected me. Peered at me as if his entire world orbited around me. Kissed me as if my lungs held the air he required for his survival. And look at him. A wild man with gorgeous white hair in total disarray, sparkling eyes, and lips puffy from my kisses. Even now, in conversation with another, he sought contact with me, pressing his hand on the small of my back.

I'd have to give up my spa, but I wasn't exactly human and had zero desire to bottle my emotions again. Something that would be necessary around humans. Besides, berserkers had pets too. I could open a new shop. Legends and Lather? Celestial Pet Spa?

Bodi glanced between us, a tinge of disgust infiltrating his features. "We should go. The goal is still to reach Deco's fortress, ja, and not be sitting ducks?" He marched ahead of us.

Viktor twined his fingers with mine and ushered me forward, staying near his brother. "Have you seen any others?"

"Ja, and I wish I hadn't," Bodi replied, his tone tight. "Kellan shifted, and we fought. I injured him, but I couldn't bring myself to slay him. But leaving him alive cost me. He came after me with Deco's men."

Shoulders rolling in, Viktor sighed. "So less than a handful of us remain."

Guilt pricked me. I'd killed four of them.

My boyfriend, for lack of a better word, sensed the direction of my thoughts, lifted my knuckles to his mouth, and kissed. "They attacked you. They deserved what they got."

Bodi missed his next step, surprised, but I nearly floated out of my body.

Suddenly Viktor jerked as though struck by a bolt of lightning. He stopped, released me, and pounded his fists into his temples before pulling at hanks of his hair. "What, what, what?" he bellowed.

Concern punched me. "What's happening? What's wrong?"

"The Valkara. Something's wrong. She's trying to speak with me," he said, his voice ragged. He swung around and slammed his forehead into a tree. Bang, bang, bang. Cracks spread through the trunk. "But she's so quiet. Too quiet. Be louder!"

On instinct, I wedged myself between him and the tree to prevent his next blow. Jagged cuts dripped blood all down his face, and the sight hurt *me*. I cupped his cheeks, cooing, "Breathe in, baby. Good. Now out. Yes, yes. Now, picture yourself throwing your frustration out of your head through your ears." Something my father

THE STOLEN BRIDE

used to say to me before I learned to bottle. "Go on. Picture it."

He frowned but gave a clipped nod. "Done."

"Now listen." I didn't want him talking to the woman, but he had to want to sever their tie. If he desired a relationship with her, well, that was on him. I refused to protest again. I just knew our relationship wouldn't last, and the mark I'd just decided to take wouldn't happen. The choice was his.

A moment passed in silence. Two. His nostrils flared. "I hear her."

I waited several moments more before saying, "Focus on her words."

His eyelids narrowed to tiny slits. "She's telling me..." He cursed beneath his breath. "She is the one Deco imprisoned. He's *harmed* her. She's weakening. Perhaps dying." Viktor pounded at his temples again. "If I do not reach her —I must reach her."

Ice spread over his expression. He looked to Bodi, to me. "Try to keep up." With no other words, he took off in a mad sprint through the jungle.

Bodi and I shared a look before leaping into action, trailing him. Though I was faster than ever before, I lagged behind. The prince hung back, keeping both his brother and me in his sights, but something gnawed at my gut.

"Your outfit is an...interesting choice," the prince said, all casual-like, as if we were merely taking a stroll in a park.

Twin circles scorched my cheeks. "Blame your brother. He picked it."

The prince flashed a smile, there and gone. "You are good for him."

"I know."

He chuckled at my swagger. I comprehended the man

responded to bravado. And Bodi hadn't even heard the half of it! I'd done the impossible and made his brother smile. "But, um, maybe be on the lookout for turul-shifters, since he's forgotten everything but his precious Valkara."

A grunting sound escaped him. "As if I'm not always on the lookout."

I scanned the canopy above our heads, through the teak and banyan leaves, unable to shake an uneasy feeling. "This could be a trap. I don't trust her."

"You are not the only one," Bodi muttered.

We experienced a surprising beat of comradery.

"She's powerful, right? Knows the secrets of the Starfire that turned mortals into berserkers. Can use a set of keys to unshift a shifter. This whole 'Deco has captured me, and I may be dying' feels a little too convenient." Something didn't add up. Maybe my suspicions revolved around Viktor's feelings for the woman. Maybe not.

Rushing off with barely a second glance at his one, true firebrand to rescue another woman in distress...

Plus

A centuries long connection...

Equaled

Some part of Viktor might love Valkara, who may or may not be in love with him, too.

Finally, the math worked out. I'd believed my hold on him was stronger than hers. And maybe it was. But any hold she had tainted mine. She wanted me dead so badly that she'd sunk to invading my dreams to convince me to willingly accept death at his hand. And she'd done this since my childhood!

Though Viktor had promised to refuse her instructions, he might change his mind. I didn't know what power she

THE STOLEN BRIDE

possessed, the strength of her influence, or the depths of his feelings for her.

My stomach churned. For too long, I'd missed the signs that Benjamin and my ex-best friend Kami bore an attraction to each other. And yet, the calculation had been right there in front of me. Stronger variables lay before me now. Otherworldly ones!

One thing was for certain. Viktor was a man with divided loyalties, and I was an all or nothing kinda girl. I had major feelings for him. I liked who I was with him. I liked him period. But I needed total devotion. Deserved it because I gave it.

An agonized groan echoed up ahead. Bodi and I shared another look before kicking into a supernaturally charged higher gear. We reached Viktor, who had stopped at the edge of an abandoned campsite.

I took in the destruction. A smashed shelter composed of mud, limbs, and leaves. A torn, bloodstained gown of multi-colors, from the darkest gray to the palest white, hung from a branch.

A dented canteen on its side, the lid several feet away.

"She was here, however long ago," Viktor rasped, balling his hands. "There are no footprints but hers. They took her from the air." He stalked about, ransacking the camp. On the hunt for something specific? "Why did she come here? For me? Did she find my key? Did Deco?" Roaring, he punched his fist into a tree trunk. His knuckles drove through the bark, leaving a gaping hole.

Bodi motioned me forward. "Well?"

I blinked at him. "Well what?"

"Calm him."

What, I was a dancing monkey on a string now?

I didn't calm Viktor because this wasn't a berserkerage,

203

but a tantrum over his precious primordial guardian. I crossed my arms over my middle and waited.

The king was panting by the time he finished.

"May we go now?" I asked.

"We may, but you should prepare yourself." He squared his shoulders.

As if I hadn't already prepared for the worst twenty times over since finding Malachi Cromwell sitting in my bedroom. Still, I had to ask, "Prepare for what?"

"I won't stop until Deco is dead, or we are."

17

Wish Granted: Making An Entrance With Your Berserker

—HOW TO TRAIN YOUR BERSERKER
By Elizabeth "Elle" Darcy-Bruce

Our trio raced through the jungle at top speed, and I didn't dare complain. The faster we reached the fortress, the better. Amidst the beauty of the tropical wilderness, I remained on the lookout for the enemy and traps.

I won't stop until Deco is dead, or we are.

Viktor's words haunted me as we plowed through dense vegetation. Though he'd once planned to do everything possible to save his former friend, he'd now set his sights on death. Even at the risk of our lives, all to save Valkara.

I curled my hands into fists. "This could be a set up," I pointed out between my huffing breaths.

Neither man responded.

The metallic clang of Bodi's machete cut through the muggy air. A sharp whoosh followed as he sliced through the thick vines obstructing our path. We ran and ran and ran, and the ongoing, never-ending hustle eventually drained me. I began to lag, until Viktor whisked me off my feet and carried me against his chest, not missing a beat.

Now this was more like it. The only way to travel, really. I rested my head on his broad shoulder, as I'd done several times before, seizing the opportunity to recharge. With my sister's life on the line–and maybe Viktor's–I must be at my best.

We whizzed past a clearing littered with bones and a field of decaying bodies. Bile frothed in my throat, and I gagged. Who were these people? Turul-shifters, berserkers or their victims?

Scavenger birds dined, picking rotting organs through the hole in each chest. Severed heads topped scarecrow bodies. The fetid stench made me gag. And that wasn't even the worst of it! The farther we went, the more gruesome the sights became. Eventually I closed my eyes and focused on my sister's rescue.

In the back of my mind, I thought I detected an invisible cord between us, growing stronger the closer we came to each other.

Viktor halted abruptly and set me on my feet. Bodi stopped too. Both royals stared at a leather poster anchored to a tree trunk, drawing my attention there. I read the words painted over the surface and ground my teeth.

Come One, Come All

King Deco's Execution Ball

Off with Their Heads

I didn't have to wonder who he referenced. His captives, Juniper and Valkara—and us. "He invited me to this ball," I said, the words fraying as I shoved them between gritted teeth. "Right before he stabbed me."

An H-bomb of rage exploded from Viktor. He spun, facing me fully. Glowing gold rings flared in his irises. "He. Did. What?"

"Oh. Um. Did I not mention that part before?" Oops? "It happened right after I woke up from my tangle with the river."

Roaring, he swept me into his arms and shot forward like a bullet. The landscape whizzed at my sides. I tightened my hold on him, hanging on for dear life. Then the jungle began to thin, and just as quickly as Vik had grabbed me and sprinted off, he came to an abrupt halt on the outskirts of a vast clearing. A massive fortress loomed less than a fourth of a mile ahead.

An unsettling current surged all around us, raising the fine hairs on the back of my neck. I searched for the source. There! Enormous metal posts planted at the four corners of a square plot of land we now occupied, each post topped with a large glass orb. But were they cameras or something else?

A bluebird flew low, and a lightning bolt shot out of the orbs, striking it. The poor creature fried and fell to the ground, dead and still smoking.

Okay, so, definitely something else. I plastered myself against Viktor's chest. "Nope. We're finding another way."

He kissed my temple and set me on my feet, keeping his arm around my waist. "Shifters are weaker than berserkers, so the fence is the preliminary defense. Meant to weaken *us* on the way in. Nothing to worry about."

"I can get us past it," Bodi said. Then he pointed. "They are the real concern."

I followed the direction of his finger. High atop weathered gray stones streaked with hints of green from years exposed to the humid jungle moss and lichen, was a parapet where an army of shifter guards patrolled. A stunning show of Deco's force for the ball. They must be on the lookout for specific intruders. Namely us.

The fortress itself was, well, a fortress, a mix of ancient and modern with thick walls designed to withstand an assault. Arrow slits broke up the symmetry, allowing sharpshooters and archers to do their thing. More armed guards patrolled the courtyard amongst the guests, while still others escorted attendees from an unused helicopter pad.

Wind kicked up, strong gusts rustling leaves. Branches clapped, and my skirt whipped at my ankles. We remained in the shadows, at the edge of the jungle.

Torches illuminated the courtyard where turul-shifters mingled awaiting their turn to enter the towering stone monstrosity. The males wore finely tailored suits. The females dazzled in flowing gowns in every color of the rainbow, and the kind of jewels that were so opulent they inspired awe rather than envy. They displayed turul feathers in their hair.

Face painters and jugglers entertained the partygoers who'd already had too much to drink. Acrobats leaped, dancers twirled and fire eaters astounded the growing crowd.

I glanced down at my genie costume and muttered, "I know how *I'm* getting in."

A muscle jumped beneath Viktor's eye. "You will..." A thousand emotions crossed over his features in an instant, none of which I could read.

"Be careful?" I finished for him. "Yes." I might not be a super-soldier who'd trained for battle all my life, but I was

THE STOLEN BRIDE

a woman determined. Nothing could stop me from helping my team. Well, other than death. But even then, I'd probably keep fighting. "I'm immortal. I won't die." I mean, not easily anyway. "Plus, I shouldn't waste this incredible outfit you picked for me. This girl has no problem working things to her advantage."

And not to brag, but I was a major asset. Look what I'd done to those shifters. Not that I remembered any of it. But still! I'd defeated ten master warriors with my bare claws.

Viktor looked to Bodi, who shook his head and spread his arms, all *not helping you with this.*

"My men are immortal, yet five have died on this trip," Viktor stated in a flat voice. "Though I wasn't going to ask you to remain behind."

"As if you ever ask me anything anymore," I muttered, with only a little bitterness. Wait. He'd intended to go into battle with me at his side?

He started opening and closing his fists again. "You won't be happy until your sister is free, and I require the Valkara to answer some questions. To successfully oversee both goals, I will make use of every weapon at my disposal."

I beamed up at him. First, he sought Valkara for questions, not romance. Second, he considered me a weapon. "Good. What's the plan?"

"We walk in together. I create a distraction, and you and Bodi proceeds to the dungeon. I'll keep Deco and his forces occupied."

"Walk in, just like that?" I snapped my fingers. "Not with those handsome faces and delicious muscles." They weren't shifters and it showed. "But as I said, I have an idea. Bodi, you mentioned getting us past the orbs, yes?"

He nodded. "With Viktor's help."

"Great. Do it. Then I'll get us in unnoticed."

Viktor sighed, the very picture of an exasperated boyfriend. We approached the edge of the invisible fence tentatively. With each step, the waft of electricity intensified until the scent of ozone singed my airways. Though I recalled the bluebird, I didn't dare give Viktor a reason to insist I remain behind.

"Stay between us," he instructed.

His protective instinct gave me a sense of security and belonging, and I soaked it up. I hadn't felt as if I belonged anywhere or with anyone for a very long time.

Bodi did some weird motions with a pair of daggers, seeming to cut through the air. Then he passed one of the weapons to Viktor, and both men held up the blade. "Now," he said.

The three of us stepped forward, with me sandwiched between the two beefcakes. Static electricity pricked my skin and lifted my hair as energy arced between the two daggers. Vik and Bodi took the brunt of the charge, their muscles flexing and straining, absorbing the worst of the onslaught. The hum of the voltage made my eardrums vibrate, and I tasted something metallic in my mouth.

We trudged forward, as if wading against a fierce ocean current. Just when I thought my eyes would catch on fire, we emerged on the other side of the invisible barrier. My fingers were a little numb, but I was otherwise unscathed.

In relief, I lifted onto my tippy toes and dropped a kiss on Viktor's cheek. "Thanks, pudding pop."

"I'm here, too, you know," Bodi grumbled good-naturedly.

I patted his head. "Thanks, Bodi. You're growing on me.

THE STOLEN BRIDE

But now it's time to put my plan into action. You two stay here, and I'll be back in a jiff."

Before either could protest, I raced toward the courtyard, quickly doing my best to blend in with the crowd. I snagged a scarf here, a hat there. My biggest achievement was swiping a palette of paints and a brush. The boys weren't the only ones good at pilfering from the enemy. Though, yes, in any other situation, I held firm to a no stealing policy.

Five minutes later, I was back with my booty—without setting off an alarm. "Yeah," I said, "I'm *that* good." I set to work, looping a scarp around Bodi's neck and plopping a hat on Viktor, King of the Turuls. I dipped a brush in paint and began dabbing the brightest colors onto their cheeks in feather patterns. They let me work without comment.

"Is this really necessary?" Viktor asked.

"Yes." Absolutely. "Can either of you juggle?"

He blinked at me.

Bodi's eyes widened, and he gave a clipped shake of his head. "No. I refuse."

Too bad. "Can you mime? Do magic tricks? Make balloon animals?"

They shared a look before staring at me like I'd come from another planet.

In the distance, horns sounded, and two wide wooden doors opened, allowing the guests to enter the palace.

"I suggest we get through the crowd as quickly and stealthily as possible," I announced. "Your expert disguises will only last so long."

"Once we are inside, you will accompany Bodi to the dungeon," Viktor instructed.

"Okay. Yes." Perfect plan. Zero tweaks necessary.

"Are you sure that's wise?" Bodi asked, and I pursed my

lips. "Deco might go with a contingency plan and kill his prisoners before we can free them."

"He won't." Confidence radiated from Viktor. "If I thought there was the slightest chance either female would be harmed, I wouldn't risk doing this. Having served him for over a decade, I know how much he thrives on pomp and circumstance. How he loves gloating. He won't be able to resist an opportunity to make a public spectacle over the Valkara's capture. In fact, I'm certain he's in the throne room, awaiting us. Once we've confirmed this, lock me in with him and his men. I won't come out until I've done what needs doing."

The flat statement drew forth a frown. And a memory. On the day we met, Viktor mentioned his love for Deco. That love hadn't died. "Please don't kill him if you don't have to." I didn't want to be a source of eternal regret for him. "Maybe, once he's in his right mind, he'll remember who he used to be and become who he should be."

Shockingly tender, Viktor grazed the pad of his thumb over my shoulder. "I will never forget the bloodstains I saw on your shirt when I came upon you in that clearing. I thought you had received the injury that caused it during battle. I hadn't realized…" Viktor worked his jaw. "He dies today. Badly."

"If we're going to do this," Bodi piped up, rolling his shoulders, "let's do it."

"Are you sure you can?" Viktor asked him.

Conflicting emotions crossed the prince's face, one after another. Clearly he wasn't keen on the idea of losing a brother today. He had probably hoped to return Deco to his berserker state too.

There was a chance Bodi possessed divided loyalties. The shifters had certainly tried to win him over. We could

THE STOLEN BRIDE

be rushing into a betrayal waiting to happen. But Viktor knew him best and trusted him, so I would do the same. Together, we stood the greatest opportunity for success.

"I can," Bodi said with a nod.

"Very well." Viktor slapped a dagger into my hand, bent his head, and pressed a swift kiss into my lips. "Stay alive, or face my displeasure."

"Right back at you, darling."

With a low growl rumbling in his chest, he started forward. Bodi and I kept pace. My heart thudded, but not with fear. Not excitement, either, but resolve. We must succeed.

The prince embraced the role of entertainer a fraction better than Viktor, which meant I had to work double time, smiling wide and giving an extra dose of enthusiastic, wish-granting-genie style magic waves to divert attention from our true aim. Several women blew kisses at my companions.

I made a growling sound, drawing the notice of multiple guards. Oops. "My bad, guys," I muttered.

From their perches, the guards squawked and excitedly flapped their wings.

"I honestly expected to be spotted sooner," Viktor said, a roundabout way of praising my efforts. "Keep going."

We reached a cobblestone walkway that led to the entrance. Still no attacks, but the crowd heading into the fortress noticed the commotion and parted like the Red Sea, creating a path. Every eye glued to us. Whispers arose, blending together, evincing glee.

Evil all but coated the air, making my skin crawl. These people *craved* our deaths. Well, except for her. She made a *call me* sign and winked at Viktor. I ground my teeth.

213

Two shifters stood sentry at the open double doors. They grinned at our approach.

"Told you they'd come," one bragged to the other.

Viktor punched both in the throat, ripping things out as we passed. He dropped his bloody bounty and kept walking. *That's my man.* And he was, wasn't he? The king who'd cared for me my first night in a foreign land. Who'd held me. Fed me. Warmed and protected me. Aided me just because I asked. Saved me when I hadn't. The warrior who calmed for me alone. The only one who calmed me.

One hundred percent, he was my firebrand. I didn't just want him to choose me over Valkara; I needed him to. Mark me? Yes, please! My knees grew a little shaky, but I didn't have time to do a full analysis of our relationship. First things first.

We would take care of Deco.

Save Juniper.

Deal with Valkara.

Either the guardian of the Starfire admitted she'd lied about me to win Viktor for herself or...something. I didn't know, but it would be terrible!

The foyer felt cool and dark, a stark contrast to the humid jungle outside. Torches lit the narrow hallways, used to light the rooms despite access to electricity. Walkways led to various chambers and corridors, designed to confuse and funnel any invaders into easily defendable bottlenecks. Even I, a war amateur, realized that. Tapestries adorned the walls, the floors of polished quartz.

Finally, we approached an arched doorway etched with mythological creatures. The wide-open doors revealed a majestic space, with a high vaulted ceiling and stained-glass windows depicting turul-shifters attacking and killing.

THE STOLEN BRIDE

The bejeweled crowd split just like they had in the courtyard, giving us a direct path to a dais made of polished stone. Atop it sat an elaborate throne, intricately carved and inlaid with gold. Gold draperies covered the walls, shimmering as if dipped in diamond powder. The room was meant to be both beautiful and impressive, but a terrible malevolence tainted the space. Shadows dimmed the brilliance of the golden hue, hinting at the shifter king's evil.

Holding a glass of champagne, peering straight at us, Deco grinned. His smile—if you could call it that—set my nerves on edge.

"Hello, Viktor," he said in the best supervillain voice I'd ever heard. I detected notes of manic anticipation, pure insanity, and stone-cold killer.

"Deco."

"I'm so humbled you fit my little party into your busy schedule."

Viktor shrugged. "When I want to kill someone bad enough, I make the time."

The shifter king appeared unfazed. "And you brought our brother and your firebrand. I was hoping you would."

Viktor shifted from side to side but otherwise remained stoic.

Deco pressed his fingers to his mouth, mockingly contrite. "Oops. Have you finally admitted her importance to you, or are you still pretending not to know?"

He hiked a shoulder. "She killed your elite with ease. How could I deny it?"

The shifter king narrowed his eyes. Finally, a reaction. He caught himself a moment later and righted his expression, grinning once again. "Welcome my guests of honor, everyone," he called, and our audience cheered. "He's going to help me with tonight's grand finale. Come, come. See what awaits you in the ballroom." Deco waved us toward a pair of gilded doors, his excitement returning and doubling. "Let me show you what I've done."

He was too happy. What did he know that we didn't?

Viktor brushed his fingers against mine in a gesture of assurance before stalking forward. With a prickle of foreboding on my nape, I notched my chin and followed.

18

Crashing the Party: Dodging Drama At the Reunion

—HOW TO TRAIN YOUR BERSERKER
By Elizabeth "Elle" Darcy-Bruce

Another set of guards, dressed formally in black tuxes with embroidered floral vests reminiscent of ancient folklore, opened the doors with a flourish. We stalked into the ballroom, and my jaw slackened.

Ornate chandeliers dripping with crystals cast the room in a kaleidoscope of hues. The polished parquet floor gleamed. Scantily clad aerial dancers hung from ribbons anchored to the vaulted, frescoed ceiling, depicting heroic deeds of the past, and the beautiful turul birds of Hungarian legend. Arched windows lined the walls, allowing views of the courtyard and jungle. Massive mirrors flanked another wall, reflecting the lavish splendor of long tables laden with food. Gleaming golden platters and bowls overflowed with succulent meats and savory

GENA SHOWALTER & JILL MONROE

vegetables. The scent of baked bread and decadent desserts filled the air.

I had to give it to Deco. He knew how to throw a party.

Despite being vile shifters, the milling guests awed. Women wore flowing gowns, the colorful and intricate beadwork on their bodices featuring bird motifs. Others donned feathered masks or headpieces. The men sported tailored suits, with wing pins attached to their lapels.

Women in simple black skirts and white shirts with golden sashes around their waists carted trays of prosciutto-wrapped melon, sushi rolls and miniature quiches. Okay, so, I nabbed a few handfuls to keep up my strength. But my last bite settled in my stomach like a lead ball when I spied an elegantly crafted stage.

Two women sat, chained to the floor with heavy links of iron. Juniper! There she was, in the flesh. My sister, my twin, garbed in a subdued golden gown that draped her restrained form. An ornamental comb secured her dark hair, the red highlights gleaming under the light of the chandelier. A jeweled collar encircled her neck, featuring a golden turul with ruby red eyes. Deco's idea of staking a claim on the prized prisoner?

She was alive and well with no visible injuries, thank goodness!

She reclined on one arm, her calves tucked behind her thighs. She hadn't noticed me yet. But. My hands. Warmth and tingles erupted from my wrists to my fingertips. Of their own accord, my arms lifted, stretching toward her like magnets drawn to metal. She must have experienced the same sensations. Her arms lifted as well. I had to actively fight to lower mine. What in the world?

The woman beside Juniper shifted and my attention swung to her. Wow. The dark-haired beauty appeared ethereal, otherworldly, as if she could meld with a waft of fog at any moment, her mere presence a blend of mystique and majesty. Attired in a luminous cascade of silver, the fabric of her gown flowed around her like tendrils of mist. She'd styled her hair into an intricate braid with threads of the ten colors of the Starfire interwoven in the strands.

Valkara. The woman who wanted Viktor for her own and me dead by fair means or foul.

There was something vaguely familiar about her. Had we met before? But where? When? I wracked my brain but came up empty. Maybe I'd glimpsed her in Viktor's varg-bane-root-triggered memories?

My sister noticed me at last, our gazes meeting. Wonder, worry and hope flittered over her expression. She tried to stand, but the chain kept her seated.

Anger and frustration collided within me, beating at my composure. Both emotions intensified as Deco ascended a set of steps and stalked across the stage.

Conversations quickly turned to hushed whispers. Even the clink of silverware and champagne glasses faded.

Still grinning, he stopped beside the women, unfurling his massive wings behind them. His meaning was unmistakable: mine.

I shuddered at the menacing sight he presented, which only made his smile grow. Dang it, I'd let him know he'd gotten to me.

"Guess we don't need to fight our way to the dungeon," Bodi muttered.

Nope. The women were here. So what was Plan B? If any of us erupted, we might kill the innocents. Perhaps that was why Deco arranged this.

Viktor remained silent, fisting and relaxing his hands, shaking his head. Hearing whispers in the fog again?

I focused on Valkara. Her eyes were closed, her lips moving. Oh, yes. She was definitely talking to him. Either she sought to warn him of some hidden danger, or she wished to distract him at a dangerous time. Because why else would she do this here at such an opportune moment?

"Who's ready for the show?" Deco called. He clapped his hands twice.

Soldier after soldier flooded into the room using every doorway, each man already partially shifted. They lined up against the walls, wing to wing, until completely surrounding us. Aggression and glee tainted the atmosphere. Next, Deco gave a quick hand motion, and the elegant guests rushed to the stage, taking up posts behind their king and his prisoners, leaving us alone on the polished parquet floor.

Well, okay then. Plan B crystalized. Fight, survive, and kill Deco. Viktor was right. The turul king had chosen his path. If it must end in his death to protect my loved ones, so be it.

Familiar heat bloomed in the center of my sternum, quickly spreading through my arms and pooling in my fingers. My nails darkened, sharpened, and extended into claws. *Careful, careful.* If I accidentally harmed my sister while she was helpless and bound...

"No, no, no," Viktor muttered, his eyes squeezed shut.

Fighting for calm, I spun in front of Viktor and pressed my palm over his racing heart. "I need you to focus on me for a moment, baby, not Valkara. Okay?"

His eyes snapped open. Glowing golden rings flared in his irises, burning away the glaze of madness. "Ja?"

"Fight to kill."

"Ja," he repeated with determination. Between one blink and the next, his body doubled in size, pieces of his

THE STOLEN BRIDE

clothing tearing. Some even fell away. Jagged flashes of lightning crackled over his skin. "Bodi," he called.

The prince understood the unspoken request and moved behind me. He, too, had doubled in size and now wore what remained of his ripped clothing. No wonder berserkers fought naked.

Viktor stepped in front of me. Together, they formed a wall of protection around me.

"You think you've won, but you're about to lose your army," Viktor stated. "Let's do this in the way of the ancients. Challenge me one-on-one. Winner is king of the House of Turul, berserkers and shifters alike."

How ironic. This was what Lena had desired all along– these two men battling for both thrones and all the power that came with them—but she wasn't here to witness the fruits of her labor.

"Ah, but I have no desire to rule your house." Hatred iced his golden brown eyes. His voice hardened, more unbendable than steel. "I intend to destroy it, piece by piece. I'll start with your firebrand." His attention slid to me but only remained long enough to blow me a kiss, throwing fuel on the fires of Viktor's burgeoning rage. "Unless you can save her." That said, he threw back his head and released a guttural squawk.

His soldiers sprang forward. The rasp of metal sliding against leather pierced the air as Vik and Bodi drew their weapons. The shifters reached us within seconds, attacking in unison. With matching roars, my teammates burst into action. A gruesome battle ensued, the combatants moving too quickly to track. I only saw bodies and body parts toppling and piling up around us. Grunts and groans blended with pops and gurgles I hoped to never hear again.

I tried to help, I really did, but my two berserker body-

221

guards worked so hard and so fast, no shifter got within striking distance of me. Except. Hmm. They were too busy to notice the newest threat headed our way. The windows above us opened, allowing additional turul-shifters to fly in from the ceiling.

"Incoming," I shouted. Internal heat intensifying, I swung my claws at a member of the flock. Mistake! He clamped his talons onto my wrist and lifted me off my feet.

He tossed me across the room. Viktor roared a denial as I soared through the air and crashed into the floor—Ahhhh! Upon impact, a trapdoor opened, and I dropped. The heart-stopping plunge didn't last long, but it might have been the most terrifying moments of my life. Air whooshed around me as I flailed about, unable to stop my momentum. When I hit the ground, I hit hard. Bones broke, and oxygen exploded from my lungs. Searing agony blasted through every inch of my body. Stars winked over my vision, and nausea churned in my stomach. Dust filled my next breath.

Groaning, I rolled to my side, coughing violently. Deep breath in, out. In. Out. Each inhalation was a gritty struggle. One moment. Two. Then the pain began to fade. The sharp stings diminished to a dull ache before vanishing completely as my bones healed. Thankfully, my stomach settled, and I pulled myself into an upright position.

Light flickered from a lantern, casting eerie shadows over uneven, cracked stone walls. Needing leverage, I slipped my fingers into one of those cracks. As I stood, I gasped, realization dawning. This wasn't a stone wall but a barrier made of stacked human skulls. My thumb passed through a hollow eye socket.

I'd fallen into some kind of catacombs. I swallowed a second wave of nausea and snapped my hand back to my side.

THE STOLEN BRIDE

The scent of decay thickened cold, damp air. Water trickled from a fissure in the far wall in a persistent *drip, drip, drip*. I grabbed the lantern by the handle, ready to find a way out of this death chamber. A glance up proved the trapdoor had already closed, ensuring no one could follow me down. Torchlight caught a crimson smear on the far wall, and my eyes narrowed. No, not a smear, but letters. Deco had painted a message for me.

Told you I thought of everything.

I pressed my tongue to the roof of my mouth. There must be an escape this place. I had only to find it.

Pace brisk, I headed down a narrow passage. Turning this way and that, I ended up back at the start. So I tried again. And again. The maze always began and ended at the same point. But no matter where else I ventured, the lantern light illuminated additional messages that peppered the walls.

There's no way out.

I'll join you shortly.

Are you having fun yet?

The things I'm going to do to you...

I was well and truly trapped, enshrined in a tomb, the only life besides mine scurrying into the shadows as I passed.

A series of noises reached my ears, and I frowned. Clinking chains. Moans of pain and snarls of rage.

I tracked the sounds, which led me to a path I'd not stumbled upon before. Racing through the skull lined corridors, I took another turn. It brought me into a massive cavern with a ceiling seemingly miles high. The air felt cooler, and it was easier to breathe. Decay didn't scent this space, but a hint of rust.

Goose bumps formed on my skin. Something told me

not to enter, but I heard another moan of pain and surged forward. Maybe it was Juniper, because she'd been dropped down here, too. Gravel crunched beneath my feet. At least I hoped it was gravel. I lifted the lantern to fill the cavern with light, my lips parting in both wonder and horror.

Chained throughout were nine colossal beasts I'd only seen in nightmares and movies. A dragon. Something that resembled a wolf, but a thousand times worse. Same for a bear and a lynx. An eagle lion hybrid. Some kind of giant sea monster, imprisoned underneath a leak in the rocky walls. A winged amalgamation of a panther and a scorpion with the quills of a porcupine. Another winged creature, but with a horn and skin of stone. And a huge, coiled adder with humanoid features and fangs the size of my pinkies. Each animal possessed glowing eyes of a different color.

The bottom dropped out of my stomach, like recognizing like. "The primordials," I rasped, pressing a hand to my chest. The original kings were exactly as my mom described them in her bedtime stories, only now they were frozen in their animal forms.

"Magnificent, aren't they?"

The unfamiliar voice startled me, and I jolted. A woman strode from behind the dragon. A creature she stroked and kissed, as if it were a beloved child. The dragon jerked from her touch, steam rising from its nostrils.

Her identity wrenched a gasp from my deepest depths. Valkara, freed from her bounds and without wounds. "How did you get free? Is the fight over?"

She motioned to the prisoners, ignoring my question. "This is what happens when an original slays a firebrand. The beast embraces hatred and takes over."

Forget them—for now. "Where's Juniper?"

THE STOLEN BRIDE

"She remains with Deco. Lucky girl, she gets to enjoy the show. I decided to speak with you alone."

Suspicions sharpened to razor points, becoming certainties. "You're working with the shifter king," I stated in a flat tone. Knew it! She'd never been in danger. Had lured Viktor here under false pretenses.

"I am. But only until I acquire Viktor. He's proved most stubborn. But in the end he'll do it. He'll slay you and turn."

The casual statement knocked the air from my lungs. "The prophesy...you didn't foresee me killing him at all. You *wanted* him to kill *me* so that he would finally shift."

"Yes, and I thought I'd covered all my bases. If you betrayed him, boom. He would've welcomed evil into his heart and killed you. That's the first thing every shifter with a firebrand does, after all. If you didn't turn him, but fell in love with him, you would sacrifice yourself when I convince you it's the only way to save him."

Find, destroy, happy.

The words Viktor had repeated like a broken record since our meeting filled my head. I'd known their sinister meaning already, but this proved they'd been Plan A, B and C from the beginning.

Find me.

Destroy me.

And finally be happy.

She'd played chess while the rest of us played checkers.

All grace and gloating, she strolled closer. When she stopped outside of the strike zone, she smiled. "Do you know why King Malachi asked such a terrible thing of you? Why he promised you an introduction to your parents?"

"Let me guess. You convinced him it needed to be done for the greater good." Just as she'd tricked Viktor.

"Actually, he did it for access to *his* firebrand."

"So you manipulated us all."

"And yet I must still go the backup route."

"Let me guess. I'm supposed to convince Viktor to kill me."

"You will," she said. "You made him fall in love with you. It's time."

Apprehension crept down my spine, new suspicions dancing across my mind in a sinister ballet. She was going to make me choose: Viktor or Juniper.

"You can't know I made him fall in love. He's never professed his feelings." But I was pretty sure I'd fallen totally, completely, and utterly in love with him. "Why don't you kill me and ignite his turning yourself?"

"I've learned from trial and error. The only way to ensure the transformation from sentinel to primordial sticks is for the king to do the slaying." Another smile flashed. "Since you won his affections, I'll give you a reward. At least in part. Allow me to introduce you to your mother." Spreading her arms, she announced, "Me."

"No you are not," I grated. I hadn't wished to meet *this* woman for my entire life. Not her, the one who'd planned my death centuries before I was even born. But, as I studied her with a more critical eye, I began to notice our similarities. The gray in our eyes. The shape of our chins. The single dimple in one of our cheeks.

"I promise you, I am." With languid, unhurried steps, she stalked a circle around me. I moved with her, not letting her stand at my back. "Did Viktor not tell you? I'm a dream-seer, able to peer into the future through my dreams. I can even reveal snippets to others in their dreams. Once upon a time, I foresaw your importance to him. Well, yours or Juniper's. I only see in pictures. From the beginning, I knew only three facts. Who I must seduce to produce you, one of

THE STOLEN BRIDE

you would be Viktor's firebrand, and the other must be used as bait. Too bad I chose wrong. Had Juniper ended up with him, he would have killed her, you would have attacked him, and he would have killed you too. Alas."

Such cold, callous words from the woman who might have birthed me. It was an invisible dagger to the gut. But now I had confirmation. She had indeed shaped my dream. "Who is our father? Why separate twins?" No doubt Juniper would've been even stronger bait if we'd stayed together.

"Your father is irrelevant. A griffin of no importance. He was of zero use to me once you were born, and I couldn't allow him to try and save you from your own mother, now, could I?"

The response hit its target: my heart. She'd killed him. All these years, what had I imagined? A mother and father unable to take care of me, who still loved the child they'd created. Now I knew my father wasn't given a chance to get to know his twins, and our mother hadn't cared about us. I pressed my fingers to the fluttering pulse in my throat. Anguish spread through me. I didn't bottle it, but I looked past it, because I must. I hadn't missed her avoidance of my other question. Why separate twins, weakening a bond she planned to utilize? Only one answer made sense. We were stronger together.

Stronger.

Stronger. The word echoed inside my head until a light bulb exploded. My spine straightened with a snap. "You fear us."

Her eyes narrowed the slightest bit, confirming my suspicions. "I fear *nothing.*"

Lie! But I set the truth aside for a moment, letting it simmer in favor of digging up more information. "Why are you collecting the primordials?"

227

She spread her arms to indicate the entire group. "Because they are mine, my pets, and humans taint everything they touch. But soon, my darling turul will return to me, and I will reclaim all that belongs to me."

I was about to reply, "Over my dead body," but that's precisely what she wanted, wasn't it?

19

Between a Berserker and a Hard Place: Finding the Least Worst Option

—HOW TO TRAIN YOUR BERSERKER
By Elizabeth "Elle" Darcy-Bruce

As those threatening words against *my* berserker rang in my head, Valkara—my supposed mother—pulled the pin on a dozen rage-grenades. Viktor was not hers. His turul wasn't hers, either. Not ever again.

She tsk-tsked, not the least bit frightened by my pending berserkerage. "Better keep yourself under control, daughter. Harm me, and both you and your sister will pay a terrible price."

"Too bad for you, complying with my enemy isn't in my wheelhouse," I retorted, but I didn't attack. Any second, Viktor and Bodi would blaze into this chamber. No way Deco and his band of shifters could overcome the royal brothers.

"Don't think your firebrand will rush to your rescue," Valkara stated.

"I don't need rescue." But backup would be nice. Viktor's presence would ensure I didn't kill someone I shouldn't. "You can't say the same."

She lowered her chin. "You think so? Let me show you what I can do."

A sharp pain cut through my head, and I grunted. In a split second, I lost sight of the world around me. A thick fog enveloped my brain, so much thicker than what I'd encountered in my dreams. My name whispered in a thousand distinct tones, becoming a scream. The sensation felt unsettling and foreign, yet somehow familiar. Sweat beaded on my brow, my nape, and my lower back.

I gripped my temples and tried to breathe. I couldn't breathe. *Come on, come on.* My lungs burned. My thoughts raced, but went nowhere. My body moved without permission, but I wasn't sure what it was doing. I couldn't...I didn't...

The whispers quieted, the fog vanished, and I blinked open my eyes, suddenly able to draw air into my nose. Noticing my surroundings, I frowned and spun. I occupied a seven-by-seven cell with three barred walls and a rocky back one. Inside was a cot draped with a ratty blanket, and two pairs of shackles. There was also a stained toilet. Hooks and shackles splattered with crimson hung from the ceiling. The floor bore dark, ominous stains, too. The oppressive air smelled of mold and hopelessness.

Small, grated windows allowed slivers of light into the cell block. Other cages stretched out beside mine. This must be Deco's dungeon. Scratches marred the cold stone back wall. No, not scratches–tick marks. They tracked the number of days of confinement. Outside the cells, in an

THE STOLEN BRIDE

open area probably reserved for guards, two wooden chairs bracketed a vertical rack. Like, an actual rack. A medieval torture device.

Nearby it, a small wooden desk occupied a corner, a bank of screens above it displaying the interior of each cell, including mine. A jarring blend of state-of-the-art tech and ancient brutality. No sign of the primordials.

I made an obscene gesture at the camera. I must have walked in here on my own, and oh, the knowledge burned. Valkara won this round.

She emerged from the shadows and smiled at me from beyond the bars. My pulse raced with both fear and frustration. To lose control of my own body...

And this was what Viktor dealt with on the daily? No wonder he'd become feral! He'd been in a fight for his free will and deep down, he must have known it.

"Do not worry," she said, withdrawing a dagger from a sheath at her waist, that smug smile still lighting her face. "Viktor will join us shortly. Be a good girl and convince him to kill you."

Ha! "You're the one who's dreaming if you think that's gonna happen."

"If you don't, your sister will die. Among others."

A twist of the invisible blade in my gut. Mother Dearest had done exactly as I'd feared. I gripped and shook the bars. Now it was my turn to play the game. "You expect me to accept death on behalf of a woman I've known, what? Less than two minutes?"

"I do, and you will. For the greater good. That, my dear, is real. Allow me to show you the future awaiting us if Viktor fails to kill you." She closed her eyes. Once again, a fog crept into my mind. This time, a scene opened up. A vision. In it, I stood in a forest, sobbing. Viktor, who looked

231

as if he'd just witnessed the end of the world, held an unconscious, or dead, Juniper in his arms, both of them splattered with crimson.

In the present, I pressed a hand over my churning stomach. No. No, no, no. What had happened? Had he...was she...?

Vision Clover screamed in anguish. Then she–

No, I began to change. I grew a beak and wings. Sprouted feathers. I developed the hindquarters of a lion, complete with a tail. The largest talons extended from my nail beds, a grotesque monster-griffin taking my place.

The vision opened further, revealing the encampment beyond our little clearing. In it I saw Bodi and others I didn't recognize, all going about their days.

The moment my transformation completed, I spread my wings, squawked–and Viktor transformed as well. He dropped Juniper and the two of us turned on each other. Fighting, raging. In the end, I won only because he hesitated to deliver a death blow. I ripped out his heart. When I finished with him, I flew into the campground, utterly wild now that I'd killed my firebrand. Though a multitude of berserkers erupted, attempting to fight me off, I killed everyone in my path. Down went Bodi, minus his head. Every single creature in my vicinity died. Men, women and children. Animals, too. And I wasn't done. I stalked off, hunting for my next victims.

The vision faded, and I doubled over with nausea. This was the world's fate if I didn't convince Viktor to kill me? "That–that's a lie," I sputtered. It must be.

"I cannot weave lies, only truth. That's the destiny awaiting each of you if you live today," Valkara confirmed. "You are linked to Viktor and when you shift–and you will– you'll become as strong as he is. Stronger, since you are

THE STOLEN BRIDE

flesh of my flesh. None of his berserkers will be able to stop you. You'll rampage, leaving only destruction in your wake. But one simple sacrifice can stop such a catastrophe from occurring. Of course, Viktor will refuse to end you. We all know he'd rather die than harm his firebrand. But I can take care of that. Confuse him in the fog so that he lashes out without thought. All you must do is accept your fate without a fight."

No. No! "If you can weave only truth, the vision you showed me throughout my life is the future, not what you've shown me today. I haven't lived that moment yet."

"What I showed you *was* the future, yes. If Juniper had ended up with Viktor. But the two of you traveled a different road, taking us to a new destination."

No! "Then today's vision proves we'll all escape," I croaked.

"Exactly. Unless you choose another path." She tossed the dagger she held through the bars. It landed on the cot and bounced. "Let him kill you with this, rather than his claws. It'll hurt less."

So doomed if I did and doomed if I didn't. "How do I know you're telling the truth about showing only the truth?"

"You don't," she said, all but bubbling over with giddiness, sensing how close she was to victory. "You'll have to take my word on it." A pause. Then, "As soon as you're dead, I'll release Juniper. I vow it."

No. No! She couldn't be trusted. Look at how she'd tricked Viktor all these centuries. How she'd used Malachi. "When you have all the primordials in your control, what's your plan?"

"Have no fear, my sweet Clover. We won't be staying on this forsaken planet." Intensity flashed in her eyes, hinting

233

at sinister intentions. "No, I have other places to be. The only reason I'm still here is because patience is needed when dealing with primordials. Rush them, and pay the price."

For the first time, I actually believed the words that came out of her mouth.

I sagged against the bars. This was bad. Very, very bad. What should I do, what should I do? I don't think I had the emotional fortitude to unleash a berserker rage-out right now. Too much sadness welled, snuffing out the flames.

Satisfied that I'd finally accepted my fate, she sauntered off and eased onto a chair near the rack, obviously waiting for something. Or someone.

My thoughts drifted to Viktor, my love. The man who might kill me–an act so horrific that it would shatter him. He'd break and forever descend into his primordial self.

By following Valkara's orders, I would condemn us both, but possibly save Juniper. Perhaps even a world. The greater good. I wracked my brain. There must be another way. An out that didn't involve our deaths. My hands trembled, and my eyes brimmed with the tears I refused to shed in front of the tyrant who'd birthed me. If I died, my only regrets would be not receiving Viktor's mark and never getting to know my twin.

And why weren't we allowed to be together? There was a reason Valkara had separated us at birth. I'd sensed it before, and I knew it now.

I popped to my feet and began to pace. That power, our connection, both had zapped between us even through a hologram. Our mother must fear what we'd be able to do if we were physically close. Yes, yes. That made sense.

My gaze returned to Valkara. Her eyes were closed, her

lips moving. Was she distracting Viktor even now? My chest clenched. How did I overcome this situation?

If I could get to Juniper, we could figure out whatever it was our mother feared we could do–something with our hands, I'd bet, because I hadn't forgotten the warm tingles or magnetic pull. Maybe, just maybe, we'd have the strength to end the reign of Valkara and Deco before they harmed my guy.

Team Good.

If the heroine I'd read about in those cozy mysteries could have Team Truth, then I could have Team Good and live happily ever after. A family.

Pounding, racing footsteps caught my attention, and my ears twitched. *Please be Viktor, alive and well, ready to take care of business.*

Rusty hinges groaned as the dungeon door burst open. It was indeed Viktor. He blazed inside the chamber, spotted me, and picked up the pace. My heart thudded. He didn't stop at the bars, but crashed into them. No. Wrong. He ghosted through. But his body seized, as if caught in the grips of an electrical shock. Dread clogged my throat as his muscles bunched and veins bulged. Then he dropped, unconscious.

With a mewl of concern, I swooped down and checked his vitals. Relief welled from an internal spring. Still alive!

A grinning Deco sauntered through the doorway, carrying an incapacitated Bodi over his shoulder. "Poor Vik. He forgot life's most important lesson. There are unseen forces far more powerful than even an original sentinel."

A third man dragged in a bound Juniper.

"Let me go," she demanded.

At the sight of her, warm tingles returned to my hands.

An urge to press our palms together grew. What did this mean? What would happen?

Valkara helped the soldier anchor my twin to the rack, rougher than necessary. Icy rage invaded my bloodstream when Juniper grimaced with pain.

"I said be gentle with her," the shifter king snapped as he entered the cell next to mine. He did this without opening a door or experiencing a shock. He simply ghosted through the bars and tossed the berserker prince to the ground. Then he ghosted out and strode toward Valkara.

How in the world? I tried to bolt after him, but the bars stopped me, solid to the touch. Impact rang my bell, slamming my brain against my skull. Dizziness flared and died as greater anger surged to the fore.

Both berserkers remained unconscious, littered with blood and gashes. Holographic scenes began to play over the air around us, courtesy of the vargbane root. A memory taken from today's battle, displayed over and over again on repeat. How Viktor had watched me fly across the throne room and disappear through a hole in the floor.

"I'm here, baby. I'm good, I promise, and you better be good, too." I returned to his side and checked his pulse. Too swift, but stronger. "I need you to wake up for me."

"Oh, he'll awaken soon enough," Deco called, so proud of himself. "After your disappearance, he and Bodi broke into a full-on berserkerage. For a moment, I feared they might overcome my forces. But Valkara did her thing, making Viktor believe he chased you and a captor, and here we are."

See! Valkara was a liar. What she'd shown him wasn't the truth. Unless she'd projected a future event. Ugh.

Deco stopped in front of Juniper. "Did you miss me,

nyuszi?" Smiling, he stroked the back of his knuckles across her cheek, surprisingly gentle.

Her eyes spit fire at him. "I hate you."

Chuckling, he stuffed a gag into her mouth. "But you want me, too."

"Don't touch my sister," I shouted.

He twisted to blow me a kiss. "Well, that depends on you, doesn't it? Is the little firebrand going to cooperate?"

"She still thinks to resist," Valkara said.

Panic frayed the edges of my composure. I darted my attention between the shifter king and my twin, asking, "How did you walk through the metal?" Could Viktor walk through when he awoke or would he seize again?

Deco spread his arms. "Valkara is full of tricks. You really should have stayed on your mother's good side."

The barb hit its target, and I flinched. "You know she intends to betray you the moment she has what she wants, yes?"

Valkara smirked at me. "Of course he knows."

Deco rolled his eyes. "The silly goddess even thinks she'll defeat me."

Goddess?

"It's true," the dreamseer stated without an ounce of remorse. "I do. And I will."

He cupped the side of his mouth, as if he was about to reveal a grand secret. "I intend to betray her, too," he whisper-yelled. "I've planned for everything, and as soon as her usefulness runs out, I'll deal with her."

"Same," Valkara said with a gleeful nod.

"Now, be a good little mouse and let the big falcon decapitate you." He rubbed his hands together. "Let's get the finale started so I can claim my ten prizes."

I truly despised this man. But all the pieces of the

puzzle finally clicked into place. Why he'd teamed up with Valkara, a woman he knew he couldn't trust. His goal wasn't just revenge against the King of the Turuls, but to reign over all the primordials. To rule all berserker and shifter factions. He would command the most powerful immortal army in this world or any other. Able to subjugate lands. Slaughter humans. Do whatever he wanted, whenever he desired.

Both Deco and Valkara must be stopped, no matter the cost. *That* was the greater good.

A moan escaped Viktor.

Deco grinned. "You understand your mission, Clover, and the consequences if you fail." He lounged on the other side of the rack while the remaining soldiers took up posts near the cells.

Fighting dismay, I patted Viktor's cheek. "Wake up for me, Tor. Come on, baby. That's it. Yes, yes, good boy."

He blinked open his eyes, then jack knifed to an upright position. His focus whipped to me, and he scanned me from top to bottom. "You are good?"

"I'm unharmed. And you?"

"Alive." He shifted to search for Bodi. A muscle jumped in his jaw when he spotted the prince, who moaned, beginning to awaken. His gaze moved to the pair at the rack, and his lids slitted. "The Valkara aids Deco."

"Yes. They're working together."

"Go ahead," Deco called. "Try to escape."

With a roar, Viktor leaped to his feet and slammed into the metal bars. He beat them with his fists, breaking bones. Slashed them with his claws, ripping off nails. Kicked and heaved with all his might, leaving his body battered and bruised. All to no avail.

"Stop. Please," I said as the shifter king laughed and

THE STOLEN BRIDE

laughed. Valkara tapped her feet, impatient. "There's more I must tell you, but I won't talk to you while you're hurting yourself."

Huffing and puffing, Viktor paused and fought for calm. The perfect opportunity. I stood and cozied up against him, petting his chest. His muscles relaxed bit by bit.

"Tell me," he croaked. "Go ahead. I can take it, whatever it is."

I could think of a thousand reasons to lie and hide the truth from him, and only one reason to tell the truth. I loved him. So, the truth it was. "Valkara is my birth mother. She gave me to Malachi as a baby, and he placed me in a home far from my sister."

Juniper made a noise around her gag. Valkara tapped her knee and snapped, "Be quiet so I can overhear their conversation, or I'll remove your tongue."

My twin went silent, and my anger neared a breaking point.

Viktor jolted, but didn't erupt again. "And? Continue, love."

More pets. "And she foresaw my importance to you."

"And?" he said, shoving the word through clenched teeth.

"She revealed to me a supposed end. How I'll murder you and everyone we love unless I let you kill me."

His entire body jerked. He flung his arms around me and hauled me firmly against his chest, shielding me from any threat. "I will not. Not now, not ever. I love you. Need you. Want you. Cannot live without you. She showed you a lie, just as she showed me lies." He didn't attempt to moderate his tone, unconcerned by our audience. "Only they will die today. Not you."

Tears stung my eyes. The declaration hit deep in my

bones, and I clung to him. "I love you, too," I rasped. So much.

"Ja, but do you love me more than the foolish Benjamin? And you must answer honestly because you owe me. This one has been in my queue, attempting to claw its way out. I might be internally, eternally scarred."

Despite the awfulness of the situation, I snorted. "It's not even close. What I felt for him is a drop of water compared to the ocean I feel for you."

"Good. That's good. But I have more questions." Viktor kissed the top of my head, then rapid-fired questions as if they were bullets from a gun.

"Will you wed me? Will you move to my world and into my palace? Will you spend forever at my side and never leave me?"

"Go ahead and say yes," Deco taunted. "Actually, I think the line is yes, yes, a thousand times yes. It'll make your death so much sweeter."

My gaze strayed to Valkara, who observed us with a smug smile. Her plan was bearing fruit right before her eyes, the players she'd set up acting exactly as she'd hoped. Then I glanced at Juniper, who watched me with wide eyes. The tingles and warmth in my hands increased by leaps and bounds.

My tears spilled over. With every fiber of my being, I longed to say yes. To marry Viktor, build a life and a family with him. Wait... did he say palace? I'd only ever seen tents and a stick shack in the forest.

Rather than answer his newest litany of queries, however, I returned my attention to him and gently told him, "First, you need to hear the rest." I didn't give him a chance to respond. "If I die, you'll transform into your primordial form. You won't be able to stop it. Valkara plans

THE STOLEN BRIDE

to add you to her collection, completing her own personal army. Deco intends to kill her and rule the menagerie."

Viktor shook his head violently before I finished my speech. "I told you. I won't kill you, not even to save the worlds," he reiterated. "And I will not apologize for that."

"If you don't do it willingly," I croaked, "Valkara will mess with your head."

"Excuse me for breaking up such an adorable reunion, but what are we going to do *besides* not kill the firebrand?" Bodi asked. "We need a plan of our own."

"My patience is gone," Valkara bellowed. "I'd hate for your last moments alive to be filled with Juniper's screams rather than tender words of love, but that is what's about to happen. You have two minutes."

20

When Three is a Crowd: Downsizing Without Bloodshed

–HOW TO TRAIN YOUR BERSERKER
By Elizabeth "Elle" Darcy-Bruce

Bile burned my throat. If I despised Deco, I positively detested the dreamseer who called herself my mother. But. Valkara had given me a clue about her downfall, at least.

I shifted my gaze to Juniper. *Come on, come on. Look at me, sis.*

A second passed–and she did. Triumph bloomed, and so did a new flare of heat in my hands. I noted the fear glazing her eyes and did my best to project a message: *I know you're scared, but try to keep Deco and Valkara occupied. Okay?*

Maybe it was the twin thing, but I was almost certain she'd understood. She gave a slight nod before erupting, struggling against her bonds. The gag fell out of her mouth just enough to allow her to shout, "You will pay for this!"

THE STOLEN BRIDE

Deco sighed and stood to reset her gag. "Must you *always* interrupt important business?"

Juniper gave him an exaggerated pout. "I'm thirsty. Give me a drink, and I'll kiss you as you've so desperately wanted."

Valkara pinched the bridge of her nose. "Deco, don't you dare give her—"

"Water," the shifter king called, snapping his fingers in the air.

While soldiers rushed to obey, everyone distracted, I took my shot. "Lure Deco to the cells," I told my guys softly. "Viktor, you're going to pretend to kill me. When someone enters to check, we strike."

Viktor scowled at Bodi. "There would be no need for such theatrics if I had my key. It allowed for the primordials escape from any lock."

The prince winced. "About that." Radiating all kinds of guilt, the prince turned his back on our spectators and slashed a claw tip through his wrist. Crimson welled and flowed, dripping to the floor.

"What are you doing?" I gagged as he dug inside the wound.

To my shock, horror and admiration, he pulled out a thin, bloody hunk of metal that was notched at the bottom with an elongated shaft and vine-like alloy strips intertwining in an ornate loop at the top. "I've never trusted the Valkara, and I doubted the key did what she said. To prevent you from giving it to her, I hid it."

"I don't understand. If this key facilitates escape, you'd be free right now," I said. "Why can't you ghost out of the cage?"

"Because it must be used in a specific way, by a specific person." Viktor stood in place, staring at his brother, anger

243

draining, replaced by shame and regret. "All this time, I blamed you. And yet you protected me. Protected our people, despite the risk of my wrath."

"You can ply me with thanks and apologies when we're home. Until then, let's win this war." Bodi wiped off the metal as best he could, then extended his arm through the bars, handing the key to Viktor.

"Bodi, I will forever love you for this," I exclaimed. "Like a brother," I added when Viktor growled. "Always like a brother."

The prince gave me a half smile. "Ja, I've grown somewhat fond of you too." He inclined his head. "You are my soon to be queen. If you agree to wed my brother, of course."

My cheeks heated as Viktor shifted the intensity of his focus to me. "When I told I was keeping you, love, I meant it. You might as well say yes."

I smiled at him, probably as goofy as a golden retriever. "Yes."

He smiled back. "Well then." He pressed the key against his sternum–and it absorbed, soon resembling a tattoo. A slight glow framed the edges. He flicked it, and it began to spin like a dial on a clock.

A frowning Deco noticed our actions and scowled, while Valkara resettled Juniper's gag in place. "What have you done?" he demanded.

At my birth mother's urging, a guard rushed over to turn a crank on the rack, pulling Juniper's limbs taunt. Her back bowed, and a muffled scream escaped her gag.

Deco's scowl deepened. "Stop," he barked. "I did not give you permission to harm her."

"Enough!" I screamed, swiping up the dagger Valkara had given me and rushing to the bars.

THE STOLEN BRIDE

Viktor rolled his shoulders, grabbed my hand, and I gripped Bodi's through the bars. We became a berserker daisy chain. Together, we walked out of the cages.

Deco and Valkara cursed. The guards rushed at us. Bodi charged at them. The rage I'd been too drained to summon earlier torched me in seconds. But this time, I didn't lose my thoughts. I remained present. Ice cold, but focused.

Knowing Viktor would deal with Deco, I locked my sights on Valkara, who paled.

"She's all yours." Without taking his gaze from the enemy, Viktor leaned down and pressed a quick kiss into my cheek. "Do whatever you like with her. I care not."

"You trust me to win?" Wonder filled me for a thousand different reasons.

"From the moment I met you, love, you have always found a way to do so." That said, he ran at Deco, who ran at him. They converged in the middle of the underground chamber, two wild animals determined to claim the title of king of the jungle. Despite everything I'd witnessed since waking up in a strange new world, their savagery shocked me.

"Consequences go both ways, mother dearest," I purred to Valkara. High on Viktor's confidence in me, I tightened my grip on my dagger and stalked toward her.

She stalked toward me, too. To block me from approaching Juniper? We stopped mere feet away from each other. I stared into gray eyes, missing only the hints of gold to match mine. We might share physical similarities, but nothing of importance. I had zero in common with this selfish woman bent on the destruction of her own children.

"Look at me, alive and well, despite your best efforts," I said, spreading my arms. Heat unfurled deep in my chest and spread along my limbs, collecting in my fingertips, where claws sprouted.

I darted my gaze to Juniper. She struggled to free herself from the rack, and my rage burned deeper. Deeper still.

"I knew it would come to this." As smug as before, Valkara added, "Just wait till you see what comes next."

Let her intimidate me? No. Enough chit-chat. I swiped out my claws. With the grace of a gazelle, she leaned back, arching her spine, avoiding contact, ensuring I only sliced through air.

She brushed a piece of lint from her robe. "Is that all you've got? Honestly, I expected better."

Must have vengeance! Must pour all the anguish I'd experienced wondering about who she was, what she was like, if she hoped to meet me as much as I hoped to meet her, into her body until she split apart at the seams. Yes!

A small, rational thought held me steady. Did she purposely antagonize me, hoping I'd lose myself in a berserkerage?

I settled for spewing a taunt of my own. "I might have mourned your loss the first part of my life, but I will celebrate your loss during the time that remains." This evil woman would never harm my loved ones again.

"You think you can win because you haven't yet read the writing on the wall. News flash. It spells doom. You cannot defeat me, Clover." Smile widening, Valkara purred, "Time for Momma to deliver her first spanking."

I blinked and suddenly she held my dagger, and I did not. Shock didn't have a chance to form. She shoved the blade into my gut. Agony seared me, and stars flashed over my vision. Grunting, I hunched over. Liquid rushed up my throat, and crimson spilled from my mouth. I was getting really tired of being stabbed.

THE STOLEN BRIDE

Juniper screamed and Viktor roared, the sounds seeming to travel through a narrow tunnel as my vision constricted. Dizzying darkness closed in...

"Love!" Viktor snarled.

"Clover," my twin sobbed.

The darkness retreated, or I stepped from its path, their voices a lifeline leading me into the light. Inhale. Exhale. Good, that was good. My head ceased spinning.

I took stock. Valkara watched me, curious. The battle between kings hadn't lessened. They used the entire space, doing laps around Valkara and me, sometimes slamming into Bodi and his opponents, the number of which had dwindled significantly. Juniper had released one leg from her shackles and fought to liberate her remaining limbs.

"You killed Lena," Deco bellowed at the berserker king. "You will know my pain!"

"*You* killed her when you believed her lies," Viktor spat.

With gritted teeth, I straightened and plucked the bloody blade free from my stomach. Never had I been more grateful for supernatural healing. "You will pay for that, too," I told my mother.

"I've wrangled primordials for centuries," she said, oh, so casual. "I'm not new to battle. As you can feel."

True, that knife thrust had hurt as if a thousand Labrador puppies tested their razor-sharp teeth on my insides, but thankfully my wound healed in a matter of seconds. "Maybe I won't kill you. Maybe I'll keep you locked up, so you can watch as I win the loyalty of the primordials. You had to chain them, but they'll adore me, their liberator."

Scowling, she swiped at me, moving so swiftly I couldn't mimic her and avoid injury. Like me, she possessed thick black claws, and the tips scraped across my cheek.

247

Skin split and blood trickled, stings erupting. My rage burned hotter.

"Hurt her good, Clove!" Juniper called.

Valkara's smile returned and widened. "Last chance to surrender."

As she spoke, I tracked Viktor and Deco from the corner of my eye. They beat at each other without mercy, ripping out organs with their hands. Both failed to do a heart amputation, but not for lack of trying. Any love between them had died.

Juniper freed her other leg.

My mother wanted me to surrender. "No, thanks," I snapped.

Valkara delivered a dramatic sigh. "Very well. I would've shown you a smidgen of mercy and let you say goodbye to your sister. Instead, I'll let Viktor experience sudden loss exactly as Deco did. The results won't be as pure, but I'll find a way. I always do."

Nothing but a blur, she latched onto my arm and flung me into the combatants. I slammed into Deco just as Viktor swung his claws at the beast's chest.

I rolled out of the way as he pulled back. The actions cost us. Deco raked his claws through Viktor's throat, and Valkara zoomed over. She grabbed a fistful of my hair and, rather than tossing me back into the fray, which had moved closer to Juniper, she threw me into a wall.

Breath abandoned my lungs, but I didn't let the lack prevent me from diving into her when she approached, driving her to the ground. We rolled one over the other, striking and blocking without mercy. Adrenaline surged until I felt nothing but the icy frost of my rage. No, no, this wasn't rage but fury, and it burned so hot it left me cold. I maintained my wits, and yet, still she delivered injury

THE STOLEN BRIDE

after injury. Strength began to drain, weakness taking its place.

I slowed gradually until my knees collapsed. Down I went, unable to do anything but huff and puff. What the—I scanned my body and gnashed my teeth. She'd cut me open from hip to hip. Things had spilled out, and the sight revolted me.

Juniper gave a cry of denial. Viktor released a guttural roar and headed my way. When the shifter king moved into his path to strike, the berserker king ripped out his trachea. It would have been his heart, but Deco repositioned at the last second. Dropping the bloody mass as the shifter collapsed, Viktor resumed his sprint to me.

How long before Deco recovered?

At my side, Valkara grinned, drawing back her elbow, claws spread. "Told you I'd win."

I spotted Juniper, sneaking up on us and smiled. "Wrong."

With a high-pitched war cry, my sister slammed into our mother. Both flew to the ground. On the way down, Valkara swiped her claws across my twin's throat, just as Viktor had swiped at Deco's. Juniper's yelp of pain died a split second after it began.

"Nooo!" Despite my weakness, I threw myself at the pair at the same time Viktor threw himself at me. My hand latched onto my sister's, who reached for me. At the moment of contact, a bolt of pure power shot through me.

Wounds healed in seconds. Strength flooded me. No part of me was left untouched. But there was too much to contain, a glowing light flickering with various colors shooting from my pores. It hurt as much as it helped, and I screamed from my deepest depths.

The same power must have hit Juniper. She reacted

similarly, the torn skin across her neck knitting back together. Our lights drew together and snapped into place like two lost puzzle pieces finally connected. A ball of light formed around us, lifting us both off our feet and blurring out the rest of the world.

My sister and I hovered mere inches apart, eye to eye. Health and vitality had returned to her cheeks. Locks of dark hair with hints of red floated around her.

"Hi," she said.

"Hi," I replied.

We shared a tentative smile. When we both reached out, offering the other our hands, a little laugh escaped me. We linked fingers.

"Any idea what's happening right now?" she asked.

"If one is good, two is better?"

Like me, she gave a little laugh, and oh, it did my heart good, seeing her happy. But she sobered all too swiftly.

The gravity of the situation sobered me as well. "I want to get to know you more than anything—except saving my future husband. Help me dial down our, um, whatever this is, so I can jump back into the fight." No telling what was going on out there right now.

"Maybe if we separate?" she suggested.

Excellent idea. Though I hated to do it, I released her, then flapped my arm and kicked my legs, as if swimming in air. I must look ridiculous, but I didn't care. As the distance between us widened, we floated to the stone floor. By the time we stood upon the foundation, the bubble of light faded completely. The chamber came back into view, and my jaw nearly unhinged. *Oh, Great Dane!*

Everyone else laid strewn upon the ground, either unconscious or—No! I rushed to Viktor's side and pressed two fingers into the hollow of his neck.

THE STOLEN BRIDE

Relief washed over me. He was alive and well.

Juniper glanced at Deco before hurrying to Bodi to check him over.

"He still lives," she called.

How long until everyone woke up? "Let's get Mommy Dearest and her fiend into the cage." They might be able to pass through the bars for reasons I didn't yet know, but they'd have a hard time getting out of their bonds.

We worked together to drag both Valkara and Deco inside a cell, shackled both, and anchored their bonds to the hooks hanging from the ceiling.

When we finished, we looked at each other and grinned at a job well done. I almost threw my arms around Juniper and hated that I couldn't. What did this mean for our relationship?

I returned to Viktor and patted his cheek. "Wake up, baby. It's time to celebrate. Your firebrand and her twin saved the day." No response. I patted with a bit more force. "Pudding pop. Come on now. Wake up and kiss me."

Again, no response. Apprehension prickled my skin. "Viktor, I mean it. Wake up."

Juniper stood off to the side, her arms wrapped around her middle, watching. "What do you want me to do?"

I didn't know. No images flashed over the walls, so this wasn't a sleep caused by the vargbane root. Plus, no one else had awakened, either.

"Viktor." I hit him hard enough to jolt.

Still nothing.

A lump grew in my throat. What had we done to everyone?

Valkara's words whispered through my mind. *You think you can win because you haven't yet read the writing on the wall. It spells doom.*

251

Something about her tone. In the heat of the moment, I'd missed it but now...My gaze flipped to the walls. The scratches I'd believed were tick marks...did they resemble letters?

I popped to my feet and raced over, intensifying my study. When the message breached my understanding, I sucked air between my teeth. On the stone, the Valkara had carved the words:

To awaken all, a twin must fall.
This deed you'll do, if goodness you eschew.

21

Brainstorming Battle Plans: When In Doubt, Berserk Out

—HOW TO TRAIN YOUR BERSERKER
By Elizabeth "Elle" Darcy-Bruce

I paced for hours, trying to work out a solution in my mind. Juniper paced, too, walking a path next to mine but always in the opposite direction. Over and over, I ran through Valkara's cryptic message.

To awaken all, a twin must fall.

Obviously, Valkara expected me to sacrifice Juniper in order to awaken Viktor. An act sure to turn me into a shifter.

This deed you'll do, if goodness you eschew.

As a shifter, I would attack Viktor, just as Deco did. If Valkara told the truth, Viktor would shift, too. One evil act would lead to another.

But I couldn't leave him in this, this coma.

But I couldn't harm my beloved Juniper, the other half of me.

GENA SHOWALTER & JILL MONROE

But I wasn't ready to die.

But. But. But. There must be another way.

"What did we even do?" I asked, indicating to those around us, still deep in slumber. Even the ball goers above us must be asleep because no one had invaded our space. Yet.

Juniper wrung her hands together. "I don't know, but whatever it was, I feel stronger than ever before."

Yeah, me too. Power crackled in my veins without a drop of rage. It made me uneasy. How was I supposed to contain all this? "Is it simply because we're together?" We passed each other.

"Should I leave the fortress, putting distance between us?" she asked.

"No," we bellowed in unison.

Back and forth, back and forth.

She massaged her nape and cast a glance at our prisoners. "You're certain you want to rouse everyone? The world will be a better place without the Valkara at the helm." She gazed down at her hands. "And Deco, too, I suppose."

"If it means Viktor and Bodi wake up, yes." I wasn't leaving without them. "I didn't mean to, I'm not sure how it happened, but I fell in love with Viktor. Bodi is his brother, and he's growing on me."

"He seems...nice," she said with a wince, and I didn't know if she referenced the king or the prince.

Hmm. I think I just jumped on Team Jodipur. Buniper? Jundi?

Focus! Back and forth, back and forth.

Again and again, my gaze landed on Viktor, and my insides twisted. What if we never spoke again? What if he'd held me for the last time? "Do you believe Valkara told the

THE STOLEN BRIDE

truth? That I'll one day shift and kill everyone unless Viktor kills me today?"

"No way! Never trust the villain."

"That's what I said!" And yet, dismay infected my every thought, and I huffed with frustration. "Maybe a change of scenery will spark an answer."

As much as I detested traipsing through the catacombs, we relocated to the massive chamber filled with sleeping primordials. We paced. Well, I paced, while Juniper checked the vitals of the ancients. They slept, too.

"What are we going to do with them?" I asked, as she examined a cut on the gargoyle's wing. Being this close to them did something to me. Agitated my insides, making my nerve endings buzz.

She bit her bottom lip. "I don't know, but they can't stay together. I can feel the energy crackling between them, and it isn't pleasant."

Yeah, but that was a worry for another day. I rubbed my sternum. How did we fix this?

Back and forth, back and forth. Minutes blurred into more hours.

Hmm. An internal tugging sensation magnified, attempting to lure me to the dungeon once more. To Viktor?

"We won't separate, but let's occupy different rooms and see what that does," I suggested, and she nodded. I ran to him. He still slept on. I began pacing at his side. Back and forth.

Okay. The hum of power downgraded just enough to clear my head. Hadn't he once told me that the greatest force in a berserker's life was his love for his firebrand? In this case, my love for him. Actually, our love for each other.

My eyes widened. That! That was the answer. I dropped to his side and focused inward, where love for him bubbled.

255

An endless well of joy, peace, and contentment. And yes, more power. So much power. It flowed from my being, as if I were a river, and straight into Viktor. Oh! His love flowed from him, into me as well. Or it attempted to. There was some sort of block at the mingling point. A fear. A fear that one of us would harm the other, deposited by Valkara's words.

I ground my teeth. That just wouldn't do. Riding the waves of love, I crashed into the fear again and again, hitting it with truth. I would not harm him. He would not harm me. We had a wedding to plan.

The block eroded, shrinking. Until…

Viktor roared, the sound echoing throughout the catacombs. Heart thudding, I watched in awe and wonder as he leaped to his feet, alive and well. Valkara, Bodi, Deco and the guards remained on the floor, unconscious.

With a whimper, I jumped up into his arms. Hot tears poured down my cheeks, and words spewed from my mouth. "I'm so sorry for whatever I did to you, and I love you so much, and if you ever almost die again, I will do something awful. I just don't know what it is yet and—"

He pressed a swift kiss into my lips, quieting me. "Your power punched into our souls, latching on. Even now, you are draining our power to fuel your own."

I was? My brow furrowed. "I don't understand."

"Yeah. Me, either," Juniper said, approaching us.

He bowed his head, greeting my sister before telling us, "My guess is, you are meant to feed off each other. But because your connection happened so late, and so suddenly, the force you generated was too intense for either of you to contain, so it reached for other sources."

Okay, yeah, that made a bit of sense. But. "How are you

THE STOLEN BRIDE

staying awake if we're still draining you? Is love really enough?"

He gave me a look, *honey please*. "I have your adoration, affection and loyalty, too."

"I think I basically Snow Whited you," I said. "Kissed you with my awesome power and broke the curse."

Juniper covered her laugh with her fingers. "More like you Sleeping Beautyed him. Maleficent put the entire kingdom to sleep."

"I don't know what any of that means," Viktor said, "but I'll agree if it makes you happy."

With what was probably soon to be a globally famous snort-laugh, I threw my arms around him again. "I love you. And yes, I will marry you and welcome your mark. I will mark you in turn, and start a family with you, and move to your world, and live in your palace, and rule our people at your side and help the primordials and match make for my sister and build another pet spa."

Pleasure flooded his eyes. "And eat all my food," he teased.

"Yes, baby. And eat all your food. That's so obvious I didn't think it needed to be stated."

He kissed me and grinned. "You will also play the violin. Probably every night."

"And you'll massage me as payment." As my pulse quickened, I decided to focus on the mission before things got out of hand. "Shall we slay Deco and Valkara, ensuring they never wake up?"

Juniper's eyes widened, as if I'd suggested something abhorrent. "Death is so...permanent. Get rid of Valkara, sure, but..."

Hmm. What was going on here? She didn't actually like her captor, did she?

"I do not know what will happen to the two of you if your tie to them is severed," Viktor said. "So, I will locate one of Deco's comms and contact Tabor, a commander in my army. He and his unit will join us and help cart the prisoners and primordials home with us." As he spoke, he bent down and draped his brother over his shoulder. "Once Deco and Valkara are locked in our dungeon, we'll marry."

"Our dungeon," I echoed. "I like the sound of that. It's a fairytale come to life."

"As a wedding gift, I offer you this realm." He spread his arms, indicating the entire dimension. "You're welcome."

"Ha! It's my wedding gift to *you*, big boy," I fired back. "I won it fair and square with Juniper's help. Juni, you okay with me sharing our realm with my husband?"

"You guys are so weird," she remarked under her breath. "But the place is yours, with my blessing. I've got my eye on a shack in the woods, where I can inspire legends about a cackling hag who is forever single."

I giggled like a schoolgirl. "Now that is a life."

Viktor's gaze met mine, and he smiled so tenderly. "All these centuries, I've only had this purpose in my head. Find. Destroy. Happy."

I peered at him through the shield of my lashes. "And?"

"And I found you. The meaning changed. We're about to destroy every obstacle in our path and move onto the happy."

I twined my fingers through his. "Yes. Happy together."

WITHIN A FEW DAYS, Commander Tabor arrived with an army of two hundred. They gathered all the sleepers and placed

THE STOLEN BRIDE

them in carts, all but Bodi and the primordials bound by chains. The shifters, plus Deco and Valkara were well and truly trapped. All would be residents of the royal dungeon. The primordials would be returned to their people, and Bodi...we would figure something out.

Juniper and I oversaw the process, directing traffic. We continued to drain the sleepers. I could feel it. One day, we would find a way to stop without harming each other. Until then, we would use our newfound strength for Team Good.

Which had a new member. Tabor was a handsome man with an abundance of rugged appeal, and I liked him immediately.

My desire to matchmake flared anew, finding Juniper's firebrand now a must. Anything to get her mind off Deco! I caught her staring at his sleeping form twice. But so far, I had only the two candidates. Bodi and now this Tabor. Surely there were a few other contenders around here.

Speaking of Tabor, he approached. "We have everyone ready for travel to the stones, Majesty."

He already treated me like the queen. "Excellent. We intend to find a way to return the shifters to their berserker-selves, so let's be extra careful with them."

Hope lit Tabor's face. He must have loved ones who'd become shifters too.

"I want guards stationed around Valkara and Deco at all times," Viktor said, joining us. That the king no longer acted feral, pulling out his hair and swiping with his claws, was not missed by his people.

My chest may have puffed with pride, all *I did that*.

The men chatted about the upcoming trip as they walked off.

"You can do no wrong in the eyes of Viktor's people," Juniper noted.

"Soon to be my people." The thought of it filled me with warmth.

Viktor returned and took a post at my side, winding his arm around my waist. "Time to go, love."

With the army and our bounty of prisoners, we journeyed to the traveling stones without problem. Every shifter we came across was sleeping. Oops. We'd knocked out everyone in the dimension.

Upon arrival at Viktor's palace, we secured the primordials and Bodi in comfort, and the shifters in chains and cells. With Valkara and Deco, we took added precautions.

In the future, we'd find Bodi's firebrand, and she would awaken him. I just knew it. Maybe Juniper? *Please.*

My sister stood in front of Deco's cell, peering inside thoughtfully.

I stood before our mother's, with Viktor behind me, his arms wrapped around me, holding me close.

"All my life, I wished to know my mother," I said. "Now, here she is. The absolute worst."

"She is terrible, ja, but you are not." He kissed the top of my head. "I must admit, I'm glad Malachi kidnapped you."

I turned and cupped his cheeks. "Yeah, me, too."

"Me three," Juniper piped up, joining us. "How about a tour of the palace?"

With the excitement of a teenage boy, Viktor showed us around, and I was not surprised to note my new home was as creepy as Deco's. It wasn't just a castle—it was a monument to immortality and a former madness, where the eternal bloodlust of a wild berserker could not die.

"Only the kind of home I've dreamed of my entire life," I breathed.

"Any changes you wish to make must be negotiated with your king," Viktor announced, a study of delight.

THE STOLEN BRIDE

"My poor ears," Juniper cried a with dramatic whine. When we showed her to her suite, she grinned at us. "I'm guessing the wedding is tomorrow."

"It is," Viktor confirmed, thrilling my heart. This guy was totally gone for me.

We left Juniper in a suite and walked the halls hand-in-hand. "I wish to take you on that date you owe me." He bent his head to nip the lobe of my ear. "So. Will you go on a date with me tonight, Clover?"

Oh yeah, totally gone. "Yes, Viktor, I will go on a date with you." I imagined a picnic dinner, candlelight and a bubble bath.

"I have everything planned," he said, eager. "We'll begin with ax throwing, then move on to archery practice, wilderness survival, building a shelter together and crafting other kinds of weapons."

I snort-laughed. "This is your idea of romance?"

An odd mix of delight and confusion infiltrated his expression. "First, that is the most magical sound I've ever heard. Second, I mentioned the part about building a shelter together, didn't I?"

"You did."

"Did I also tell you that you get to design it, and I'll put it together while I'm shirtless?"

"Mmm. Yes. I'm liking the sound of this." I rested my head on his shoulder. "Shirtless is always a good look for you."

He winked. "That is only the beginning. We'll eat, obviously. The cook has prepared two dozen dishes for you to sample. To start. We can serve your favorites at our wedding reception. There's also a new litter of puppies in the stables, as well as a box in the attic that someone suggested has sheet music handwritten by Mozart."

GENA SHOWALTER & JILL MONROE

I blinked at him. Then blinked again. My hand fluttered to my chest. "You do know me, don't you?"

He flashed me a smile so beautiful that it made me gasp. "Know and love."

We spent the rest of the day traipsing through the rolling hills of the Hungarian countryside that surrounded Turálvár Kastély, my new home, searching for the perfect spot. Which we found inside a secret passage in the garden. As we fed each other, we discussed the wedding.

"The nine kings will come tomorrow. We'll tell them about the primordials then." Eyes glinting like polished emeralds, Viktor reached out and glided his fingertip along the line of my throat. "I had decided to wait until our wedding night to mark you, but I've changed my mind again. I should do it now, before we're surrounded by royals." With his free hand, he motioned to a window. "The moon is full, the world practically begging me to do this."

My heart fluttered. "All right. Yes."

In a blink, he had me on my feet, with my back pressed into a rocky wall. I grinned and traced my palms up his chest as he leaned into me. "Don't forget, I'll be giving you my mark, as well." I wanted this. Badly. Because I was a berserker, too, and our people should know I belonged to Viktor as much as he belonged to me. Harm my man and pay the price: War.

"I won't be satisfied until you have done so." Anticipation and heat radiated from me. So much heat. Our quick, ragged breaths accompanied the scrape of metal against leather as he unsheathed a dagger.

My heart pounded. "I know there will be blood and a hint of pain."

"Ja." He handed the blade to me and offered his hand, his eyelids hooded. "But I will ensure you don't mind it."

My chest clenched as I made an incision in the center of his palm, blood welling. His only reaction was a soft, proud smile. A pride that bloomed in me, as well.

After he claimed the knife, he made an identical incision in the center of *my* palm. At the first sight of crimson, he dropped the weapon and linked our fingers, pressing our wounds together. A jolt of pure, undiluted power shot through me. An energy like I'd never experienced, even while swimming in the river of our connection. I gasped.

Viktor captured the noise with his lips, his mouth fully covering mine. In seconds, I was lost. Lost to him, in him, for him. This beautiful berserker was all I'd ever desired in a partner. Strong. Honest. Generous. Devoted. He'd trusted me with his heart, and I would do everything in my power to guard it.

The kiss picked up speed and intensity until we were gasping and kneading and straining together. But only a few seconds into the frenzy, Viktor wrenched up his head.

"The ceremony must be finished," he rasped. Then he spoke in Hungarian. "A világ véget ér, de a szeretet és a béke örökké tart."

I interpreted the words and melted against him. *The world will end, but our love and peace will endure.* "A világ véget ér, de a szeretet és a béke örökké tart," I repeated, slurring the last syllables. Suddenly the most delicious intoxication washed over me, pulling me inward into the most sublime oblivion.

22

Wedding Bells and Battlecries: When Cake and Combat Mix

–HOW TO TRAIN YOUR BERSERKER
By Elizabeth "Elle" Darcy-Bruce

I awoke the next morning, expecting to be cuddled in Viktor's arms. Sunlight streamed in through the lacy curtains covering the floor to ceiling windows of our suite, but he wasn't anywhere nearby.

Disappointment struck. At least I could hold his words close.

The world will end, but our love and peace will endure.

Tomorrow had officially become today! My fiancé must be overseeing final details for our wedding.

A note waited on his pillow. Grinning, I snatched it up and read.

I will give you time to enjoy your sister. After the ceremony, we won't be leaving our bed for weeks.

What a darling man. And sexy!

Barely able to contain my excitement, I raced to my

THE STOLEN BRIDE

sister's room. She slept, but I shook her awake. "I'm getting married today! Up, up, up!"

She groaned as she opened her eyes. "Are you always Miss Chipper Morning Sunshine? Let me fetch a gallon of coffee or you can expect nothing but complaints from me."

I wrinkled my nose. The one subject we disagreed on. "Fine. Get your motor oil. But bring me back a kifli. And some biscuits and gravy. Also, add rantotta, szalonna, some kind of sweet pastry and kefir." My bottomless stomach had more demands than ever.

"Yeah, yeah, yeah," she muttered, lumbering to her feet. She was a total grouch in the morning, and for some reason, I adored that about her. "By the way, I can totally feel Viktor's energy radiating from your body, and it's as freaky as it is savage. If I don't get marked one day, I will revolt."

I giggled as she exited, yes giggled. Unable to sit still, I returned to my private bathroom to shower. My excitement amplified with every minute that passed. After I dried off and donned a robe, I returned to Juniper's room. She arrived soon after with food. We ate and drank and laughed, then prepared for my big day.

Juniper applied my makeup and curled my hair, then helped me into my wedding dress. A masterpiece so elegant, I couldn't believe a seamstress had created it overnight, without taking any measurements. Embroidery in subtle golden hues adorned a fitted bodice. The full-length skirt flowed to the floor, the train a full five feet long, and it too possessed golden hues.

She teared up as she looked me over. "You are the most beautiful, amazing woman in the world, and I'm so glad you're in my life now."

Before I teared up too and ruined my face spackle, I hugged her close. "I'm so glad, too."

I felt as if I'd waited for this moment my entire life. Never had I experienced such contentment. Such satisfaction. I had won the love of my life, forged a relationship with my twin, and defeated the enemy, who just happened to be our mother. Normally, a girl's mom helped in times like this.

My shoulders slumped.

As if she'd read my mind, Juniper reached over and hugged me. "Valkara is nothing to us."

Yes, today was a day for putting the past in the past and walking into my future. And Valkara was definitely in my past. But I wanted her to know I saw her vision of doom for what it was. A lie meant to manipulate me. "Let's go see her, one last time."

If any staff and guests thought it odd to spot a bride in full regalia gallivanting down the steps toward the dungeon of Turálvár Kastély, no one said a word.

Juniper chuckled. "Told you. You can't do anything wrong in the eyes of the turul kingdom. If you decreed every day to be Broadway musical day, the people would learn how to choreograph, guaranteed."

Lights triggered by our motion illuminated the corridor that led to the dungeon. Cameras followed our every move. Foreboding hung heavy in the air. Considering the time I'd spent behind iron bars in Deco's fortress, I was chilled to the bone in seconds.

Two armed guards with grim expressions reluctantly stepped aside after giving each other an oh-no look. What in the world?

We quickened our steps. An unexpected flurry of activity greeted us as we passed them, entering the other side. A handful of soldiers scurried about in a constant state of motion. Searching for something? Swinging my

THE STOLEN BRIDE

gaze to the left, I gasped when I spotted my mother's cell. Empty.

"Explain," I demanded of someone. Everyone.

Commander Tabor stepped from a cluster of warriors examining a set of bars, his handsome features fixed in a blank mask. "She escaped this morning."

My blood curdled. "Does Viktor know?"

"He does."

Wait. He knew, and he hadn't told me? We'd have to have a talk about sharing info right away.

Where was she? How had she done this?

"Deco's still here, though, right?" Juniper picked up her skirt and dashed toward the iron bars. She huffed with relief as I came up beside her. The shifter king still slept on his cot.

I returned my gaze to the slightly rumpled blanket where my mother had once slumbered, the chains open and empty on the ground. "Why did no one tell me?" I demanded.

"No one wished to ruin your special day," Tabor said. "But we are also forbidden from lying to you or refusing to give you whatever you seek."

Well, that was something, at least.

The commander gestured toward the entrance. "Come. I'll escort you to the traveling stones. The time has come."

I motioned to the empty cell. "Shouldn't we postpone and, well, do something?"

He shook his head, beseeching me with his gaze. "The people need this ceremony. We are excited to cement you as our queen. Citizens have dreamed of this for centuries. Don't take it from them."

Well. I swallowed past the lump in my throat and stepped forward, with Juniper at my side. We peppered

267

Tabor with questions about the investigation as he guided us out of the dungeon, through the castle, and to the round driveway, where he stopped in front of a large glass carriage.

"Seriously?" Juniper chuckled. "My sister is Cinderella."

"Only your sister and members of the Ten will be witness to your vows," Tabor explained. "This way, your new subjects can see you in your finery as you head toward the traveling stones."

Sunshine bathed me as I settled inside the vehicle beside my grinning sister. The commander mounted a horse. Not one of the beauties pulling the carriage, but a black and white stallion. We eased into motion, and he remained at our left.

As he predicted, thousands of people lined the cobblestone road to wave and throw flower petals as we passed.

Juniper practically jumped on her cushioned seat, joining in the revelry. "You're the one they've come to see. Give them a show."

Commander Tabor's words echoed. *We are excited to cement you as our queen.* Very well. I threw myself into my new role, waving and smiling, thrilled to include these people who wished me well on my happy day.

"Do all royal weddings take place at the traveling stones?" Juniper asked.

Did her adoptive parents not explain, even hiding truthful information in fairytales, as my mother had done? "Each house is different, but all royals must meet a peer's firebrand and that firebrand must prove capable of calming the royal's beast. The only requirement is that each meeting take place on neutral territory. Hence, the traveling stones."

Her features scrunched up with confusion. "How do you prove you're Viktor's firebrand?"

THE STOLEN BRIDE

That, I didn't know. I glanced Tabor's way.

From his perch on the horse, he told us, "All but two royals remain in their doorways and consume gelu root to deaden their emotions. The groom and the royal best able to rouse his temper. Rage then sparks between the two, and a fight follows. If the groom doesn't erupt in a berserkerage, the union is accepted. But that isn't what's happening here. Viktor is an original. His chosen is already accepted. The royals serve as witnesses for the union only."

My spine straightened, and I knew I projected a queenly air. "I'm okay with that." With my mother on the loose, I wanted my man battle ready, not in recovery mode.

We passed through the barbican gates, and the horses picked up speed. Juniper and I chatted until fog settled over the land. We were close.

Nervousness overtook me the second we halted. The time had come!

The commander helped both me and Juniper exit the carriage, and the three of us aimed for a circle of large black stones. Not the stones we'd used to enter Deco's world, but bigger and more menacing.

Tabor stopped at the threshold and motioned us on, not speaking.

I didn't speak, either, the moment thick with anticipation. Arm in arm with Juniper, I walked forward. The fog parted, revealing eight males and two females standing in the stone doorways. Though one of those women occupied a spot with a black-haired blue-eyed hottie in a kilt.

They must be the other royals, since Malachi stood among them. But oh, wow, I had never seen a more ferocious bunch of people. Aggression seeped from their pores. Especially the woman who stood alone. A tendril of smoke curled from her nostrils. Embers flickered behind her, each momentarily displaying an outline of wings.

A weird mix of anger and gratefulness sparked as I focused on Malachi. He was the one who'd started me on this journey. But where was Viktor?

Juniper and I marched to the king of griffins, already irritated by all his gorgeousness and Hollywood charm.

"Hello, ladies," he said with an unrepentant grin.

Juniper pointed a finger at him. "I owe you big time."

I glared at him. "Yeah! What she said."

"I agree," he said, perfectly at ease. "You both owe me. I introduced you to each other and your firebrands."

My hands fisted. "Juniper hasn't met her firebrand yet probably." *Don't be Deco. Anyone but Deco!* "But don't play the innocent. You instructed me to turn Viktor evil, knowing he'd have to kill me to lock in his primordial form."

Malachi lifted his arms in innocence, projecting, *who me?*

"That's the worst acting I've seen since your last movie," I snipped.

"Ouch," he said, though he remained unoffended. "I knew the Valkara plotted something awful against the primordials. I also knew a woman from the House of Griffin would see right through her and overcome for us all. I played my part. Expertly, I might add. You believed me."

"Hmph." Maybe he'd told the truth, maybe not. But I'd let it go because this was the happiest day of my life (so far), and he had, in fact, introduced me to my firebrand.

The beauty with Mr. Kilt raised her hand, as if seeking permission to speak. Long brown hair flowed over an elegant shoulder. "I'm Elle," she announced with an American accent. "This guy's wife." She hiked her thumb at Mr.

THE STOLEN BRIDE

Kilt. "I'd like to officially welcome you into the wonderful world of berserkers."

"I'm Clover."

"I'm Juniper."

"Let's do tea and cookies after my honeymoon," I said. "And pancakes. And sausage patties." Now where was Viktor?" No way he'd changed his mind, as Benjamin had.

"I'm here," his familiar voice called as he stepped from the only open stone doorway, seeming to appear out of thin air. "I wished to recapture your mother and offer her as a gift to you. Alas."

My knees went weak at the sight of him. Where once his white hair stood out in spikes, it now hung in soft waves that invited my fingers to touch.

His once wild eyes devoured me, taking in my gown, and he went predator-still. He looked me over a second time, slowly, savoring. Instead of displaying a face frozen in rage, he smiled, sending shivers over my spine.

I kissed my twin's cheek and rushed to him. He caught me with strong, steady arms and kissed the air from my lungs.

"You'll agree to take him as your own, then, I assume," Malachi piped up with a dry tone.

With a growl, Viktor wrenched his face from mine. He didn't glare at the other king for daring to interrupt, as I expected, but stared down at me. "Well? Do you?"

"Yes, I take you as my own," I called with a laugh to one and all. "And if you or anyone ever threatens Viktor Endris again, I'll destroy you, super-villain style."

"We both will," Juniper said, chin high. She cracked her knuckles before waving her fingers. "These little babies can do damage."

271

The griffin king held up his hands in a gesture of innocence.

"I take Clover as mine and accept responsibility for the world's worst mother-in-law," Viktor announced, still staring down at me. He flashed me a grin. "And now, by decree of the King of the House of Turul, we are wed. This has been witnessed. Everyone go home." He swept me into his arms. Without another word, he carried me from the crowd.

I grinned up at him. "We're going to get a happily ever after, aren't we?"

"Love, I won't settle for anything less. But first, I'm going to give you many—*many*—happy endings." He winked at me and shouldered his way into our bedroom.

The Fire Bride–Coming Soon
Book 3 in the Kings of Fury Series

More About Gena and Jill

You can hang out with Gena and Jill on their Patreon where they share exclusive content: http://patreon.com/genaandjill

Books in the Kings of Fury Series

The Wrong Bride

The Stolen Bride

The Fire Bride–Coming Soon

Books in the Jane Ladling Series

Romancing the Gravestone

No Gravestone Left Unturned

Game of Gravestones

Twelve Graves of Christmas

Conrad: Falling For the Gravekeeper

Grave Wars

Grave New World

Books in the Writing Fiction Series:

All Write Already

All Write Already Workbook

The Write Life

Write Now! An All Write Already Journal

About Gena Showalter

Gena Showalter is the New York Times and USA TODAY bestselling author of multiple series in paranormal, contemporary, fantasy, and young adult romance. She's also written romantasy, and co-writes the Jane Ladling Mystery series with Jill Monroe.

Learn more about Gena, her menagerie of rescue dogs and cats, and all her upcoming books at genashowalter.com

ALSO BY GENA SHOWALTER

No Monsters Like Hers

Start with: The Great and Terrible

Book of Arden

Start with: Kingdom of Tomorrow

Gena's Complete List of Releases:

GenaShowalter.com/books

About Jill Monroe

Jill Monroe is the international best selling author of over fifteen novels and novellas. Her books are available across the globe and The Wrong Bed: Naked Pursuit has been adapted for the small screen for Lifetime Movie Network.

When not writing, Jill makes her home in Oklahoma with her husband, enjoys exploring creativity, texting with her two daughters and collecting fabric for items she'll sew poorly.

Learn more about Jill at jillmonroe.com

Also By Jill Monroe

Sworn Series:

Sworn Promises

Sworn Duty

Sworn By A Kiss

Sworn Protector

Sworn Enemies

Sworn Instinct

.

Wrong Bed Series

Naked Thrill

Naked Pursuit*

*(Now a movie from Lifetime Movie Network)

.

Formally From Hallmark:

At The Heart of Christmas

.

Spicy Romance:

Fun & Games

Treasure in the Sand (novella)

.

Jill's Complete List of Releases:

https://jillmonroe.com/allbooks/

Printed in Great Britain
by Amazon